TWENTY AND OUT
Mickey Duff

TWENTY AND OUT
Mickey Duff

with Bob Mee

CollinsWillow

An Imprint of HarperCollins*Publishers*

First published in hardback in 1999
by Collins Willow
an imprint of HarperCollins*Publishers*
London

The HarperCollins website address is
www.fireandwater.com

1 3 5 7 9 8 6 4 2

A CIP catalogue record for this book is
available from the British Library

ISBN 0 00 218926 7

Set in PostScript Sabon by
Rowland Phototypesetting Ltd,
Bury St Edmunds, Suffolk

Printed and bound in Great Britain by
Clays Ltd, St Ives plc

Photographic acknowledgements
All photographs are supplied courtesy of the
author unless otherwise stated.

Action Images plate section page no. 15t and bl;
Allsport 6c, 9tr and c, 13c, 16t; Allsport/Hulton
Deutsch 2t, 4c, 10b; Colorsport 14t; Express
Newspapers/Archive Photos 2br; Hulton Getty
3c, 4t, 12c; Doug McKenzie 6b; Mirror
Syndication International 3t, 7t, 8t, 11t and b,
12t and b, 15br; Patricia A. Orr 16c and b;
Popperfoto 2bl, 4b, 5, 7b, 9tl, 13t and b;
Topham Picturepoint 8b

Contents

Acknowledgements		vii
Introduction		1
1	A Polish Refugee	5
2	In the Ring	14
3	Making a Living	21
4	The Underworld	28
5	Sweet Like Sugar	38
6	Fighting Solomons	46
7	Heavyweight Heroes	53
8	Legends of the Ring	70
9	The Greatest	83
10	Taking Control	105
11	Lawless Men	126
12	The Middleweights	144
13	Outside Boxing	153
14	The Fighting Business	162
15	Ragamuffin and the Gifted One	181
16	Little Big Men	191
17	Bruno	201
18	Iron Mike	224
19	America and Television	235
20	End of an Era	246
	Epilogue	262
	Career Statistics	267
	Index	273

Acknowledgements

There are people in the public eye – boxers, managers, trainers, promoters and other colleagues – whose contribution to my story is well documented in the pages which follow. However, behind the scenes others worked tirelessly to assist me over the years and this seems a fitting moment in which I can pay tribute to their loyalty and dedication.

Firstly, my secretary Eileen Allen has been with me for 20 years. In all that time, while we may have had disagreements, we have not had a bad word to say to each other. When I interviewed her for the position, we talked and I said I would let her know because there were other applicants I had to consider. She looked at me and said: 'You won't choose anybody else.' She was right – and her appointment was one of the most sensible decisions I have ever made. I would also like to place on record my appreciation of the efforts of David Jones, who was a general factotum for us for 25 years. He gave valuable and loyal service, was always helpful and carried out the kind of work that would otherwise have taken up too much of my time.

It is also appropriate to thank my son, Gary, for his help and assistance in recollecting some of the precise details of my story on the occasions when my memory failed me.

Introduction

I stood on the stage at the International Boxing Hall of Fame in Canastota, New York, and looked down at a sea of faces. Some of them I had known for years, some of them I had never seen before but who knew me, and some of them I had long forgotten and never dreamed I would see again. I accepted the ring signifying my induction with immense pleasure for somehow it represented a lifetime's effort in this most demanding and enjoyable of sports. I am proud to say I am a boxing man through and through, and have been for more than half a century.

I was not sure what I was letting myself in for when I accepted the invitation. I need not have worried. I was in Canastota for five days – and it was fantastic. The weather was hot, the atmosphere extremely pleasant. One of the annual procedures is that every inductee has to put his hand in a pot for a mould of his fist. When my turn came and my hand was lying fixed in the cement, I said: 'I boxed as an amateur for three years, a professional for four and a half years and this is the first time one of my fists has made a real impression!'

I enjoyed doing the rounds, talking and telling stories and I had pictures with Ray Leonard and Marvin Hagler, two of the greatest fighters I have ever seen, on either side of me. I saw Alexis Arguello, whom I've known for years, and men like Gene Fullmer and Carmen Basilio, old men now who were my idols and who constitute part of my lifetime in boxing.

The others who were inducted alongside me were world champions Khaosai Galaxy and Eusebio Pedroza, whom I had promoted 14 years earlier in his classic 15-round battle with Barry McGuigan in London; promoter Bob Arum, who isn't one of my greatest friends but with whom I've done many a backstage battle over the years; publicist Irving Rudd and the great heavyweight of my youth, Jimmy Bivins.

It was especially heart-warming to see Bivins, who had been forgotten, almost presumed dead, a couple of years ago when he was discovered living in the attic room of a member of his family. The old man was apparently skin and bone but by the time he was honoured he had been restored to health. I looked at him and saw those fabled names of my youth, men he had fought: Ezzard Charles, Charley Burley, Archie Moore and the greatest of them all, Joe Louis. For some reason Bivins referred to Louis, whom I met several times in the sixties and seventies, as 'Big Red'. The man fought them all but never had a shot at the title and it was nice to see him given credit for what he had achieved.

Posthumously honoured were the former lightweight champion Lew Jenkins and another man I promoted, Vicente Saldivar, the world featherweight champion from the 1960s. Saldivar, who died of a heart attack in his early forties, twice fought the wonderful boxer from Wales, Howard Winstone, on shows we promoted in London and Cardiff. Winstone was there to receive the award for Saldivar.

As I heard other names honoured from the past – legends like Johnny Coulon, a bantamweight champion from before I was born, and heavyweight Sam McVey – I let my thoughts drift back over the years spent in this most entrancing and enduring of sports. And I felt not only was it a privilege to be there but it had been a privilege to spend my life in such an activity and with such people. I had never been to Canastota before. Now I am going every year which God gives me.

Also at the Hall of Fame celebrations, in the audience, was the last of my fighters, Billy Schwer. I have called this book *Twenty And Out* because of him. At the time of writing I have been directly involved as manager, matchmaker or promoter in the careers of 19 world champions, beginning with the great 'Dashing, Crashing, Bashing, Terry Downes' in 1961. Billy Schwer will shortly fight for the world lightweight title and I sincerely hope, for his own sake not mine, that he can become the 20th on my list. Nobody will deserve it more.

This story goes back a long way, to my roots in a community of orthodox Jewish people in a small Polish town before World War Two, and it travels on through a life which has allowed me to see more than most and mix with some great people. I could talk about the famous celebrities I have met but frankly it doesn't impress me and so I would not expect it to impress you. I am, and always have been, a boxing man. I am moved by boxing, by boxers and by boxing people. I may not have liked them all – in fact, I firmly believe that a man who has gone through life without creating enemies is a fake – but I have attempted here to recall things as they were.

Memory is a strange phenomenon. I have tried very hard to get things right and this is, I believe, the truth as I saw it, and as I see it now with retirement approaching. I promised myself when I set out to tell this story that I would do it as honestly as possible. I owe it to all of you to tell the truth. I think I have done that and if you enjoy reading my story half as much as I have enjoyed living it then I'm sure you'll find it worth your interest.

CHAPTER 1

A Polish Refugee

I don't know of a worse pain than fear.

I felt it first at Passover, 1937, when I was seven years old and with my parents and elder brother Lewis in our home in Poland. After the Passover meal we sat and talked as families do, until Lewis eventually went to bed. I wanted to stay up longer but in time was so tired my parents laid me on the couch. They must have believed I was asleep, for I heard my father, Sindel, who was extremely intelligent and wise, say: 'We have got to get out of here. It's dangerous to stay. There is going to come a day when a Jew will be unable to walk the streets.'

I lay there shivering. I was petrified.

My family lived in Tarnow, a small town to the east of Krakow, which had been a centre for Jewish people since the 15th century and had a magnificent synagogue, which was gutted by the Nazis in 1939. I was raised speaking Yiddish, not Polish, and Jews made up – I am told now – about 40 per cent of the population. My parents had a dairy shop in the Jewish area, selling milk food: butter, eggs and cheese. In orthodox Jewish society there is meat food and milk food. You don't sell both from one shop.

My father's great grandfather, Moishe Rokach, was the original rabbi of Beltz, another Polish town with a massive Hebrew university, which he founded. The orthodox Jewish people, the Hassidin, did not register their marriages with the government. They married in the synagogues, which gave the marriage authority in Jewish law, and the government didn't really mean anything to them. As a rule, children took their mother's name. So my father, whose mother was called Deutsch, took that rather than Rokach. When my father married my mother, they never bothered to register it and, as her maiden name was Prager, we had to take that. I've said many times that I come from a long line of bastards!

I was born Monek Prager on 7 June 1929 in Tarnow and, as my father was a rabbi, my early years were steeped in the strict, Hassidic religion. You see the young boys now dressed in black with the ringlets in front of their ears? That was me in those days! Jewish laws were all in favour of the man, and as marriages weren't registered with the government, men only had to get a religious divorce to be free to marry again. My mother Tyla – pronounced Tillie in England – was the second of his four wives. As he changed wives, he became more modernised but when I was a child he was still very strict and traditional. I still have my brother Lewis and a half-brother from my father's first marriage, Norman Rokach. Both have homes in Britain and Israel.

I remember Tarnow better than what I had for breakfast this morning. Maybe these early memories stay in your mind because they are there first. It's possible they change conveniently to suit what you want to believe as you get older, but they do seem fresh. Later memories have to be tucked away in a different compartment where there isn't so much room!

We were Jewish, not Polish. Poland was simply where we were born. When I first went to school at six, I could hardly speak any Polish at all but to this day I am amazed how quickly children learn. I learned it without, it seems now, any effort and spoke it for three years, then when I came to England I forgot it all within six months.

Those days in Tarnow must have been terribly difficult for my parents because Poland was mostly Roman Catholic. Jewish people had a very hard time. If the government felt you owed them income tax, they sent people without warning and confiscated your possessions. I remember them doing that twice to my father. I also remember walking across a bridge with my grandfather when he was attacked by a gang of men. They knocked him down and cut off half of his long, flowing beard to ridicule him. They knew he would not shave (because of his religion) and would have to wait years for the beard to grow back to its full length.

A month after I heard the conversation at Passover, my father was smuggled out of Poland. He couldn't get permission to leave because at the time they were not giving passports to Jews. Ironically, he was taken out not through the nearest border, which was south over the Carpathian mountains into Czechoslovakia, but west through Krakow and into Germany. Once he was there, he found conditions were not as bad as they were in Poland and again, because he was a rabbi and a cantor who led the synagogue services, he was allowed to come on to England because of the influence of people in synagogues here. As far as I know, he was allowed out of Germany without any real problem.

I idolised my father as a young boy. He was a strong disciplinarian and could be heavy handed but I hung on his every word. He was a rabbi by qualification and faith, but was always business-minded. He liked to get into other things. He was a rabbi in Dunk Street in the East End and was a cantor in the Great Garden Street synagogue, which was fairly large. But he also got himself a job as a travelling agent for the Rickett Smith Coal Company. They hired him because he spoke Yiddish, had a beard and could go around the Jewish areas taking orders for coal. Altogether, he just about scraped a good enough living and by 1938 he had permission from the British government for my mother, brother and I to travel here. We beat World War Two, and almost certain extermination, by a year.

I remember us leaving by rail, from Tarnow to Krakow, and then taking another train – a much longer journey. It was probably to Danzig, which at the time was the major Polish port separating Germany from the old state of East Prussia. Then we were on a boat for eight days – the first and last time I travelled anywhere by boat – before we reached London on August 8, 1938. My father was waiting for us at East India Docks. When we disembarked he was on the quay but I walked straight past him. Then he saw us and, needless to say, we were very pleased to see each other. I think that was probably the last time he hugged me.

My father's flat was in Gore Road, Hackney, right opposite Victoria Park. On almost my first day in London, I found myself playing in the park with the other Jewish kids, who made a big fuss of me. They made me feel at home. I couldn't speak English – in fact I could only say one phrase, 'Thank you', which someone had taught be on the boat – but two weeks later when we went to school, I had learned enough from the other children to take part in lessons.

The state of Europe didn't have much effect on me. I was a boy who was excited by all of the new things that were happening to me. Children settle and adjust very quickly and I don't remember any particular worries once we had come to England. However, my mother brought her favourite sister,

Helen, out of Poland – miraculously only two days before the German troops began their 'blitzkrieg' invasion at dawn on 1 September 1939. My mother lost a brother and two more sisters in the concentration camps, and I don't know how many of the family's little ones died. The Nazis created a ghetto in Tarnow to the east of the old town, destroyed the synagogues and between June 1942 and September 1943, 40,000 Jewish people were killed, either shot in massacres or sent to the camps, mainly Auschwitz. There are memorials there now.

Soon after the war started I was evacuated to a tiny village in Northamptonshire called Crick. I stayed with a non-Jewish family, Mr and Mrs Shepherd and their son and daughter. I was a novelty to them in my strict orthodox Jewish clothing and their way of life was strange to me. I wouldn't eat their food – all they could do was give me bread and toast it – but necessity is the mother of invention and knows no law. The alternative was half-starving, and by the end of my stay I ate everything apart from the stove! After eight or nine months my parents took me back because the bombing they had feared hadn't happened. I don't think I'd missed a bomb, but as soon as I went back home it all began.

My brother, mother and I slept in the Underground at Whitechapel when the air raids were on. We were children and I suppose the adults did their best to make it fun. We used to hear the bombs and see the damage of course, but we were very fortunate. Our house was never touched.

When I was 11 I was sent with my brother to Gateshead in the north-east of England, to a religious college. Lewis was far more religious than me even then. He finished up getting rabbinical qualifications. He never took them up but completed the course. I lasted four months. I came home for the Passover holiday and my mother received a discreet letter saying they were short of beds and perhaps it was best if I stayed at home. They still had beds for everyone else, of course. Even then I was a non-conformist and it just wasn't my scene. I didn't have the capacity for it.

From Lorriston Road school in Hackney, I went to Deal Street, but at the age of 13 years and eight months I got myself a job at a clothing factory, two doors away from our house. You couldn't officially leave school until you were 14 but I kept producing a doctor's certificate and they left me alone. I was taught to use a sewing machine and became a plain machiner. Plain machiners do the mundane jobs. Essentially, I made linings for clothes. I worked there for almost six months, but I was sacked because I was always late. I only lived a few steps away, but was usually 20 minutes or half an hour late. As we all had to start together for the system to work, it threw everybody else off. Everybody would have finished their work, but the chain would then break down because they would be waiting for me.

After that I had several jobs. I was a plain machiner in another factory, I worked on the markets – Petticoat Lane on a Sunday. I sold batteries for torches, which were obviously vital in those years of the blackout. In the war you couldn't get a battery anywere but I found a supply. I don't remember exactly where I bought them but I would have paid black market prices and sold them for about five times their value.

By 1941 my parents' marriage had broken down and they had divorced. My father remarried and he and his third wife opened a restaurant in Mortimer Street W1, which was the textile area of London at the time. It was called the Textile Restaurant. My mother continued to work in a kosher restaurant in Great Garden Street. He always had the capacity to put his wives to work, while he used to sit around and play cards. My mother worked bitterly hard.

My mother lived to a good age – 80 – but after all those years working at the restaurant she became worn out. She had nowhere to go, and my wife Marie suggested we invite her to live with us. She did, in Mile End and Stamford Hill, but unfortunately she eventually had to live in a home because her mind had gone. I was very close to her but at the finish, for the last three or four years, it broke my heart to go and see her. For the last year she no longer knew me.

However, back to those days in the early part of the war. I was 12 years old when one day I went to see my father. While I was visiting, I heard an argument between him and his new wife. When I got home, my mother was inquisitive and persistent and I volunteered the information that I had witnessed what I thought then was a terrible row. There was a great deal of animosity at the time between my mother and father and she chose to tell the world that he was not getting on with his new wife – as if to make the point: 'You see, he can't get along with anybody.' Naturally, this reached my father's ears and when I went to see him a few days later, he told me icily to get out and not come back.

As well as the fact that I had told my mother about his domestic life, he did not approve of the way I was conducting mine. He could see that I was not as religious as he would have wanted, but it was a rejection that hurt me then, and possibly in an indirect way still does now.

We never spoke again. I was in his company for barmitzvahs and weddings, but we never said a word to each other in the next 35 years, until he died in April, 1977. He refused to attend my own barmitzvah, which of course was on my 13th Jewish birthday. I missed my father. He would have helped me learn my barmitzvah and would have been there for me. I am not sure whether his absence at the actual ceremony hurt me at the time. I was probably too full of myself. People would have been telling me how well I had done and I would have been the centre of attention. But in retrospect, it hurt.

Once, years later, my brother rang me to say he would like to come to a show. 'By the way,' he said. 'I am bringing father.' I sent him four complimentary tickets, they came and I said hello to my brother and ignored my father. To be honest, I thought he might have said hello and, if he had, I would have talked to him and made the peace, but he didn't.

I may seem confrontational – and there are some people in boxing who will certainly believe it – but I am not naturally that way. I am quite soft. I am concerned about fall-outs and I tend to give in first. Maybe that's as a result of the experience I had with my father. And it would be fair to say that in later years my power emerged to some extent out of uncertainty, as a counteraction to a lack of confidence. I think I was fighting a slight inferiority complex, born out of having to struggle. I grew up with a mother who was far too busy trying to make a bare living, and a father who chose to decide I did not exist after the age of 12½.

My father lived until his mid-eighties but we never mended our relationship. When he was on his death-bed my half-brother, Norman, telephoned to tell me my father was dying and wanted to see his children – all of us. I said: 'You know, I never did anything wrong to him in my entire life that I am aware of, other than telling my mother something when I was 12 years of age that she shouldn't have heard. I will come, but *he's* got to ask me and not you. Just put the phone to his ear and let him say "I want to see you."'

He didn't. And I didn't go.

I don't know for sure whether my half-brother passed on the message. We have never got on all that well. We are different types of people. We have different priorities. I'm not saying better or worse, simply different. However, I regret not visiting my father at the end of his life and when he died I was sorrowful. I did fly to his funeral in Israel. He was buried on the Mount of Olives, the sacred place in

Jerusalem set aside for the holiest of rabbis, on a lovely day. My elder brother and I were very much the odd men out. We stood out like sore thumbs among the Hassidic community and I heard someone say as we passed: 'Look at this. Beltz grandchildren. Disgraceful!'

As I attended the burial I realised that I should have gone to see him when he asked because he was dying and I was not. I have always tried to practise in life the saying that two wrongs don't make a right. What my father did was really disgraceful but I should have gone to see him. I have regretted it ever since.

CHAPTER 2

In the Ring

Boxing came into my life when I was 12 years old . . . and it's still here almost 60 years on. A boy named Kossowitzky had two pairs of gloves and used to challenge everybody at school to fight him. Other boys did, and he would beat hell out of them. He used to goad me, but I would never box him. I remember shaking my head and insisting: 'No, no, no.'

I was fascinated, though. I kept watching him and in time I realised what he was doing. All the other kids were swinging away at him and he was punching straight. It was so simple. After a while, I said I would box him. We put the gloves on and instead of swinging, I did exactly what he did, but fortunately I was a little quicker. And I beat hell out of him. That was it. I wanted more.

I went to Oxford and St George's Boys Club in the East End, which was run by a man named Basil Henriques, who was a Justice of the Peace and very well known. I attended the boxing classes, but the standard of the team was very high. The club had a rich tradition and had produced one of the finest boxers of the 1930s, Harry Mizler, and Benny Caplan. Mizler represented Great Britain in the 1932 Olympic Games in Los Angeles and fought Jack 'Kid' Berg and Jimmy Walsh for the British lightweight title, while Caplan went 15 rounds with Jim 'Spider' Kelly for the British featherweight title in Belfast. Both would have been champions today.

Some time later I left to join Brady Street Boys Club, where there was less talent and where I could be more respected. Legend has it that Harry Levene, later of course our promoter, once had his nose broken in a bout there in the early days of the century. I got in the team in no time and improved, because your confidence grows as you win a few fights.

I moved on from Brady Street to West Ham Amateur Club. The chief trainer there, Les Maddison, felt he could improve me and I think he did, but I could never get enough contests. I was impatient and took to turning up at amateur shows with my bag on the off chance that I could box as a substitute. I used to take the prize, which might be as much as a canteen of cutlery, and flog it for ten shillings. Maddison didn't like me sorting out bouts for myself and after a couple of warnings I was ordered to leave. During war-time clubs were sometimes disrupted by the bombs, or were short in some other way, and the Glacier, Caius and Hendon clubs were combined in order for them to share facilities. If you boxed for one, you could box for all three. I joined them for a while.

I must also point out that a story which did the rounds at one time that I was a London Schoolboy finalist was false – although my decision to enter the championships did lead me to discover the name which has made me famous. To enter the championships you needed written permission from your parents or a schoolteacher. My mother and father would have been horrified and so I took some headed note-paper from the headmaster's desk at school, asked one of the older kids to write the note for me and changed my name. I was already being called Mickey instead of Monek and chose Duffy because I had just seen James Cagney play the character Jackie Boy Duffy in the movie, 'Cash and Carry'. I shortened it to Duff. It didn't help. I lost my first contest.

I was barely 14 when I found my way into a pro gym in the West End – Bill Klein's in Fitzroy Street. I went because I heard Harry Lazar from Aldgate trained there and I was introduced to him and his brothers Davey, Eddie and Lew. None of them were as good as Harry, who was a contender for the British lightweight title.

In the gym I also met Dave Crowley, who had boxed Mike Belloise in New York for the world featherweight title in 1936 and had been British lightweight champion in 1938, the year I had arrived in London. Crowley was a brilliant boxer from Clerkenwell, and at the time I met him in the summer of 1943 he was 33 years old and on about his 15th comeback! I got in the ring and boxed with him one day and he liked what I did. Or tried to do. As a result I used to go down there almost every day. He used to say to me: 'I'll pay for you to go to the pictures if you can hit me.'

Sometimes I went five days without going to the pictures!

Eventually, Crowley had 180 fights spread over 17 years, but it took its toll. When he was an old man he was almost blind.

I was an amateur until I was 15 years and four months old. Then a man named Jack Henning, who managed a few professional fighters, told me he thought I was good enough to box as a pro. I agreed with him. I went to Watford Town Hall to box a fellow named Sid Beech from Dunstable, and before the show an inspector from the British Boxing Board of Control asked to see my licence.

'I haven't got one.' I said.

'Well, we'd better sort that out,' he said, put one in front of me and charged me five shillings for one year.

I didn't have a medical, and upped my age by eight months to conform with the board's limit of 16. They probably still think I was born in October 1928. Anyway, under age or not, I beat Sid Beech in the first round. I also won my second fight in one round, but any illusions that I might have had about being a heavy puncher quickly disappeared. In the rest of my career, which lasted for 69 fights, I only stopped one other opponent.

You could say I wasn't the most colourful of boxers. I was very defence-conscious. I was never sufficiently physically developed to be a boxer. I didn't have the physical strength or athletic energy. I depended on skill and was a fairly good boxer, but basically I survived by ducking and diving. I was also bright enough to manage my managers, Jack Henning and then later Alf Jacobs. I turned down a lot of matches because I made sure I watched my opponents before I accepted fights with them. I did take contests at the last minute but only if I knew the opponent and had seen him. It was a caution I was to carry on into my career as a match-maker, manager and promoter.

I carried on boxing until 1948, when I was 19, but the highlights of my career were lowlights. I was ambitious to start with, and I kept saying to myself: 'If I keep on picking the right opponents I will eventually go a long way.'

But fairly quickly I realised that while I was quite talented, I had neither the physical energy nor the punching power to succeed. There was nothing I could do about it. I adore aggressive, attacking fighters but I was a counter puncher. I hit and I ran. As a matchmaker, rest assured, I would never have booked myself! I did get knocked down by a big punching kid called Kenny Green at Mile End, but lasted the distance. That was when I understood what it meant to be knocked out, even though I didn't go down for the full count. I remember being on the floor and having no idea how I'd got there. I didn't feel hurt. It was as if I was floating through a dream. I got up and boxed on, and remembered nothing of the next two rounds, which were the fourth and fifth. I came to properly when I heard the timekeeper call out 'Sixth and final round!'

Overall, I made sure I didn't come to any harm. On one occasion, I was matched with Eddie Thomas from Merthyr Tydfil, who had won an ABA title and would go on to become British and European welterweight champion. My manager accepted the match and I declined – but not before I had purloined a pass into the show. I had a spell out with a damaged nose which needed an operation in 1946 but nothing more serious. There was also a rare photograph of me in the ring published in a book by one of my former opponents, Harry Legge, named *Penny A Punch*. Legge and I drew at the Prince of Wales baths in Kentish Town in January 1948. I knew Harry well and for his book, from somewhere, he found a picture of me at work in a boxing booth in Bournemouth run by a man named Bob Parkin.

I worked the travelling booths for years starting when I was a boy of 14. It was a marvellous life. Wherever we travelled I was always Billy Jones. If we were in Bournemouth, I was Billy Jones of Bournemouth. If we were in Brighton, I was Billy Jones of Brighton. And so on. I would be a stooge in the crowd because they very rarely attracted genuine challenges. After the barker had done his spiel, I would shout out: 'I'll have a go', and push my way to the front. Whoever was the Master of Ceremonies would say: 'You only look a young lad. Are you sure you know what you're doing? All right, you can fight, but mind yourself.'

We travelled around the south coast and down into Corn-

wall, sharing good times with good fighters like Jackie Rankin, Davey Lazar and Ivor Thomas from Wales, who was
good enough to fight champions. I carried on working the
booths even during the slow times as a professional. They
were exciting days, if not always comfortable. I once fought
13 times on a booth in Norwich . . . on Boxing Day! And
on a freezing cold night there were eight of us in a caravan
and I couldn't sleep because it was so cramped. I went for
a walk because it was more restful. The next day's papers
said it was the coldest night for 40 years.

I wasn't destined to be a star inside the ropes, but had
regular mentions in the trade press. I dug out the *Weekly
Sporting Review* for 1947 and 1948, to refresh my memory
of those times, and was pleasantly surprised at the impression
I created in those six and eight round battles so long ago in
small halls around Mile End and Kentish Town. They called
my points win over Doug Harnett of Wales 'a splendid exhibition of left hand hitting', going on to say that I presented
my opponent with 'a very elusive target who used the ring
to the utmost. Duff never missed an opening to flick out his
rapier-like left. Occasionally he loosed a stinging right hook,
giving the impression that his stock would rise considerably.
Duff won by a comfortable margin.'

And again, in a drawn fight with Al Wilburn from Hickleton Main in Yorkshire:

'Wilburn forced the fight throughout and Duff had to bring
out all his ringcraft to prevent an early termination. Fre-
quently when cornered he manoevered out of danger in
almost miraculous fashion, and on several occasions when
he appeared to be at the mercy of his rugged opponent, he
was just not there when the intended decider came over.'

So, I couldn't have been that bad, could I?

However smart I was at finding a way out of trouble, I
could never claim to have made crowds want to rush to see

me perform. There was one fight against Dick Levers at Mile End when I did think my display had been honoured by the quaint tradition of nobbins – that's money tossed in at the end as a bonus from the delighted punters. I said to my trainer, Danny Vary:

'Great, they're throwing nobbins in.'

Vary gave me a withering glare and pulled me out of the ring. 'That's not nobbins son, that's stones!'

I had my last fight at West Ham Baths in 1948. I said to myself: 'That's it. I am never going to box again.' I realised I wasn't getting anywhere and I knew it was time to do something else with my life. Once I retired, I never put on a pair of gloves or a pair of shorts again. With years of amateur boxing, booth battles and 69 professional fights – 55 wins, eight defeats and six draws – I had done my whack . . . I was all of 19 years old.

CHAPTER 3

Making a Living

Although I had curtailed my boxing career, I knew I would never be able to shake off the sport – and nor would I want to. It was like a religion with me. I knew all the boxers, and knew their strengths and weaknesses. I went back to earn a living in a clothing factory for a while because I could use a machine. But I kept myself involved in boxing, hanging out at gyms and gibbing into fights. I rarely, if ever, paid at the door!

Joe Bloom had an office at one end of his gym in Earlham Street and, to help keep his costs down, he rented out a cordoned-off space at the other end to two East End promoters, Morris Bodinetz and his younger brother Harold. The Bodinetz brothers ran a show every Monday at Leyton Baths. I got quite friendly with Harold in particular, and used to suggest matches to him. They had used several matchmakers and weren't happy with any of them, and one day they asked me to do the job.

'But I haven't got a matchmaker's licence,' I said.

'Well,' replied Morris. 'I've got a licence to make my own matches. You can just tell me what to do.'

He gave me £7 and 10 shillings a week – very good money in those days – and a percentage of any profits. I became their matchmaker for a while and at the end of the year collected £85. It felt as if I had just broken the Bank of England. It was obvious to the British Boxing Board of Control what was happening and eventually somebody at the board suggested I apply for an official licence.

At the time, the chairman of the Southern Area Council was a promoter, Victor Berliner, who had also managed the great Jewish fighter of the 1930s, Harry Mizler. He quite liked me, but the biggest British promoter of the era, Jack Solomons, did not. In fact, even in those days he hated my guts. He knew I used to gib into his shows and bet at ringside, which he disliked because he felt it was disruptive and, of course, beyond his control. He had stooges on the area council – Jack Hyams, Mike Milligan and his main trainer, Nat Sellers, who worked with world light-heavyweight champion Freddie Mills. The council were ready to refuse me. They must have asked me every question it was possible to ask in a sustained attempt to catch me out. But I was young and unbelievably keen, and knew every answer. Morris Bodinetz was there as a council member – obviously supporting my application – and he told me what happened after I had left the room. Apparently, Sellers spoke first.

'I don't know what we're doing here,' said Sellers. 'Are we mad – talking about giving a licence to a snotty-nosed kid like this?'

'Well,' replied Berliner in my defence, 'he answered all your questions and he's going to make the matches anyway. If we give him a licence we will have some control over him.'

At first they gave me a provisional licence. I had never heard of one of those and consulted a lawyer, who went through the rule book of the Board of Control and said there was no such thing. He wrote to them and without argument they changed it to a full licence.

It might be hard for modern sports fans to understand just how powerful and successful Jack Solomons was in the 1940s and 1950s. He had boxed very briefly as a professional during the First World War, had been a fishmonger in the East End of London and had begun promoting in the 1930s when still a comparatively young man. He had also made matches for Sydney Hulls, who ran shows at Harringay Arena. Solomons rose to power with the sporting boom which occurred so dramatically in the golden years immediately following the Second World War.

They were the years of Bradman and Compton in cricket, of footballing giants like Sir Stanley Matthews and Tom Finney and of fighters like Freddie Mills and Bruce Woodcock. There's an old saying that boxing's state of health is reflected by the credibility of its world heavyweight champion. And when Solomons reached his peak, the 'Brown Bomber', Joe Louis, had been heavyweight champ for a decade. Boxing was already big. Under Solomons' influence it became huge, and to be fair to him he knew how to put on a show. He staged the great outdoor spectaculars of the time at White City Stadium in west London. Nearly 50,000 people saw Freddie Mills outpoint Gus Lesnevich for the world light-heavyweight title there. The two world title fights between Mills and Lesnevich were fantastic successes, and Woodcock was a national hero who some felt could succeed Louis as heavyweight champion – when the great man decided to retire. In fact, Solomons billed a fight between Woodcock and Lee Savold for the heavyweight championship, and received some support, but Savold won when the Yorkshireman suffered a horrible curving gash the length of his left eyebrow in the fourth round. It drew a vast crowd, estimated at 60,000. Solomons must have felt he was king of the sporting world.

With the benefit of hindsight, we can also now see how ruthless he was. He thought nothing of booking Mills to fight Lesnevich in 1946, meanwhile also tying him into a contract to box Woodcock three weeks later. This was the first time Mills challenged the American and he was badly beaten, stopped in ten rounds. He was ill in the dressing room and, later that night, on the way to the home of his manager, Ted Broadribb, he vomited twice. There was no doubt that Mills was seriously concussed, yet 21 days later he boxed Woodcock, conceding weight of course, and lost on points over 12 rounds. Both men finished with the marks of battle only too visible – they each had an eye swollen shut. Some say Mills suffered headaches as a result of his career. He died from gunshot wounds in his car at the rear of a club he owned in the West End in 1965. The verdict of the coroner was that he killed himself. Woodcock, meanwhile, finished his career virtually blind in one eye. As well as great days, they were hard, gruelling times.

I was still a teenager when Mills, Lesnevich, Woodcock, Savold and the big Polish-American Joe Baksi were filling those arenas, but I was very much a part of the circuit, of course, as a boxer and then in my early years as a match-maker. It was a struggle. The Bodinetz brothers gave up on Leyton Baths and around six months later I applied for a manager's licence and began to build up a small stable. For the whole of the 1950s it was a hard business, but I hustled along. I made matches for Dave Braitman and Ronnie Ezra, who tried running shows in opposition to Solomons in the Empress Hall and at Earls Court. Later I worked with Jarvis Astaire who, to this day, remains the greatest friend I have in the business.

In 1951 life changed direction when I married Marie Sim-

mons, whom I had met through her brother Henry. He was
Jack Solomons' office boy from the time he left school. I
was about 20 and he would have been 17 when we became
friendly, and consequently I met Marie. I also knew their
father, who came to all the boxing shows, and their mother.
About six months after meeting Marie, I took her out and
we courted for around 18 months before we were married.
We rented two rooms and a kitchen on the top floor of a
house in Cephas Avenue, Mile End. The people we rented
from, Max Sinclair and his wife Rita – who was a good
singer under her maiden name of Rita Carr – also rented it.
Like me, Max was struggling to make a living, and he needed
our £1 a week. To this day, every time I see Rita she laughs
and says: 'You still owe me two quid.'

Marie was a tough lady – too tough for me! She had to
fend for herself because I was away from home so much
over the years, but then she had learned to do that from the
age of 12 or 13, when her parents divorced and she had been
housekeeper for her father, with a younger brother to look
after as well. She ran a home even then.

My matchmaking work at this time was far from a reliable,
or large enough, income so after we married, I went to work
for my wife's uncle, making duffle coats – nothing to do with
my name – donkey jackets and corduroy trousers.

The best boxer I managed in those early years was Solly
Cantor, a Canadian whose real name was Solomon Bona-
parte. He used Cantor because his father was a cantor in the
synagogue. He had fought in Madison Square Garden and
had previously been managed by the famous American manager Bill Daly, but their contract ran out and he signed with
me. He was living in London and when I was matchmaker
for the Bodinetz brothers I put him on for them at Leyton
Baths. Then, in 1953, I took over as his manager. He was a
handsome boy, a lovely boxer with a beautiful left hand and

a good chin. He was stopped a couple of times because of cut eyes, but was never knocked out.

One day Sam Burns, who was Jack Solomons' office manager, asked if I wanted to take a fight for Cantor in Johannesburg (by then Solomons was tolerating me). The purse was £400, which was a fortune in those days and in spite of being married with a baby son, Gary, I went to South Africa in the summer of 1953, six weeks before Solly's first fight with Tony Habib in the Rand Stadium in Johannesburg. It was unbelievable. At the time there were half a million Jews living in the city and the fight drew 16,000 people. Solly won, no question, but didn't get the decision. He was robbed. We made a return, then he drew with Johnny Van Rensburg, and they offered us a fourth fight, which we took. There was no point in going home in between, and altogether I stayed for eight months.

Of course, this long absence from home was bound to affect my relationship with my wife. In fact, during one telephone conversation Marie said: 'You're not coming back, are you?'

She was serious. She thought I had left her. But when I finally returned to her in February 1954, I had £600 in my pocket, which was enough to start us in our own business. I opened my own place, 'Cut, Make And Trim', and used to take in work. The manufacturer would give you the cloth with the pattern, you would make it up and give it back to him. You didn't have the hassle of selling it, or of buying the cloth. I did that for several years. It was regular money when we needed it.

I was anything but a family man, but then if we had lived together as a normal couple I don't think our marriage would have lasted two years because we were really incompatible. I think it's like a lot of relationships. It was great at first, but when the passion faded, coupled with my frequent absences from home, we had only friendship to fall back on. And we soon realised we had little, if anything, in common. I was never the most attentive of husbands and had a tendency to become pre-occupied even then. I think I'm being kind on myself – let's call it forgetful. A perfect example was the day I took my son out for a walk in his pram.

At the time we lived at 123 Clapton Common, which leads on to Stamford Hill. I had just come back from South Africa with Cantor and Marie said to me: 'Do you know, you have never taken the baby out?'

It was true, I hadn't. So, dutifully, I walked him out and down the road in his pram. On the way I met some of the boys on the corner by the ABC Cinema, which has gone now. We all got talking and eventually I went home. I was about to go through the door when Marie put her head out and shouted: 'Where's the baby?'

I had forgotten all about him. I had to sprint back to Stamford Hill to fetch him. He was all right – just had the chocolate I'd given him all around his mouth. Somehow I don't think I was cut out for minding babies!

As for married life, I wasn't absolutely great at that either. Men's priorities, and what was expected of them, were far different in those days. I think it's much tougher to stay married now than it was in the 1950s. Nevertheless, I can say quite honestly that if I hadn't been in the boxing business, my wife and I would have been divorced many years ago. Now we are old, we can't be bothered. We have been separated for the last seven years, but I would say that of the 38 we were together, I spent half of them away from home. It was the only thing that kept our marriage together.

I suppose that's sad.

CHAPTER 4

The Underworld

It would have been impossible to have been around boxing in London in the 1950s and not meet an assortment of tough, heavy operators. Fortunately, boxing had given me a solid grounding in what life had to offer and physical intimidation never worried me in the slightest. I have never had any time for tough guys. I don't think there is a lower form of life than a person who trades on fear. I've been afraid a few times in my life, but of situations of which I had no control or knowledge, not of physical aggression. As any former fighter will tell you, once you've faced punches in a ring, nothing else bothers you.

Nevertheless, over the years my association with boxing served up some of the worst as well as the best of characters.

Jack 'Spot' Comer was one of them. From Aldgate, he considered himself a self-appointed Jewish representative in the underworld, a flipside 'King of the Jews' if you like. Not a pleasant individual. He once said to me: 'Where would the Jewish people in this country be without me?'

Incredibly, he was serious.

They called him 'Spot' because he always seemed to be on the spot when something nasty occurred. As my career improved, I began to attract some publicity and he seemed to resent the fact. Why, I haven't a clue, but all of these people were very publicity conscious. At the time the Government had introduced a 33 per cent entertainment tax against the takings from shows. The loophole was that if you ran a show for charity, you were exempt. It will come as no surprise then, when I tell you that charity shows suddenly seemed to spring up everywhere. I used to run shows for various charities and give them a share of what we made. On top of that we would hold auctions for the charity and pass collection boxes around.

One night Solly Cantor was topping the bill at Leyton Baths and Jack Spot came to the window of the box-office with a companion, a non-Jewish guy, just a tearaway. I happened to be there.

'Give me two tickets,' said Jack.

'What price?' I asked.

'You think I came all this way to *pay*?' he scoffed.

I have never liked bullies and thought quickly enough to say: 'But, it's not my show. It's a charity night.' Spot was ready to lean on us, but the guy with him saw sense and realised there wasn't much of a point to be made. 'Come on Jack, it's not worth it,' he said, before turning to me. 'Give us two tickets.'

He put £5 in the box. Ringside tickets were two guineas each, and so I gave him the 16 shillings change. Afterwards Spot wanted to make a pal of me, but I would have none of it.

Another heavy character of the time, Albert Dimes, was disenchanted by the result of the second Terry Downes-Paul Pender fight at Wembley in 1961. Presumably he had a substantial amount invested on the American and didn't take kindly to Pender's decision to retire on his stool at the end of the ninth round. Dimes and his henchmen followed Pender's manager, Sam Silverman, to the Pigalle club in the West End, called him outside and gave him a kicking. The police arrived when the dust had settled but Silverman said he was unable to identify anyone. Maybe that was so, and maybe it wasn't. Dimes was an Italian, Alberto Dimeo, and there was a famous fight in the West End when Jack Spot went for him with a razor. I think Spot got the better of it, but it was like half a draw – broken up before they went to the judges' scorecards!

Bobby Ramsey, a lightweight during the 1940s and one-time manager of a West End club, was another who considered himself a big shot. He was a minder for Jack Spot and was an influence on the Kray twins when they were young. After shows at Leyton Baths, I would go to an all-night restaurant in Aldgate Avenue because it was one place where you knew you could get a meal. I walked in with a fighter I managed called Jimmy Cardew, and as I did Ramsey, who was sitting down, said sneeringly: 'Here he is, with his tuppenny ha'penny fighters.' I was furious.

'You were supposed to be a good fighter,' I said. 'What have you got now?'

'What are you talking about?' he replied. 'I've got property.'

'What, you mean that place you served 18 months in. They let you keep it?'

Ramsey didn't appreciate the joke and wanted to take the matter outside. Things turned ugly.

'Don't you threaten me,' I said, 'because I've got the best minders in the world. They all wear blue uniforms. And if you try anything with me, you'll find I'm the biggest copper's nark that ever lived.'

In the mid-1950s Ramsey was jailed for seven years for

grievous bodily harm. Along with Ronnie Kray and another villain named Billy 'The Fox' Jones he had attacked a man in an East End pub ... with a bayonet. When the police stopped their car afterwards, they also found an axe, a gun and a crowbar. Kray and Jones got three years. Ronnie Kray was actually certified as insane while in jail for that spell.

I knew the Krays as teenagers. They were boxing during the time I was making matches at Leyton Baths. Let me tell you, the story which they told about them being unbeaten prospects was a load of rubbish. Their elder brother Charlie was an accomplished fighter, a tough guy and very capable. Of the twins, Ronnie was really useless. It was hard to find him a win. Reggie was more useful, but only in comparison to Ronnie, who lost more than he won, even when I was picking his opponents! They were managed by Jack Jordan, who never became famous as a manager, but who had trained Dick Corbett and Harry Lazar. We had no idea what would become of the twins, and even in the 1960s when they were at their height we knew the nature of their business but not the extent of it, and we certainly were not aware that they were such cold-blooded killers. I remember Danny Vary, who trained me and later looked after the twins, saying: 'They are nice lads, good to their parents and always polite,' adding without a sense of the irony that the words would later assume. 'Mind you, Reggie can be a bit spiteful . . .'

In their early days they worked for Jack Spot and Ramsey, then of course branched out on their own and became the most famous gangsters in British history.

I hadn't been in contact with either of the twins for years when, in 1964, at the height of their terror, they tried to attend the opening night of our newly-formed Anglo-American Sporting Club. Jarvis Astaire, Ivor Barnard, an optician who liked to dabble in boxing promotion, and I started the club at the London Hilton in Park Lane. This was especially prestigious because it was the first Hilton to be built in this country and we naturally wanted our club to reflect the status of its surroundings. We were in the process of building membership before the first show on 12 October 1964, with the legendary Sugar Ray Robinson top of the bill against Johnny Angel, a Nigerian who was living in London.

I had a man working for me, Archie Kasler, who hustled membership for us on a 10 per cent commission basis. For example, if he sold a 50 guinea membership I paid him a fiver. Archie was a gambler with a great sense of humour but was always short of money. I liked him. One day he sent me the name of a prospective member which I didn't fancy. I said to Archie:

'I am worried about this guy . . . about the kind of person he will bring along.'

'Why?' said Archie. 'He's fine. There won't be a problem.'

It must have been a quiet time, a day where nothing much was coming in so, reluctantly, I let it go. It turned out to be a gross error of judgement.

We had a system whereby we sent out cards for members to fill in, confirming their attendance, telling us how many guests they were bringing and the names of the guests in order for us to place name cards on the tables. They also enclosed the cheque for the tickets for the guests. I received the card from this man for a table of ten, with a cheque, about a week to 10 days before the opening night. I looked through the guests and saw the name 'R.Kray' twice. You didn't need to be Einstein to realise, and so I rang Archie to give him a broadside. He seemed puzzled at my reaction. 'They're all right, Mickey,' he said. 'They'll behave themselves.'

But I wasn't happy so I rang the guy involved:

'I have received your form with your guest list and cheque.' I said.

'Yeah, looking forward to it.'

'I see you are planning to bring Reggie and Ronnie Kray.'

And he used exactly the same words that Archie had used. 'Well, they're all right. They behave themselves.'

'I have got nothing personal against them,' I said 'but people will object to their presence. It's our opening night and I don't want anything to go wrong.'

'But I've already invited them,' he said. 'I don't want to tell them they can't come, but if you want to phone them . . .'

I was perfectly happy to do that. They had boxed for me as kids and didn't scare me. I took Reggie's number from the man who had invited them and rang. After I had told him who it was, I came straight to the point.

'Reggie, it's nothing personal, but you are well known guys and a lot of straight people will object to you being there.'

'Why?' said Reggie. 'We go to the Palladium.'

'The Palladium is a public building,' I said. 'You don't have to be a member to go there. But this is a private members' club. To show you it's nothing personal, I have got a show at Wembley coming up. If you want to buy [and I stressed the word] ringside seats, I will put you in the first row, facing the TV cameras. That's a public show and anyone who wants to can come.'

He wasn't convinced so we eventually agreed to meet in a pub in Vallance Road, Stepney, near their family house. After shaking hands, they drove me to the Blind Beggar pub. They bought me a drink and we sat at a table. Reggie did the talking.

'Why have you put the block on us?' he said.

'If you are allowed in the hotel management are bound to ask what kind of a club we are running,' I replied.

'Well,' said Reggie. 'The Richardsons are on your guest list.'

I didn't know them at the time, but I promised to look at it. They accepted the position and Reggie said: 'If we can't go, we can't go. We wanted to do business with you and you gave us the blow out. We have friends who are stars, like Judy Garland, and we don't need to go to your club.'

Even so, they invited me to see Miss Garland and her daughter Liza Minelli, who were in concert that night in London, but the last thing I needed was a social evening with the Krays. I talked myself out of it. When I returned, I found the guest list included Charlie and Eddie Richardson and one of their leading heavies 'Mad' Frankie Fraser. I satisfied myself that we didn't need them either and cancelled their tickets.

The Richardsons, officially scrap metal dealers but in reality gangsters who controlled the south London under-world, eventually received huge sentences in a notorious case known at the time as the Torture Trial. Charlie Richardson was sent down for 25 years, Eddie Richardson 15 and Frankie Fraser 10. Other gang members were also jailed. In a bizarre twist, Fraser later offered to give evidence in defence of the Krays at their trial.

The day after I had resolved the situation with Reggie Kray, George Whiting from the London *Evening Standard* rang me at the office in Wardour Street. I liked George – he was a character and of course an extremely competent boxing writer.

'I heard you barred the Kray twins from the opening night of the Anglo-American Sporting Club,' he began.

'George, are you telling me your readers are interested in that?'

'Son,' he said, 'Let me decide what's of interest to my readers.'

'In that case,' I told him, 'I have no comment to make at all.'

The next day the Standard headline was 'Don't Come To The Hilton' and Whiting's story began: 'Two famous ex-boxers, Reg and Ronnie Kray, have been barred from the opening night of the Anglo-American Sporting Club at the London Hilton Hotel.' It was no surprise to me at all to receive a telephone call.

'Hello. You know who this is,' the voice said. 'Why did you have to put it in the paper?'

'Reg, I didn't,' I insisted. 'In fact, I tried to keep it out. If you look at the story, I had no comment to make.'

'Well, we have put it down to you. And none of your friends will be able to help you.'

'Do what you like,' I said. And I put the phone down.

The opening night went off well, with Sugar Ray Robinson and without the Krays, and soon afterwards I had to fly to Miami to see the American promoter Chris Dundee regarding the world light-heavyweight title fight between Terry Downes and the champion, Willie Pastrano, we had planned for Belle Vue arena, Manchester, at the end of November. (Pastrano knocked out Downes in the 11th round of a good fight.) Marie and I were living in Tenterden Grove, Hendon, at the time in a flat called Raymead. In those days when I travelled I always called Marie every day to see how things were and check what had happened. One day she seemed a bit off-hand. She was impatient to end the conversation. The next day it was the same, and finally I said:

'Look, what's the matter with you? I don't like your attitude.'

'Oh' she sighed, 'now it's all over, I might as well tell you. The morning you left, the postman delivered a parcel, wrapped up as a present with paper and ribbons. I took it, opened it ... and there were four dead rats inside.'

It was a message, of course. I suspect there were four rats because they had been misinformed that I had two children, not one. Marie had obviously been upset, but she is a strong person. She immediately rang Jack Manning, who was head of the murder squad at Scotland Yard. She knew I was friendly with him and that he was a guest at our shows. In later years he became a regular at the Anglo-American. He put a police guard on our flat, and on the shop which we owned and which my wife ran in Hounslow. It was a fancy goods store, 1001 Bargains. We used to call them swag shops. Manning also told her to take the same route to work each day – in other words, they tailed her, and he placed a guard on Gary at his boarding school. A police officer took away the rats. When I came back, I saw Jack and thanked him very much for taking it so seriously and acting so thoroughly.

'I don't think you'll have any more trouble with them,' he said. 'They were on my manor and I pulled them in. I told them, "If anything happens to Mickey Duff or his family or anyone he is connected with, I will close down every drinking club in the West End."'

The Krays used to take protection money from clubs and if an owner refused to pay the place was routinely smashed up. I heard no more from them, although they enjoyed a celebrity lifestyle and were often photographed in the company of boxers and people from high society. Ironically, the twins were arrested after an investigation led by Leonard 'Nipper' Read, who is now the chairman of the British Boxing Board of Control, and in March 1969, they were sentenced to life imprisonment with a recommendation of a minimum of 30 years for the murders of George Cornell, who was shot in the head at the Blind Beggar, and Jack 'The Hat' McVitie, who was killed in an East End flat. When they arrested Ronnie, they found a piece of paper in a coat pocket which contained a chilling message. Under the headline 'These Men Must Die' was a list of names. Mine was on it, and so was Terry Downes'. When a police officer told me, all I could think of to say was: 'I hope they were going to kill us in alphabetical order!'

I went to watch the closing stages of their trial at the invitation of David Hopkin, who was then in the office of the Director of Public Prosecutions and who was later chairman of the British Board of Control before Nipper Read. I had a good seat behind the jury where the twins could see me. Ronnie looked at me as if he could kill me on the spot but Reggie mouthed 'All right?' as if we were old friends.

Ronnie, who was eventually committed to Broadmoor, died inside and Reggie has never been released.

CHAPTER 5

Sweet Like Sugar

Who is the greatest pound for pound fighter of all-time? That's a question I'm often asked and, due to the length of time I've been in this business and the number of fighters I've been involved with, I'm probably as well qualified as anyone else to make a judgement. But it's impossible to say for sure whether Jack Dempsey, for instance, would have beaten Mike Tyson and how could you equate the nimble brilliance of Willie Pep with the sheer power of George Foreman.

But, if I was forced, I'd have to say Sugar Ray Robinson was the greatest fighter *I* ever saw. He had everything a boxer needs: he had style, skills, combination punching, a phenomenal chin, a champion's heart and the ability to take a man out with one shot. I was fortunate enough to be involved with him in the 1960s when he was in the twilight of his career. It was a privilege. Like most other people who saw him as a middleweight in his thirties, I wish I had watched him when he was welterweight champion in the second half of the 1940s.

He was the best welterweight in the world long before they let him fight for the title, but sadly no film exists, or at least has been discovered, of his 147lb championship battles.

Look at the champions he beat in those early years: Sammy Angott, Fritzie Zivic, Jake La Motta, the great Homicide Hank – Henry Armstrong, Marty Servo and Izzy Janazzo. La Motta, the Bronx Bull, was the only man to get a decision over him in his first decade as a professional. That was in Detroit in 1943, and three weeks later Robinson put the record straight in the same town.

When Robinson came to Europe in the summer of 1951, he was like a movie star. He had a pink Cadillac, an astonishing entourage which included his personal barber and a midget who acted as his interpreter in France and a kind of resident clown everywhere else. Before he arrived in London to fight Randolph Turpin at Earls Court in July, he had taken in Paris, Zurich, Antwerp, Liege, Berlin and Turin . . . and had fought in every city. Only nine days before he defended his middleweight title against Turpin, he stopped Cyrille Delannoit in Turin.

Of course, very few expected anything but a glorified exhibition from the great man against Turpin. I was still struggling along in those days and Jack Solomons promoted the fight. Was I there? Is the Pope a Catholic? On that night if you were a fight fan there was nowhere else to be. The atmosphere was amazing as the fight unfolded and it gradually dawned on everyone that Turpin was winning. It was a magnificent night. It's possible that Robinson was jaded from his summer tour, but that didn't matter to us. Turpin won. Strangely, when I saw the tape of the fight a short time ago it was fairly tame, but of course the atmosphere on the night made it all very exciting. Only 64 days later at New York Polo Grounds, Robinson was losing again and badly cut when he produced the kind of barrage of punches in the 10th round that made him the great champion he was. Turpin was knocked down and then stopped while swaying on his feet. Robinson took him out when he had to. That was the kind of thing he could do.

Robinson was already 31, but eventually held the world middleweight championship five times, fighting the greatest names of his day like Carmen Basilio, Gene Fullmer, Carl Olson and, when he tried to win the world light-heavyweight title, Joey Maxim. That night in front of 48,000 people in Yankee Stadium he almost became a three-weight world champion, but was unable to come out for round 14 because of heat exhaustion. He couldn't lift himself off the stool. It was so hot and humid that referee Ruby Goldstein was replaced after the tenth round because he was close to collapse. His substitute, Ray Miller, took over and said Goldstein's scorecard was so sweat-soaked that his score for the previous three rounds was illegible. Maxim, the naturally bigger man and a very good fighter in his own right, had been able to conserve his energy better than Robinson, who was eventually carried from the ring.

Sugar Ray was fighting in world class company for 20 years and was almost 41 when he took Fullmer 15 rounds in a National Boxing Association title fight in the city I would come to have a special affection for, Las Vegas, Nevada. I met Basilio and Fullmer at my induction into the International Hall of Fame in June 1999.

I didn't like Robinson's manager George Gainford, but through an agent we used at the time, Dewey Fragetta, we did manage to persuade Ray to come to England in the early 1960s. Fragetta, an old style hustler who had worked with people like Rocky Graziano when he was middleweight champ in the forties, was helpful to us for many years until we had a fall out. We discovered he was making his money twice, charging us and the fighters he was sending over for us. He was a thief with a licence.

Nevertheless, through Fragetta I met Gainford and I was able to make a deal for Ray to come to Britain in September 1962 to box Terry Downes at the Empire Pool, Wembley. By then, I was working in partnership with Jarvis Astaire, with Harry Levene as the figurehead of the promotion. We offered Robinson a guarantee of $30,000 and he accepted. He arrived in Southampton on the 'Queen Elizabeth' and almost as soon as the great liner docked, he held a press conference. Inevitably, the journalists wanted to know if, at 42, he was fighting for money alone. In other words, was he broke? He was amazingly open with them. 'The dough I can use,' he said. 'None of us ever gets too much money.'

He added that he was also fighting for pride and because he genuinely believed he could be middleweight world champion for a sixth time. He told George Whiting that the Inland Revenue Service in America had left him 'nickels and dimes' and were withholding payments against future tax amounting to more than half a million dollars. By then, Peter Wilson had already written a dreadfully negative story in the *Daily Mirror* demanding to know how we had the cheek to bring a pathetic, old Robinson over to fight Downes, who was 25 years old and had lost the world middleweight title back to Paul Pender in Boston only five months earlier. Wilson ended his story by declaring pompously that he was fortunate in that he would not be present to witness the debacle because he would be covering another event.

Harry Levene panicked as soon as he read it. Wilson was one of the most powerful writers in Fleet Street. 'I am going to cancel the show,' said Harry. 'My reputation is at stake.'

It was a lot of rubbish. The tickets were selling like wildfire. But Levene's nerve had gone. Jarvis knew that Levene had a lot of respect for the great American promoter, George Parnassus, who worked in Los Angeles and Las Vegas but was at the time in London. Jarvis had breakfast with him at the Dorchester, explained the problem and then escorted George to Levene's office in Soho. Parnassus said, in his thick Greek accent: 'Harry, when was the last time Peter Wilson bought a ticket to see a fight? When the newspapermen start buying their tickets, then you start listening to them.'

Levene could have a childish attitude, but to be fair to him he was an elderly man when he worked with us. I didn't know him in his prime and he must have been far more capable then than he was when we dealt with him because he would never have succeeded in any kind of business!

As it turned out, Wilson was almost right. Downes knocked hell out of Robinson for nine rounds. At the end of the eighth, the corner were forced to use an inhaler to revive the old champion. Then in the last session, Ray found something from somewhere, opened up and did a number on our man. Downes survived and won clearly and we were vindicated . . . just! The crowd gave Robinson a standing ovation as he left the ring and, typically, he did not complain about the decision. George Gainford, his manager, lacked that kind of class. He was quickly whingeing about a robbery, but people ignored him. I was very pleased to see Downes's reaction.

'It would be a liberty to say I beat Robinson,' he said. 'I won, but I didn't beat the real Sugar Ray. The name was the same, but I beat a 42-year-old man who was going through the motions. I cannot imagine what it must have been like fighting him at his peak.'

Ray stayed in Europe for a couple of months on a tour which we helped organise and won fights in Vienna and Lyons. When we brought him back to Britain, it was September 1964 in Paisley on the outskirts of Glasgow, with a

Coventry-Irishman, Mick Leahy, as his opponent. Leahy was a tough guy from Cork who was by then a naturalised British subject. He was British middleweight champion when he fought Robinson, but was in the middle of a bad run with three defeats in his last four fights. Even at the age of 44, Robinson had lost only to world champ Joey Giardello in his last 15 outings. I had actually been involved in the promotion of his most recent fight in, of all places, Omaha, Nebraska, where he drew a 10-rounder with a local prospect, Art Hernandez.

We felt Leahy was a reasonable opponent, who would stand up but who was unlikely to win. Leahy was a popular, aggressive fighter whose style was a perfect blend for the cultured boxing skills of Sugar Ray. Before the fight there was a piece of controversy when Robinson came in overweight, even after trying to shed pounds with a run around a park. Leahy's manager George Middleton, who ironically had managed Randolph Turpin, claimed a financial forfeit, as he was entitled to do in the terms of the match contract. At the end of 10 hard rounds, I thought Robinson had won, but referee Ike Powell gave it to Leahy. It was one of those things, although once again Gainford was yelling at anyone who would listen and, for that matter, anyone who wouldn't. 'It's a disgrace,' he said. 'Boxing will die in Britain if you get more decisions like this.'

Robinson took the verdict with dignity but was terribly disappointed. He told the press he thought he had won but praised Leahy for his persistence. However, when he spoke to me he was extremely despondent. It seemed to him that he was somehow jinxed here. He had lost to Turpin, Downes and now Leahy. We had already booked him to top the bill on the opening night of the Anglo-American Sporting Club the following month, which was of course very important to us. He was in Europe picking up exhibition money and also had a contest in Paris lined up, after which he was scheduled to return to London, fight for us and at the same time be our guest of honour.

Robinson was the sort of guy who needed to be busy, who liked to have a fight every ten days or two weeks, but he looked shattered as he said to me: 'Mickey, I am going home. I'm not going to your show at the Hilton. I can't win a fight here.' I needed to say something quickly, and came up with: 'Ray, you will win your next fight even if I have to go in there and take a dive myself.'

The joke turned him around. He laughed, and agreed to stay. Even then the fighter I picked, Johnny Angel, looked like beating him for three rounds. In the end, Robinson won in round six . . . to my great relief.

By this time Sugar Ray was staying in hotel rooms rather than suites. His fabulous entourage had been reduced to his wife Millie and about five others, including his trainer. He was living almost from fight to fight. After the Angel job he was contracted to box for us once more in Newcastle, but he said he could not honour it because his mother was sick. He said he had to fly home immediately. 'You only have one mother,' he said, sadly.

I knew he didn't like flying and accepted the severity of the situation at his word. We understood and wished him well, then discovered some time later that he had taken the boat, which took five days to reach New York. He wasn't that desperate to see his mother, after all – he had simply had enough.

He fought on until a world class fighter, Joey Archer, outpointed him in Pittsburgh in November 1965. It was his 202nd recognised fight and he made his retirement official at a great celebration at Madison Square Garden the following month. He was given a big party by Pennsylvania promoter Don Elbaum around that time. Elbaum has been hustling around for years – and I always said if he took a job as an undertaker people would stop dying. Elbaum somehow found Robinson's first professional opponent, whom the record books tell us was named Joe Echevarria, and produced a beautiful cake with candles.

Ray was in tears when Elbaum also pulled off one final, sensational move – he produced the great man's gloves from that far off night a quarter of a century before. Robinson looked at those battered horse-hair gloves and the memories must have come flooding back as he turned them over in his hands. Then a photographer asked him to put them on for a picture and Elbaum began saying 'No, no.' Robinson went to put one on his left hand, only to find both were right hand gloves. Part of him crumbled with the humiliation and part of him was furious at having been used as a promotional tool. Elbaum fled the room.

Looking back on those days when we dealt with Robinson they did not seem especially sad. We can all use hindsight and say of course they were – a 44-year-old man going on way past his magnificent prime – but it didn't come over that way to us at the time. Boxing was what he did, and what he wanted to do. I was glad, and still am, to have been a small part of his story.

CHAPTER 6

Fighting Solomons

My friendship with Jarvis Astaire has been one of the great, enduring pleasures of my life. I met him first when we both spent time in Bill Klein's gym in the West End when we were young men. Jarvis, who is a few years older than me, at one time managed Billy Thompson from Hickleton Main in Yorkshire. Thompson held the British and European lightweight titles in the five or six years after the war and moved on when his contract was bought by Benny Huntman, when Jarvis became too busy with his other business commitments to concentrate on a championship-class boxer.

Huntman, incidentally, was a fantastic character and a great motivator in a corner. He was also unscrupulous. He once sold far more than 100 per cent of the contract of Eric Boon, when the crowd-pleasing lightweight was boxing in South Africa towards the end of his career, to a variety of excited South African backers. (Boon was involved in one of the greatest fights I ever saw against Robert Villemain of

France at Harringay Arena in 1948. Today he would have made millions.) Huntman's own career ended when he upset Jack Solomons. One of Benny's fighters was beaten and he said: 'Jack, I will build them up – and you knock them down.' That was the end of him professionally. Solomons froze him out.

I don't think Jarvis and I have had more than two arguments in all the years we have known each other. We shout at each other all the time and anybody listening to our conversations might think we were sworn enemies. But we have retained our independence and freedom of thought and if we don't agree, we say so. We don't fall out about it. He has never wanted the limelight and boxing has remained primarily a serious hobby for him. Most of his business interests are, and always have been, outside the sport.

We began to work together properly when he managed the British welterweight champion from Clapham, Peter Waterman, in the 1950s. Jarvis needed somebody to provide or check the rank and file opponents Waterman was facing on the way up. I think I can say that even as a young man I taught him a lot about boxing – and he taught me a lot about life and about right and wrong.

I was invited by Jarvis to work in Waterman's corner with Snowy Buckingham, Peter's main trainer. Buckingham, who had snow-white hair, was a big name at the time but I felt he was a fraud. Although he had handled Larry Gains in the old days, he did not know that much. Peter thought a lot of my opinion and from then on I was with him through the whole of his career, which ended in 1958. He had two fights with the former world welterweight champion Kid Gavilan.

Peter won at Harringay in February 1956 and Gavilan outpointed him in the return at Earls Court two months later. The verdict in the first fight caused a storm with sustained boos and cat-calls from the crowd of more than 10,000. Most of the national press said the verdict of referee Ben Green was an outrage. I didn't see anything terribly wrong with it, and neither did the trade paper, *Boxing News*, who felt Gavilan slapped and cuffed too much with the inside of the glove. These punches don't count. However, in the rematch Waterman was well beaten, knocked down and decisively outpointed. It was his first defeat in 33 contests.

Way back in those early days I worked with the Bodinetz brothers, Curley Carr and later Harry Grossmith. Carr, whose daughter Rita was my landlady at the start of my married life, ran Curley's Cafe in the Whitechapel Road and Grossmith had a millinery business. We built up talent there and then moved to Shoreditch Town Hall when the season ended. Carr dropped out, Grossmith was joined by his son Bernie for a time, and we made some headway. Jarvis and I were partners with Grossmith, although Jarvis never worked with Carr or the Bodinetz brothers. I received £15 a week wages and I think 15 per cent of the profits at the end of the season. I don't think Jarvis ever bothered with his share from Shoreditch – we all thought it was a joy to work there.

Shoreditch was a fantastic venue with a wonderful atmosphere. The closest arena London has to it now is the York Hall in Bethnal Green, but Shoreditch, a smoky, compact fighting pit with an old-fashioned balcony which almost overhung the ring, had a magic that was impossible to define or explain. They were wonderful days and were responsible, more than anything else, for my evolution into a successful matchmaker, promoter and manager.

The opening night at Shoreditch on 14 May 1957 was incredible in that two future world middleweight champions topped the bill ... for a total of £195, including expenses! Terry Downes received £135 and Dick Tiger £60. Eighteen months later it would have cost me ten times that outlay. I thought I had done my homework. Downes, who was managed by Jarvis at the start of his career and later co-managed by Jarvis and Sam Burns, was our star. I had seen Tiger lose to a nobody in Liverpool and thought he was a perfect opponent – one who would make a show but wouldn't be good enough to win.

Like many other African fighters of the day, Tiger had travelled to Liverpool a couple of years earlier and had not made much impact. He was already 27 years old, only a couple of months younger than me, and had lost almost as many as he had won in Britain. We had absolutely no idea that he would go on to be first the middleweight and then the light-heavyweight champion of the world.

In Downes we knew we had a sensation. He was a brash lad of 21 from Paddington who had moved to America when his sister, who was working there in a circus, lost an arm in a traffic accident. Terry had joined the US Marines and was being considered for the 1956 Olympic team when the authorities discovered he was British. He turned professional, managed by Jarvis but with Solomons having first promotional claim on his services, in April 1957 and scored quick wins over Peter Longo and Jimmy Lynas.

Then of course Tiger stunned everyone. He was a revelation. By the end of round six, when Terry was retired by his cornerman Snowy Buckingham, the 'Paddington Express' had been well and truly derailed. His right eye was badly swollen, he had a jagged cut across the bridge of his nose and he had been floored three times. Jarvis tried to do a salvage job in the dressing room, pointing out to writers that Tiger had come in unexpectedly heavy at 11st 11lbs and, even after being forced to shed a couple of pounds, had a weight advantage of more than five pounds. A reporter asked Downes whether he had been aware of Tiger's size in the ring. 'Yeah, he did look a big middleweight to me too,' said Downes. 'Then I realised I was lying down and he was standing up!'

Even at that stage Downes had a way of making people like him, and he went on to become one of Britain's favourite fighters of the day. At the same press conference he told writers: 'I'll just have to go back and start again ... with flyweights!'

Following on from that theme, a reporter asked him who he would like to fight next. 'The bastard who made this match,' he said. Which was my cue to slide away!

After that fight, however, I was in his corner in almost all of his fights. Downes was a wonderful character to deal with. In March 1958, he did me a favour by stepping in as a substitute at Leyton Baths when the former Olympic flyweight gold medallist Terry Spinks had to withdrew from the main event. I made a new top of the bill and persuaded Downes it would be an easy job against a Tunisian named Ben Salah Fahrat. He was introduced as the 'Dashing, Crashing, Bashing Terry Downes' and the crowd gave him a welcome roar. Everything was going nicely when Fahrat suddenly landed a right hand in round two, and Terry went down. He came back to the corner at the end of the round and said: 'Where did you get this geezer from?'

Then, in the fourth, it happened again and Downes fell down by the corner, stuck his head under the ropes and yelled at me through his gumshield: 'Nice easy job this is, innit?'

Eventually he won in the fifth when he pounded Fahrat with such a furious bombardment the referee had to step in. Terry had a cut lip and a bashed-up eye, and a couple of loose teeth, and when he climbed down from the ring, he looked at me sideways and said: 'Mickey, do me a favour. Don't get me any more of these easy jobs in the future.'

By the end of that year Downes was British middleweight

champion. In January 1961 he lost a world title challenge against 'Fighting Fireman' Paul Pender in Boston because of cuts and then on a wonderful night six months later he forced Pender to retire after nine rounds at the Empire Pool, Wembley. The Americans made the excuse that their man was suffering from a cold and they had considered pulling him out of the fight, only to be dissuaded by Pender himself, who had trained for six weeks and did not want to disappoint his fans – or delay collecting his guaranteed payday of around $100,000 including expenses. Maybe it was true, and maybe not. Frankly, I couldn't have cared less. What mattered was that Terry Downes became our first world champion. We were by then presenting Jack Solomons with a significant challenge – and British boxing with a serious alternative.

Incidentally, at a press conference the day after Downes won the title, a female reporter from the *London Evening News* called out what she thought was a clever question. 'Mr Downes, I understand boxers look at either an opponent's eyes or feet when they are in the ring. Which do you do?' Terry looked at her for a moment before saying: 'To tell you the truth, darling, I always look at his gloves – because I haven't been clouted by anybody's eyes yet.'

Terry always had a wild sense of humour – he once played a practical joke on me on a visit to Massachusetts by having his old friends in the local police force 'arrest me' for a supposed gambling offence. It was some time before they revealed it was a wind-up.

Downes did well out of boxing. He lost the title back to Pender on a 15-round decision in Boston in 1962, and retired after losing in the 11th round to Willie Pastrano in a world light-heavyweight title fight at Belle Vue, Manchester, in 1964. He was winning that one until Pastrano received a slap from his trainer, Angelo Dundee, at the start of round

11. It woke Pastrano from his lethargy and he found the punches that saved his title.

During the build-up to that fight, I became friendly with Tommy Steele, the Cockney showbiz star who had made his name first as a rock 'n roll singer and then in cabaret with shows like 'Half A Sixpence'. He was performing at a theatre in Manchester and I was working at promoting the fight. He was often kicking his heels during the day, we started hanging around together and he got a kick out of coming to the gym to watch the fighters train. At nights, if there was nothing much happening, I quite enjoyed going to see his show. He was a smashing guy.

Downes retired and, with Sam Burns, ran a string of high street betting shops. Burns, who was Jack Solomons' office manager until 1955, was by then working with us. They were eventually bought out at a substantial profit by the Hurst Park Syndicate, owners of the Surrey racecourse of the same name. In turn William Hill bought Hurst Park and Jarvis was a board member there for many years.

By then we had developed into a major force in British boxing with Mike Barrett our partner at the Royal Albert Hall and Harry Levene as our promotional figurehead at Wembley. The great years were approaching.

CHAPTER 7

Heavyweight Heroes

The heavyweight division is the promotional gemstone of boxing. Fans love the big guys, even though their skill levels may not be as high as fighters from lower weight divisions and consequently promoters love them because they sell more tickets than anyone else.

Henry Cooper was by far the best British heavyweight of his generation and the 1960s also gave us one of the biggest ticket sellers of the time in the 'Blond Bomber' from West Ham, Billy Walker.

Cooper had big fights with men like Brian London, Dick Richardson and Joe Erskine, a beautiful boxer from Cardiff who would have been a great fighter if he'd been blessed with a punch to match his speed and ringcraft. Erskine was managed by Benny Jacobs, a short, stubby, portly Welshman who was one of the characters of the time with a dry sense of humour. He knew boxing, and he knew the strokes he could pull as a manager, but while he did very well for his boxers, he could get a bit mixed up about money. He also happened to be a serious gambler who won and lost sizeable sums on the horses and in casinos, so he was often in need of cash. I think he stole from promoters. Promoters can look after themselves and I have no sympathy if a manager overcharges on, say, expenses to get to the show. A favourite trick of unscrupulous managers is to skim money off the top of a fighter's purse. They take the gross, take a cut for themselves, then tell the fighter the gross is less than it actually is – and then charge what the boxer believes is the correct percentage. The fighter is none the wiser unless contracts are in writing, which all too often they are not. This may or may not have been what Jacobs was up to, but really he was a robber by necessity, not nature! I liked him even though he was a rogue. At the end of Erskine's career he left Jacobs, whom I remember quite clearly protesting: 'How do you like him leaving me after all the years I've been stealing from him?'

I never got along with Jim 'The Bishop' Wicks, who managed Henry Cooper and trained his boxers at the Thomas a' Beckett in the Old Kent Road. The general picture that has been created of Wicks as an avuncular, genial old man is only a part of the story. Cooper will not have a bad word said about him and was loyal to him from start to finish. I admire that. In fact, for years I think they worked without even bothering with an official contract. Wicks in turn did a wonderful job for Cooper, taking some risks but not others. He would never, for example, let Henry anywhere near Sonny Liston. However, Wicks was aggressively jealous of anybody talking to his fighters. If anybody tried, he would say: 'I'm the manager. You want to talk about boxing to any of my fighters? You talk to me.'

He never remembered anybody's name. We used to call him Jim Whatsisname. I got on with his son Jackie, who was box office manager for Harry Levene, but not Jim. Jackie must have taken his personality from his mother! I never built a good relationship with Wicks. He tolerated me because if he wanted fights at Wembley he had to talk to me. I stood back and was quite happy for him to make his end of the deals with Levene. Jarvis and I had rehearsed Harry well before he ever went in to talk with Wicks anyway and I was happy to keep him at arms' length. He wasn't one of my kind of people. Years before that, in 1954, he had joined Solomons in talking darkly about the supposed threat of a 'syndicate' which hoped Jack would soon leave the game. He even put his name to quotes in a story in the *Daily Herald* which claimed: 'Only Jack Solomons can save the sport from this menace.'

Eventually he saw that his best business position was outside the Solomons umbrella. Henry was skilful and could punch of course with the left hook which Wicks labelled 'Enry's Ammer', but he wasn't quite big enough. He was tall at more than six feet, but his best weight was about 13st 7lbs, which by today's standards would have made him a cruiserweight, and at the very top level even in those days you needed to be bigger.

By the time he beat Brian London for the British and Empire heavyweight titles at Earls Court in January 1959, Cooper was already established as a world class fighter. He had proved that the previous October by outboxing the world number two, Zora Folley, which was his first appearance on a Harry Levene promotion at Wembley. The story goes that Levene had already lined up Sonny Liston as Cooper's opponent for that fight after talking to Chris Dundee, the elder and more influential brother of Angelo, in Miami. Wicks hadn't seen Liston, but had already been warned off him by Jim Norris, the American who ran the International Boxing Club in New York. Eventually, Zora Folley came in as a substitute, wasn't properly fit and was outpointed.

Henry lost a rematch with Folley, in two rounds, in 1961 but by then was well established. He fought for us and for Solomons in the early days and then stuck with us more as our power base increased. Over the years he defended against the best British heavyweights of the time: Joe Erskine three times, Dick Richardson, Brian London, Johnny Prescott, Jack Bodell and Billy Walker. And of course, he fought Muhammad Ali for the world heavyweight title in 1966, three years after their controversial first fight when Henry floored Ali, or Cassius Clay as he was then, near the end of round four.

Incidentally, I don't hold with the view that Cooper almost knocked Clay out or that he would have beaten him if that big left hook had landed earlier in the round. Look at the tape and you will see that Clay was on his feet at the count of two or three and walking back to his corner because the bell had gone. They gave him smelling salts and worked on him hard, but he really turned it on in round five and his right hands made the cut, which Henry had picked up earlier, so bad that referee Tommy Little had to stop it.

People have made much of the tear in Clay's glove which bought him a little extra time at the end of round four and a legend has developed that Angelo Dundee was somehow responsible for either making the original tear or worsening it. I think that's rubbish. In my opinion Dundee wouldn't have been prepared to do something like that.

Jack Solomons promoted the first fight at Wembley Stadium in 1963, and we staged the rematch for the heavyweight title at Highbury in May 1966. It was a huge night for us financially of course but also very important in the long term as it took us into the big league, where we stayed for three decades. Cooper boxed well, but Ali was too quick for him and when Henry's eye cut again it was stopped in round six.

By then our team was established with Jarvis Astaire and Harry Levene as the unofficial joint promoters – Harry's name was on the official licence – and me working as match-maker. We worked similarly with Mike Barrett at the Albert Hall. Levene had been a very successful manager who had worked in the business, as I had, since his teens. He was, shall we say, somewhat tight-fisted. He had been in New York as a very young man and had seen the Jack Dempsey-Luis Firpo world title fight in 1923. I can guarantee you somebody else would have paid! At one time he had managed the Bagatelle club in Piccadilly where the Queen, then Princess Elizabeth, used to enjoy a little respectable night life. He lived in Park Lane, and then moved into an apartment in Great Cumberland Place near Marble Arch. Many years later I was to take a flat in the same building. I think he would have turned in his grave at the thought!

Levene had managed the great black Canadian heavyweight of the 1930s, Larry Gains, and the world class Manchester middleweight Jock McAvoy, who couldn't get a title shot in his own weight division. Jock eventually lost on points to light-heavyweight champ John Henry Lewis after fighting with a broken hand. Gains really was a star who would have fought for, and possibly won, the heavyweight title if he had not been frozen out of the picture during his peak years. Anyway, whatever the truths of that particular time, Levene's experience was considerable. He had run shows at the Albert Hall for some years but was unable to challenge Solomons effectively and had virtually drifted away. However, when he negotiated a promotional contract for the Empire Pool, Wembley, in 1956 it became possible to stage shows that could rival anything Solomons could do.

Harry was past his prime when I got involved with him. I am at an age now that I realise he could only think at a certain pace and consequently I can appreciate and understand him better, but he would always talk about what he did 25 years before. However, he never refused me anything

I thought I was entitled to, financially. That wasn't because he liked me, it was because he valued me. If he could have found somebody as good as I was for £4 cheaper, he would have given them the job. As far as we were concerned he was a weapon we could use to tackle Solomons, an ideal name which we could use in order to compete.

Solomons realised what a threat we would become, hated the thought of anyone opposing him and promptly named us 'The Syndicate', a term he had first used when he felt similarly threatened in the early 1950s. It was ridiculous. Our system was no different to the one he had operated for years. To make any business work, people have to work together in their different capacities, and that's all we did. Solomons eventually became very bitter, especially when Jarvis and I were instrumental in having his stooges voted off the Southern Area Council and so cut away some of his power base. Solomons, through the Board of Control, had once made a ridiculous attempt to drive me out of the game because I was not a British citizen. On another occasion, the Board restricted for a time the number of promoters for whom I could match fighters to four, which was scandalous. I never got on with Levene, but it was a relationship which succeeded, which is all that mattered.

As well as our promotions involving Henry Cooper, our development of Billy Walker was hugely important to us. His elder brother, George, boxed for the British light-heavyweight title in 1953, but lost to a Welshman named Dennis Powell. I was friendly with George when he was boxing under Sam Burns, when Sam worked for Solomons. He had a fairly successful career, then went into business and did well. Eventually, Billy came along and began to attract a lot of publicity. He was good looking, charming and could punch, and his career was launched for us by his starring role in the November 1961 amateur international when Great Britain whitewashed the USA 10–0 at Wembley. Walker flattened a big American named Cornelius Perry in the first round – laid him out cold like a scene from a movie. The knockout was the highlight of the BBC television coverage.

I went over to George, congratulated him and some time later he phoned me. 'I think my kid's ready to turn pro,' he said. I met George for lunch at Graham's in Poland Street, just off Oxford Street, and he really had no interest in Billy signing for Solomons, whom he felt had treated him badly during his own career. George asked for an initial three-fight contract for £5,000 a fight. I told him he must be crazy. We ended up making a deal for £10,000 for three fights.

'On one condition,' he said. 'I want the money up front.'

'What are you talking about, up front?' I said. 'Nobody does that.'

George explained that Billy wanted to use the money to back a restaurant venture which was to be known as Billy's Baked Potato. I went away, sat down and discussed it with Jarvis and Harry, and agreed to pay him what he wanted. Levene met him at the Dorchester Hotel and Billy signed a three-fight deal and topped the bill at Wembley in his professional debut over eight rounds on 27 March 1962. I knew he would be a tremendous attraction and we got our money back and were comfortably ahead, even after that first bout, a one-sided fifth round stoppage of a Belgian named Jose Peyre. On the same show we had good champions like Wally Swift, Terry Spinks and Mick Leahy, but Walker was a star from the beginning to the end of his career.

George Walker, who later made a fortune with the Brent Walker empire, was the toughest man in the world to deal with. He always gave you little stumbling blocks which made things dearer but never anything that bordered on the immoral. And he never broke his word. He continued to work with us because he had great confidence in my ability to select the right opponents for Billy. He knew I understood Billy's strengths and weaknesses and he appreciated my basic theory that it is impossible to develop fighters with hard fights. You will never succeed if you give a man wars all the time because by the time he has learned his trade he has little left. He's burned out. Sam Burns had a great saying, which I always tried to apply: 'The best way to manage fighters is to keep yourself in high society and your fighters in low society. Tell the world they are world-beaters but tell yourself they are nothing.'

George very cleverly always preferred, if he could, to finalise terms with Harry Levene because he felt he could get a better deal out of him – and usually he was right. He was, and is today, a smart man.

Once, the press slaughtered me over a bad performance by one of Walker's opponents, Charley Powell. He went over in a couple of rounds at Wembley in 1965. Some remarks even suggested it was a fix. I replied publicly: 'I know people sometimes suggest a fighter could have gone on after being floored, but boxers have varying degrees of courage. All right, I am in the hot seat. I made the match. I judged that Powell would be a good opponent for Walker. And he turned out to be inadequate, but it's easy to be wise afterwards. How many of the critics who have made such a fuss now said anything before the event?'

Walker was powerful, exciting and could punch, but he couldn't have beaten Henry Cooper. He didn't have enough skills. Eventually we made the match because we had taken Billy as far as we could in terms of building him up. The public wouldn't come along to see him fight ordinary opponents any more, and so there was nowhere else for us to go but into championship class. We hadn't protected him completely – he had ended Joe Erskine's career with a points win in 1964 and the previous year had slugged out two tremendous battles with another rising star, Johnny Prescott, a handsome, talented kid from Birmingham. Billy won the first fight on a stoppage and Prescott won the rematch on points.

By 1967, however, Billy was 28 and we had to push him forward. It was the right time for risks. In March he challenged German southpaw Karl Mildenberger for the European heavyweight title in front of a capacity crowd of 10,500 at the Empire Pool and was stopped in round eight. He was never in the fight. Mildenberger cut him over the left eye in the first round, outboxed and outpunched him and when the Dutch referee, who had already given Billy a standing count, stopped the fight blood was gushing out of the cut.

He took a rest of six months, then fought Cooper for the British and Empire titles. It was the same story as the Mildenberger fight, with Walker soaking up shots, refusing to give ground and forcing the pace. It was nowhere near enough and although Cooper was cut first, the fight was stopped when Walker picked up a much worse injury over his right eye. By the end the fans at ringside were yelling at referee George Smith to stop it. Looking back at the weights for that fight, it shows just how comparatively small our heavyweights were in those days: Cooper scaled 13st 5¾lbs and Walker 13st 10lbs.

That was the end of the 'Blond Bomber' as a championship level fighter and he retired in 1969 after packing out Wembley one last time. Jack Bodell stopped him. That night contained a moment of black humour at which the British excel. During the preliminary bouts the bandleader Billy Cotton, whose catch-phrase in his chat with audiences was 'Wakey, wakey!', collapsed at ringside and died, if not then, shortly afterwards. He was a huge sports fan who thoroughly enjoyed his boxing, but as he was stretchered away, the inevitable happened. He left the arena to cries of 'Wakey, wakey!' If he could have heard them, I'm sure he would have appreciated the gag.

Walker had met Her Majesty the Queen and Prime Minister, Harold Wilson. He had earned well and invested wisely. The year that he turned pro with us, he and George each bought a one-third stake in a garage, and also made money with the Billy's Baked Potato restaurants and other investments, including a taxi firm. After his retirement from the ring he lived in the Channel Islands for a long time and is back in England now. He has renewed his involvement in boxing by taking a position with the British Boxing Board of Control. I see him quite often and he's a charming man. It doesn't seem possible that he celebrated his 60th birthday in 1999.

Of the fighters in other weight divisions in the 1960s, I would say the Dartford lightweight Dave Charnley was by some distance the best British fighter since the war not to have won a world title. Charnley was exceptionally talented: short, strong and skilful – and a southpaw. He lost a bad decision to world champion Joe 'Old Bones' Brown on a Jack Solomons promotion at Earls Court. Referee Tommy Little had the needle with Charnley's manager Arthur Boggis – they had fallen out as young men – and wouldn't do him any favours. I thought he had won and the protests at the decision were so angry that some of the normally phlegmatic British press were provoked into losing their cool. Later, we promoted a rematch at Belle Vue, but Brown had lost his title by then and was well past his best. Charnley won easily in five rounds.

You could fill a book with names of world champions who were not as good as Charnley. He had bad luck – and Boggis. Arthur was the gamest manager who ever lived. When he was offered a match he never used to say 'Who?', he would say 'How much?' He put Charnley in with several unsuitable opponents along the way but by far the worst was the one which finished Dave's career against world welterweight champion Emile Griffith. It was absolutely ridiculous. Griffith was on the heavy side for a welterweight and would go on to be middleweight champ, while Charnley was a small lightweight. Fancy giving weight to a man like Griffith. There has to be co-operation between a boxer and a manager, and between them and a promoter. When you are talking about the moving and placing of boxers, you are talking about how many times they are going to get hit, or how many times they are going to hit another guy. It's a tough business and nobody should try to look at it any other way. We are capable of taking punches – more than we are sometimes led to believe, perhaps – but nothing is guaranteed. Boxing is dangerous. Charnley survived his career despite Boggis. He always negotiated top money and he did create a lot of precedents as far as the size of purses for smaller boxers is concerned, but the cost was obvious. Charnley was not protected as he should have been, and would have been if we had looked after him. Solomons used to have a saying: 'If you name the price, I name the opponent. If you name the opponent, I name the price.' I believe the proper line is somewhere between the two.

The 1960s produced some wonderful British fighters, some of whom we were involved with, and some of whom we were not. But as well as the champions I have always felt a great affinity for the bread and butter fighters who have no hope of winning a title, but who make some kind of living and work the circuit, often stepping in at late notice to save a show.

One of my all-time favourites was Joe Somerville, who was billed from Berkhampstead. Actually, he lived in a caravan in Hemel Hempstead but he fought so often and with such modest success that nobody bothered too much about the finer details. If you wanted a middleweight, Joe was your man. A light-heavyweight? Joe would be there. He wasn't a superstar, wasn't even a star for that matter, but I admired him. If he was overmatched he would work it out very quickly and get himself out without coming to any harm, but if he found he had half a chance he would fight as if he had a personal grudge.

One night he fought a headstrong prospect from Liverpool, Pat Dwyer, and frustrated him to the point where Dwyer hit him low, way down in the orchestra pit! When Joe heard the referee threaten to throw Dwyer out it was music to his ears. He clowned and goaded Dwyer again, boxing beautifully as the youngster lost his temper. In the next round another one sank in low and Somerville collapsed in a heap. Dwyer was disqualified. This so impressed one of the old doyens of the British national press, Desmond Hackett, that he made a foray into the dressing room to talk to Joe, whom he had somehow not noticed before.

'How old are you?' said Desmond.

'Thirty,' replied Joe.

'You were late turning pro.'

'I've been a pro ten years,' explained Joe, patiently.

'Well, how many fights have you had?'

'About 80.'

'How come I've never heard of you before?' said the suspicious Desmond.

'My manager's bringing me along slowly . . .'

My favourite moment with Somerville was a night at Shoreditch Town Hall when I was let down at the last minute and was in terrible trouble. I needed somebody to fight a local lad who had sold a bucketful of tickets and naturally thought of Joe. But it was 6.30 in the evening and Joe didn't have a phone in his caravan. It was too late to send a telegram and all I could think of was to ring the local police station, talk nicely to the sergeant and see if anyone could pop round to Joe's and ask him to ring me on a reverse charge call. Amazingly, a constable was dispatched, Joe happened to be at home and sure enough the call came through. His car had broken down, but he accepted the job without asking any more than where it was. I told him to take a cab both ways, for which of course he would be reimbursed. He rang off and all I could do was hope he made it in time. Needless to say, I had nothing to worry about. The taxi pulled up outside the hall and out stepped Somerville, wearing his shorts and with his hands bandaged ready to be slipped into his gloves. He had changed in the cab and was ready to fight. I cannot tell you how pleased I was when he won on points.

Joe retired in 1969 at the age of 35 after 102 fights. I suspect the majority of them had been at relatively short notice. To mark his services to boxing we were delighted to invite him as a special guest to the Anglo-American Sporting Club and present him with a gold watch as a token of our thanks.

I love stylish boxers and one I really enjoyed watching was Howard Winstone. We were involved with Winstone's career at the highest level of course. He fought the Mexican southpaw Vicente Saldivar for the world featherweight title at Earls Court in September 1965 on our show, we also made their second fight in Wales when the decision in Saldivar's favour was hugely unpopular, and it was on our show at the Albert Hall that Howard won partial recognition as featherweight champion by defeating Mitsunori Seki of Japan in 1968. Saldivar, whose retirement had left the title vacant, congratulated him in the ring as the massed Welsh fans who had travelled to London saluted him by singing their anthem.

When Winstone lost the championship in his first defence

in Porthcawl against the flashy Spanish-based Cuban, Jose Legra, it's fair to say we were not thrilled. I had a contract for Winstone to defend the title at the Albert Hall which should have presented no problem, until Winstone's manager, Eddie Thomas, who was notoriously difficult to deal with, went back on his word. The financial terms for the defence were omitted by mutual agreement at the time because we were not certain who the opponent would be, which left Thomas or us room for negotiation over the purse. Behind our backs Thomas then signed for Winstone to fight Legra in a rematch for Solomons. We took the case to the British Boxing Board of Control but they decided there was no binding contract because we had not stipulated the purse money beforehand. They also went on record as disapproving of Thomas's conduct, but that was of little use to us.

Fifteen years later we were still not seeing eye to eye. We could have brought the world welterweight title rematch between Colin Jones and Milton McCrory, Emanuel Steward's fighter from the Kronk gym in Detroit, to England or Wales, but Thomas wouldn't even give us a chance to bid. We had promoted Jones at Wembley on the way up but he signed a contract with Don King for Las Vegas. If that fight had been in Britain, I believe the home advantage would have tipped the fight in Jones's favour and he would have become world champion.

Shortly before Legra knocked out Winstone and ended the Welshman's career, I had travelled to Paris to see a French-Australian, Johnny Famechon. Although he drew his fight, I was impressed, and retained a fondness for him, perhaps because his uncle, Ray Famechon, was one of the idols of my youth. Ray boxed one of the best world featherweight champions of all time, Willie Pep, and lost a 15-round decision in Madison Square Garden, New York, in 1950.

When Legra beat Winstone, I thought of Johnny

Famechon, who by then had returned to Australia and was winning again. Johnny was actually born in France and christened Jean-Pierre but the family had moved to Melbourne when he was five. At 16 he persuaded his father Andre, who was also a good fighter, to allow him to turn professional. By the age of 23, he was as seasoned as any featherweight in the world and in fact I felt in time he was actually better than his uncle Ray. I cannot pay him a bigger compliment than that. It occurred to me that Famechon could beat Legra and on 21 January 1969 at the Royal Albert Hall he did just that. Legra was hot – on a winning streak of more than 50 fights – but Famechon boxed on the move, never giving him a free shot at his chin and generally frustrated him for the full 15 rounds. Legra felt he was unlucky, but whatever the ringside opinion, Famechon was champion. He made good money in a short time, boxing for us in London in three non-title workouts and twice successfully defending his championship against the rugged, attacking Japanese star 'Fighting' Masahiko Harada.

Jarvis Astaire recounts an incident at one of the Famechon-Harada fights which sums up the honesty of our relationship. I was in Japan, representing our interests, when at the last minute a local businessman gave me $20,000 in cash to advertise his company around the ring. There is no way Jarvis could have known about it but as far as I was concerned it was our money, to be divided between us. I told him the moment I arrived home and he has never forgotten it.

Eventually, Johnny lost the title to Vicente Saldivar, who had come out of retirement, in Rome in 1970 and immediately retired. Famechon kept his money and was doing well for himself before he was badly hurt when he was struck by a car. He received serious head injuries but fought back with typical courage. I have nothing but good memories of the man.

Alan Rudkin, the bantamweight from Liverpool, fought for the world title three times. He had great 15-rounders with Masahiko Harada in Japan and Lionel Rose in Australia but was overpowered in two rounds in Los Angeles by Ruben Olivares. As he was about to leave the dressing room at the Olympic Auditorium, a bodyguard tried to reassure the pale, boyish-looking Rudkin. 'Don't let the crowd worry you,' he said. 'They'll have to shoot *us* before they can get to you.'

Very reassuring.

One of the toughest characters of the time was the brooding middleweight Rubin 'Hurricane' Carter, who became a *cause celebre* for almost two decades after being wrongly imprisoned for triple murder. We brought Carter to London in the spring of 1965 for two fights with Harry Scott of Liverpool. Carter won the first on a cut and Scott pulled off a shock points win in the rematch.

Carter could fight, had fought Joey Giardello for the world middleweight title and had knocked out Emile Griffith in one round, but he was not the nicest of characters. I am sure that the courts were right to grant him freedom and I feel sorry for anyone who is locked up in jail for a crime they did not commit. However, when I met him he was certainly not a saint. At the time I was well known by immigration officers at London Airport and as things were far more relaxed than they are now, I was allowed to meet boxers on the tarmac as they left the plane after their transatlantic flight. Carter arrived and I offered to carry one of his bags. I took him into London and left him at his hotel, the Regent Palace, while I returned to our office in Wardour Street. The same day I took a phone call from the hotel. 'Could you come over right away?' said the hotel manager. 'Nothing's terribly wrong, but we need to talk to you.'

I went round and to my absolute horror discovered that a gun had gone off in Carter's room. Nobody was hurt, but there was a hole in the wall. For whatever reason, the hotel had not taken the matter further and I sat down with Carter, who didn't seem bothered by the fuss at all.

'Do you know what would have happened if they had caught you bringing a gun into this country?' I said.

'I didn't bring it in,' he replied.

'What do you mean?'

'I mean I didn't bring it in. *You* did. It was in the bag you carried through.'

Carter was a difficult, outspoken man who had made a name for himself in and out of the ring in his home town of Paterson, New Jersey. He spoke out at one time, saying black people should have died in the street protecting their children from the New York police. That was after a child had been killed in riots in Harlem. A year after the incident in London, he was arrested and in 1967 convicted of the murder of three people, along with a man who was with him at the time he was picked up. Carter spent most of his sentence in solitary confinement and eventually Bob Dylan and Muhammad Ali became embroiled in the fight to free him. He was released in 1976 but jailed again after being found guilty a second time on a retrial. Eventually Carter and the man convicted with him, John Artis, were freed. Today 'The Hurricane', who once made me an unwitting gun-smuggler, lives in peace in Toronto.

CHAPTER 8

Legends of the Ring

Before Muhammad Ali 'shook up the world' in February 1964, the heavyweight division had, since 1919, been dominated by four great champions: Jack Dempsey, Joe Louis, Rocky Marciano, and Charles 'Sonny' Liston. I feel privileged to have met them and worked with them all during my early matchmaking career.

Liston, of course, was the master of menace. Although he had a bad reputation, I actually liked him and found he had a good sense of humour. But he was a complex human, who had a voracious appetite for women, and he could be an ogre if he didn't get his own way.

He came to Britain in 1963 when he was heavyweight champion of the world and people flocked to see this big, powerful man who had been raised in the cotton fields of Arkansas and on the mean streets of St Louis. One of 25 children, Liston was a boy of about 12 when he followed his mother to St Louis. The police found him wandering the streets looking for her, took him in and fed him until they discovered where she lived and handed him over. He was in jail as a youth and again, for beating up a policeman in an alleyway in the mid-1950s when already a rising professional heavyweight.

There were rumours of underworld connections and the California State Athletic Commission went so far as to vow that Liston would never be permitted to fight there because his manager of licence, Joseph 'Pep' Barone, was merely a front for mobsters. Liston bought out Barone, but at the US Government enquiry into boxing run by Senator Estes Kefauver in 1961 it was stated that Sonny's undercover manager was Frank 'Blinky' Palermo, the right hand man of the notorious John Paul 'Frankie' Carbo, both of whom were handed down substantial jail sentences for muscling in on the contract of the former world welterweight champion Don Jordan.

Liston was probably the best heavyweight in the world for several years before he knocked out a terrified Floyd Patterson in the first round in 1962. In those days return clauses were almost automatic – I don't agree with them by the way – but nobody should have enforced the one which existed between Liston and Patterson. The outcome was horribly predictable: another first round win for Sonny. With a potential defence against Cassius Clay still being talked about, Liston came to Britain to enjoy himself. Jarvis and I met him and his wife, Geraldine, at the airport and he was given a suite in the Mayfair Hotel. For some reason Mrs Liston returned to Denver within a day or two. He appeared at a press lunch and trained in the ring at Wembley on the night of the first Billy Walker-Johnny Prescott fight in September 1963. He used to work out to the classic blues tune 'Night Train', skipping or working the speed ball to the rhythm. Those engagements went well but his temper was uneven and his demands for female company became increasingly menacing. He had a tremendous magnetism that was quite astonishing, even to the point of taking women from their husbands. He would wait until the woman was on her own for a few moments, sidle up, begin talking and then five minutes later invite her to his room, leaving the husband wondering where his not-so-good lady had gone.

The worst moment came on a Sunday when London was three-parts asleep but Liston, bored and restless, wanted women.

'What do I do today?' he said. 'This place is like a morgue.'

'Well Sonny, it's Sunday,' I replied. 'Everything's closed. Why don't you relax?'

'How about some broads?' he persisted.

'That's not my racket,' I said. 'I don't know what I can do to help you.'

He was so insistent that eventually I told him I'd see what I could do. One man who was there was a member of the Stork Room, a club which was sometimes used by hookers where drink was served in coffee cups. Off we all went with Liston, his trainer and sparring partner, only to find it deserted except for two women. One was a massively built girl and the other, tiny and Scottish, must have been about 4ft 8in. I asked them if there would be more action later as I heard Liston muttering: 'Where are the broads? Where are the broads?'

The big woman said it was the day most working girls took off because it was always so quiet. I asked about the girls who danced and sang in the show, which didn't begin until later in the evening. 'Well, they're not hookers,' she said, 'but they do like a party. After the show, they'll probably be happy to come with you, if one or two can bring their boyfriends to meet the heavyweight champion.'

We decided on a party in Liston's suite, arranged for sandwiches and gave one of the girls enough money to buy chicken from a late night place nearby. Liston went back to the Mayfair in a vile mood and it must have been around 2 a.m. when everyone else arrived. As I entered the room Liston was sitting in some short pyjamas, plainly very unhappy indeed. One of the girls found a record player and turned it on and they began to dance. Everyone was eating the food and drinking . . . and ignoring Liston. Suddenly, he got up, switched off the record player and snarled: 'What the hell is going on? I sent you out for broads and you come back with fags.'

I asked Sonny to step into the corridor and explained. 'Charles, you've got to play it smart,' I said. 'You can wind up with any broad you like, but you've got to be nice.' He gave me his stare, marched back into the room, looked at the women and said: 'I'll take that one, that one and that one.'

The impact was dreadful. The room emptied, including the fat hooker, who went off with his sparring partner, which left only the 4ft 8in Scot. I felt it an appropriate time to leave.

We had a noon press conference planned for the next day and so at about 10.30 I went to Sonny's suite. As I approached I heard the most terrible screaming and I rushed inside to find the Scottish woman yelling obscenities. Liston stood with his arms folded, still in his pyjamas, staring gloomily at her. 'What's the matter, darling?' I said.

She was in no mood to play at niceties.

'That big ape has been fucking me all night long and now he wants to give me a tenner.'

'Charles,' I said, 'that's only about 24 dollars.'

Liston scowled at her. 'What about all the sandwiches you ate?'

'I don't fuck for sandwiches,' she said.

There seemed nothing to do but leave.

In London, he was more relaxed with reporters than he

was in America. One time he was arguing with Reg Gut-teridge – who wrote for the *Evening News* at the time – about the characteristics of black people and white people. Stereotypes, I suppose. The details are vague now, but eventually Liston wanted to bet that he had less hairs on his leg than Reg. They agreed on £10. Liston rolled up his trousers. The general consensus was that there were two on his shin, just below the knee. At that point Reg pulled up his trousers to reveal a shiny false leg. Nobody had let on that he had lost the lower part of his left leg when he jumped off a tank on to a mine in Normandy in the Second World War. Sonny burst out laughing and called him a 'cork-legged conman limey son of a bitch'.

When he was in London he was also a guest of the Krays one evening and they were pictured with him. The story was that they had offered him £500 to visit one of their West End clubs, which he did. It was of course absolutely nothing to do with our arrangements.

He flew to Scotland, where he was met off the plane by a pipe band. The Scottish part of the visit was jointly pro-moted by Peter Keenan and I. Keenan had fought the South African Vic Toweel for the world bantamweight title a decade earlier and was extremely popular. When he retired he took out a promoter's licence and staged shows in partner-ship with me – we shared the billing on all of Jim Watt's world title fights. During one of the press conferences, a reporter asked Sonny:

'Have you any interests outside boxing?'

'Yeah,' said the champion. 'Broad jumping.'

'Really,' asked the reporter, 'what distance have you jumped?'

'From one broad to another.'

One man who did stand up to him was Keenan himself. One time in Liston's suite at the Central Hotel, Peter was smoking a small cigar and Liston told him rudely to put it out.

'You're ignorant,' said Keenan. 'Say please.'

Liston walked towards him and growled: 'Never mind about ignorant. Put it out.'

Then he knocked the cigar out of his mouth with a cane. Keenan threw a left hook, which Sonny completely ignored, but the Scot had drawn the battle lines and would not retreat. 'You may be the heavyweight champion of the world but I have never lost a street fight in my life. Come outside.'

They didn't go.

Generally, however, Liston and Keenan got on well and the champion became very fond of Peter's son, Peter junior. He invited him to the States to spend Christmas with him and his wife, Geraldine, took him to Disneyland, Las Vegas and on to Denver. They had a local community competition for the best decorated Christmas tree and Sonny had little Peter dressed as an angel and sat him on top of the tree. They won.

After the tour of Scotland, Liston went on to Newcastle, where he was famously photographed riding a white horse through the streets. He also boxed an exhibition at St James Hall.

Liston, as every sports fan knows, lost his heavyweight title in 1964 to Cassius Clay, who changed his name to Muhammad Ali and knocked Sonny out with embarrassing ease in a return the following year. There were all kinds of strange claims about Liston taking a dive after receiving threats and the story was never quite allowed to rest. The secret, if there was one to tell, went with Liston to his grave. He was found dead at his Las Vegas home in the first few days of 1971 when his wife returned from a brief holiday. She found the body and pathologists estimated Sonny had died on 30 December 1970. Nobody knew for sure, just as nobody really knew when he was born in those Arkansas cotton fields. One theory I do not buy is that Liston died from a self-inflicted drug overdose. I firmly believe he was killed.

There could be no greater contrast between Liston's brooding suspicion and the uncomplicated generosity of Joe Louis, even though late in Sonny's career, Joe worked in his corner and they spent nights out together in Las Vegas and Denver: two extremes with a common ground that remained barely acknowledged by a judgemental outside world.

Of course I have only seen Louis fight on film but he was the heavyweight champion from 1937, when I was eight years old and not yet interested in boxing, until 1949 when my professional career was over. He was revered.

I met him in 1959 at Jack Dempsey's restaurant on Times Square, when I went there with the agent Dewey Fragetta. Joe was a lovely man. That was my first trip to New York and to this day I remember the thrill of seeing the Manhattan skyline. It's still a marvellous city.

In my capacity as general factotum at the Anglo-American Sporting Club, as well as making the matches, one of my missions was to make the club successful by attracting popular guests of honour. We played host to both Dempsey and Louis, and of course I met Joe several times in his later years when he worked as a greeter at Caesars Palace, where I always stayed when in Las Vegas. Incidentally, I travelled to Plymouth to book one guest for the Anglo – Sir Francis Chichester, who arrived home in May 1967 at the end of his epic voyage around the world in his yacht, Gipsy Moth IV.

Louis has sometimes been unfairly perceived as politically and racially naïve by boxing historians, but he was nothing of the sort. He was certainly kind-hearted. I recall taking Joe into a Manchester clothing store, during one of his visits to

England. He had wanted an item but only had a $100 bill and so asked a young shop assistant to change money for him at a bank. He gave the lad a £2 tip, which was huge. He saw the boy's amazement and asked him what he planned to do with the money. 'I am going to pay something off my suit,' he replied.

Joe looked a bit non-plussed so I explained to him that the boy would be paying for his suit on a hire purchase agreement.

'How much will it cost you?' said Louis

'Twelve pounds,' replied the boy.

Joe immediately gave him another £10.

'That was very nice of you,' I said as we walked away.

He looked at me and said calmly: 'That's one kid who won't hate niggers.'

In his later years Louis came to London as our guest with his wife Martha, who was a highly respected lawyer. She was combining the visit with a short trip to Italy to conduct some business and while she was gone, asked me to help Joe as and when necessary. It was a privilege. I went to his suite in the morning to check that he was all right, let myself in and looked in through the bedroom door to find the bed turned completely around. Only when I peered over the head-board could I see the former heavyweight champ was sleeping soundly. I tiptoed out into the living room and had not been there long when the phone rang. It was Mrs Louis. I told her there was no great problem, but explained that Joe had turned the bed around in his room. She wasn't in the least surprised, assured me there was nothing to worry about and said she would explain when she arrived. I didn't mention it again until she brought the subject up while Joe was not present. She said he was plagued by an obsessive delusion that he was on a Mafia hit-list and his only way of escaping his killers was to turn the bed around so that they would not see him. The poor man's mind was letting him down.

In 1970 he was committed for treatment at a psychological hospital in Denver on the signature of his son, spent several months there and the following year was hired full time by Caesars Palace to stroll around the hotel, chat, sign autographs and play with house money at the tables. He enjoyed it, but his health declined and he was only 66 when he died in 1981.

Jack Dempsey, another of the sport's greatest heavyweights, was an awesome man. I have a fabulous photograph taken with him at his famous restaurant which he opened in the mid 1930s, after his fight career had finished. In fact, I can still picture him sitting there. He had a rule that people could have his autograph, but they had to eat first. On the night I sat with him people kept coming over to him. After a while, I said:

'I know it's business, but doesn't this ever get on your nerves?'

'Never forget,' he said. 'Sign an autograph and you make a friend. And always remember – it's nice of them to ask.'

You felt the greatness in Dempsey. Even as an old man he had an aura about him and spoke about boxing with such authority. Of course, he was heavyweight champion for seven years after the First World War up to 1926, when Gene Tunney beat him in the rain in Philadelphia. They drew a crowd of 120,000 people, and in the rematch in Chicago they grossed more than $2 million – the first fight ever to do that, and a live gate record that wasn't broken until the Muhammad Ali-Ken Norton fight in 1976.

Dempsey was a huge star – and was wise enough to make his fame work for him in retirement. Somebody described him in those days as the longest running show on Broadway. He eventually closed the restaurant in 1974 because the rents were raised to an unreasonable level and they wanted to use the building for something else. Sadly, a piece of boxing folk lore went with him because it was a meeting place for fight people from all over the world.

When he came to the Anglo-American Sporting Club in 1967, he asked if he could bring a guest. Naturally, we said he could and when he arrived it was with J. Paul Getty, the American oil tycoon. Apparently they used to spar together when they were youngsters. It was the birthday of one of the great British boxers of all time, Ted 'Kid' Lewis, who was then in his seventies. We got Dempsey to present Lewis with a birthday cake. They had known each other as fighters in the 1920s and it was a very emotional moment when they met and embraced.

Human beings have all kinds of different wants and needs and Rocky Marciano, the heavyweight champion from 1952–1956 enjoyed money – having it and keeping it. He didn't like to spend it either. A good example of his attitude came in November 1963 when we were promoting a fight between Terry Downes and Mike Pusateri in Manchester. Downes had lost his world middleweight title by then but was still a good fighter and we were hoping for another chance. Pusateri was from Brockton, Massacusetts, Marciano's home town, and was managed by Rocky's cousin, Allie Colombo, who had trained the champ alongside Charley Goldman.

Pusateri had been something of a knockout artist on his way up but seemed to have reached his level. He was a respectable opponent but had been outpointed in three of his last four fights, which made him a reasonably safe bet for Downes. The public obviously thought so too because the fight wasn't selling at all. I thought an invitation to Rocky might help sales and so I spoke to Colombo, explaining that the arrival of the former world heavyweight champion might be just the boost we needed. Al said he would talk to him, but added that Rocky would obviously need paying. I said $1,000 was all we could afford and he said he would do what he could.

I heard nothing more and didn't feel able to press it, so I assumed nothing had come of the idea until three days before the fight when I received a dawn phone call to say Marciano had flown into Manchester airport and was wondering why nobody was there to meet him. Obviously, he had no idea where he was supposed to go. I persuaded the customs authorities to keep him away from the public until I got there. 'Please don't let him leave,' I said.

I phoned all the newspapermen I knew in the north of England and got to the airport as fast as I could. When I saw him, I couldn't believe it. He looked like a tramp. His jacket was full of holes. We sorted him out with something a little better and held a press conference, which immediately injected some life into the show. Later that day, I remember sitting in one of the restaurants in the Midlands Hotel in Manchester when we heard that President John F. Kennedy had been shot in Dallas. We were all moved and upset, but Rocky more than most. He said Kennedy had been instrumental in helping him make up his mind to retire from the ring in 1956.

After the fight, which was a success, with Downes winning in five rounds, Marciano stunned me by asking for $2,000, instead of the $1,000 agreed, in cash. We were in a club at about three in the morning and he said he wanted to catch the first plane home the next day. I said $2,000 was not the deal, managed to borrow enough cash for the sterling equivalent of $1,000 and handed it to him. He peeled through the bills, accused me of short-changing him and grabbed me by the collar.

'You rotten son-of-a-bitch,' he said.

'Rocky, you have three seconds to take your hands off

me,' I said, 'or you'll be forced to make a comeback.'

'Don't ever speak to me again,' he said as he let me go.

I told him it would be a pleasure.

We did meet again some time later through an acquaintance and shook hands. Eventually the incident was forgotten and we became friendly. He also came to London on a visit we arranged, and while he was here we persuaded him to attend a function at the pub in Fulham belonging to the Mancini family, who have been in boxing for many years. At the end of the evening, he was asked to make a speech and got up shyly. He had been the world heavyweight champion who had boxed in front of thousands of people in great arenas in New York, San Francisco, Philadelphia and Chicago, yet found it hard to speak to a gathering of admirers and fans in a small room in an English pub. He stood up and said in his own unpretentious way: 'I don't know why I'm up here in front of you all. I can't sing and I can't dance. But if you like, just to be sociable, I'll fight the best man in the house.'

They loved him for it. Out of the ring he was the most modest and charming of men . . . unless he thought you had short-changed him!

His obsession with hoarding money and his fear of going broke, which is an understandable fear in a man who had grown up poor and then had earned millions of dollars, cost his family a considerable fortune. When he died in a plane crash in August 1969 near Des Moines, Iowa, he left no will – and left no clue as to where much of his money was invested or hidden. 'Something's gone out of my life,' Joe Louis said, when he heard of his death. 'I'm not alone. Something's gone out of everyone's life.'

Liston – who was to die in equally tragic circumstances only 16 months later – and Dempsey also paid public tributes.

These were different but great men, a great quartet of heavyweight champions and in their own ways a tribute to the best things boxing can offer. I knew them all in small ways and I am proud of it.

CHAPTER 9

The Greatest

If Sugar Ray Robinson was the greatest pound for pound fighter of all-time then Muhammad Ali was unquestionably the best heavyweight. More than that of course, he was also one of the great men of the century, not to mention one of the greatest publicists. In the ring, the man had everything: height and reach, unbelievable reflexes, tremendous ability, was hard to hit in his prime and, if he had to, he could take a punch as well. He was a heavyweight with the foot speed of a fast middleweight and the hand speed of a lightweight. On the first of his trips to England, he beat Henry Cooper in 1963 at Wembley Stadium when he recovered from that famous knockdown to win in round five. We were not involved with that promotion – it was a Jack Solomons show – but we did stage the rematch for the heavyweight championship at Highbury Stadium in north London, the home of Arsenal football club, in May 1966. Obviously, it was and remains one of the high points of my career.

By then the great man had dispensed with his original

name, Cassius Marcellus Clay, and become Muhammad Ali. He was a member of the Nation Of Islam and I think was a genuine believer. I don't know how deeply he actually thought about his politics and religion, but of course the basis of its creed appealed to him. It seemed to him to be the solution to a lot of the social and religious problems affecting black people, especially in America, and he was a big help to the Muslim movement by promoting it. Whatever the truth of the matter it was his business and should have been nobody else's.

The Ali who arrived in London in 1966 was a far more mature and serious individual than the 21-year-old who was here as Cassius Clay three years earlier. His two wins over Sonny Liston had been perceived as controversial and mysterious – Sonny had quit on his stool in the first fight, then folded in the first round of the return. Following that, Muhammad had angered sports fans by ridiculing Floyd Patterson who, for all his limits as a champion, was a dignified, gentlemanly guy. Then, in March 1966 he refused to serve his country in Vietnam because of his religious beliefs. It was a time of war, when sensitivities are heightened, and political pressure was growing in America to oust him as heavyweight champion. When he fought George Chuvalo in Toronto and won easily over 15 rounds, some American states had refused to stage the contest and the closed circuit film of the fight was barred in others.

In effect, although it was not until the following year that he was banned from fighting, he was already being forced to look for work outside America. When he arrived in London – billed by us, incidentally, as 'Muhammad Ali, formerly known as Cassius Clay' – he was tired because the flight had been delayed and forced to take an unscheduled stop at Shannon. As he stepped off the plane he addressed the British writers, and the emotion was evident: 'I have been driven out of my country because of my religious beliefs. All that I ask is the same treatment that other boxers and athletes get. My religion is against war and because of that I am within my legal rights to be a conscientious objector.'

His religious zeal had also cost him his first marriage because his wife, Sonjie, apparently would not, or could not, adjust her ways to fit in with his expectations. He said he did not want to be plagued by constant questions over the draft issue or his divorce and took exception to one question which referred to him as a Black Muslim.

'I am not a *Black* Muslim, I am a Muslim. I am not here to answer questions on religion,' he said, then marched straight into the racial issue.

'Is this a fight between a black boxer and a white boxer to you?' Ali continued. 'You should be ashamed of yourself.'

He tried hard to lighten the mood after that, but the change in him as a person was plain to everyone who had watched his crazy, ebullient behaviour when he astonished British sports fans in 1963. Before that fight Ali, or Clay as he was, had insulted Cooper by calling him a bum and a cripple. This time he referred to Henry almost reverently as an English gentleman and a worthy challenger for the title. After the difficulties which were pressuring him in America, I think he enjoyed life here.

Our fight produced a huge row because Jarvis Astaire's company, Viewsport, had the exclusive rights to screen it live and had 32 closed circuit venues around the country. Jarvis offered a deal to the BBC and ITV, who had protested to the Government only to be informed that they had no case. Jarvis asked for £32,000 in return for allowing them to show the fight the following day. They refused.

Quite rightly, Jim Wicks tried to drive a hard bargain for Cooper. He asked for £30,000 and I helped persuade him that a percentage deal made more sense from his point of view. He finished with a lot more than that, I think more than £40,000. Ali's end came to about half a million dollars.

When Ali arrived in his limousine at the Piccadilly Hotel there must have been 500 fans waiting outside. The scenes were amazing as he made his way through them. He ran every morning in Hyde Park with his friend and sparring partner, Jimmy Ellis, who would hold the World Boxing Association title during Ali's three-year exile. They worked out in a gym at White City.

For one newspaper stunt I arranged for Ali to spar with East End light-heavyweight Jimmy Tibbs, who at the time combined boxing with a job in one of Terry Downes' bookmakers shops. Ali faked a knockdown and pulled the trick well, which of course drew more good publicity. It also helped people believe that Cooper had a realistic chance of knocking Ali out, which in turn was good for business. In reality, though, there was never any chance of that.

They were the days when the race was on in earnest to put a man on the moon. Before he won the title, Ali had created that very funny rhyme about knocking Sonny Liston out of the ring and into space – the first human satellite. Now he told writers after one workout: 'The way science is moving forward, maybe I'll even end up defending my title on Mars!'

Ali was a magnificent publicist. He never tired of meeting people and we even arranged for him to have lunch with Prime Minister Harold Wilson. Jarvis also took him to a Test match between England and the West Indies at Lord's. Some said he fell asleep but that wasn't true. He did watch the morning session, then, after lunch, he asked who was playing now. When Jarvis told him it was the same game and that it would go on for five days, he was horrified: 'Five days?' he said. 'You guys must be crazy. Let's get out of here.'

Henry Cooper and Jim Wicks played their parts by appearing on TV and radio and on the night a crowd of around 43,000 poured into Highbury Stadium. The cheapest seats cost two guineas. To be ringside, you had to shell out 20 guineas. We made a substantial profit, even after Ali, Cooper and the undercard boxers had been paid and all of our other expenses had been dealt with. Ali was paid the precise sum of £148,400 – and nine pence! Why the nine pence ? I have no idea.

The public might have believed Henry had a chance, but the cold, analytical forecast of the boomakers suggested otherwise. They put Ali at 1–10 and Cooper at 6–1 – in other words, they considered an Ali win a formality. We had three former world champions at ringside: Rocky Marciano, Ingemar Johansson and the legendary 'Orchid Man' from France, Georges Carpentier, who had fought Jack Dempsey for the heavyweight title way back in 1921. Carpentier was still sprightly at 72 and posed for publicity photographs with Ali in the build-up.

Ali had demanded a big ring, which he was entitled to do, and we had to have it made specially. He used it well, moving magnificently without really opening up until round six when Henry's eye burst open. Ali knew it was over as soon as he saw the blood and seemed content to move around, as if he didn't want to inflict any more harm than was necessary. The blood splashed down on Henry's chest and I think at one point Ali asked the referee to stop the fight. I can't think of a worse cut eye in all my time in the business. 'Man, I could hear him bleeding,' Ali said later.

On a personal note, it was after the Ali-Cooper fight, on my 37th birthday, 7 June 1966, that my British citizenship came through. For years I had considered myself British but had officially been stateless. Only when my international travel began to increase did it become obvious to me that I had to go through the formalities.

Ali's second fight in London that summer was for Jack Solomons at Earls Court against Brian London. We had first refusal on it, but didn't believe it would sell and turned it down. We were proved right. It was a flop. The arena was half-empty. Jack felt the British public would want to see Ali no matter who he boxed but his booking of London was beyond the credibility line. It was a total mismatch. In fact, *Ring* editor, Nat Fleischer later complained: 'London got $100,000 for doing nothing ... it was a stinker, booed by the fans who endured it.'

Although London was a poor opponent, the slow sales probably had more to do with other factors. Inflation was beginning to run out of control and most of the more casual sports fans had probably exhausted their budgets by following England's progress in the World Cup in July. England's victory in the final over West Germany was only seven days before Ali fought London, which made it one of the most disastrous pieces of judgement Solomons ever made. He had no time to get any real publicity and people were already emotionally and financially drained. It stands as a piece of hard evidence that the one-time East End fishmonger was losing his grip on the business that had made his fortune.

London was nowhere near ordinary world class, and certainly not in Ali's league. He had once tried to interrupt Sonny Liston at meal-time to offer his services as a sparring partner and had been completely ignored. He had fought Floyd Patterson for the world title in Indianapolis in 1959, against the wishes of the British Boxing Board of Control, and had been knocked out in round 11 of a bad fight. The Board fined and suspended him for disobeying them.

Now in 1966, Solomons wanted people to believe that London could put up a show against Ali. Even Brian knew he had no chance and refused to travel from his Blackpool home for the pre-fight press conferences. Not surprisingly,

My record of 55
wins out of 69
professional fights
wasn't a bad record,
but I soon realised
my talents lay
outside the ropes.

y father (far right), to whom I
dn't speak from the age of 12.
vill always regret not mending
ur relationship before he died.

With the legendary
'Manassa Mauler'.
I spent time with
Jack Dempsey in his
restaurant where he
was known as 'the
longest-running
show on Broadway.'

The Kray Twins with their mother. Ronnie and Reggie liked to called themselves 'former boxers' but in truth they were useless.

Right: Jack Solomons controlled British boxing ... until we beat him at his own game.

Left: With Harry Levene at Wembley. 'It doesn't matter if you're rich or poor', Levene used to say, 'as long as you've got money.'

Below: With Mr 'Only in America' himself ... the always controversial Don King.

Left: Henry Cooper and his manager Jim 'The Bishop' Wicks were close. I didn't like Wicks at all.

Far Left: The self-styled 'King of the Jews', otherwise known as Jack 'Spot' Comer.

Right: Billy Walker made a fortune during his career without ever winning a title.

Sugar Ray Robinson – quite simpl the greatest boxer I ever saw.

Right: Dave Charnley (right) against Joe Lopes in 1958. The Dartford southpaw was desperately unlucky not to become world lightweight champion.

The end is close for Henry Cooper in 1966. Muhammad Ali said afterwards: 'Man, I could hear him bleeding.'

Terry Downes (left) after winning the world middleweight title against Paul Pender, the fighting fireman from Massachusetts.

Above: Sharing a joke with 'The Greatest' during one of Ali's visits to London in the 1970s.

Left: Ali trains, Angelo Dundee watches. Dundee should have taken a stand during Ali's all-too-obvious decline.

Right: Old friends. I brought Ali over recently for the opening of Planet Hollywood in London.
Sadly, he's a shadow of his former self, but there's still a twinkle in the eye.

Ali gives Joe Bugner a boxing lesson in Kuala Lumpur in 1975. Two hours later a far from distraught Bugner was splashing about in the hotel pool. His conduct disgusted me.

Bugner ended Henry Cooper's long career in 1971 with a controversial points win at Wembley. Joe said he didn't love the game, but he was still fighting 28 years later!

Jarvis Astaire. My friendship and association with Jarvis has lasted more than 40 years

Jonathan Martin, the BBC Head of Sport, who turned down Naseem Hamed and told me: 'No more Frank Bruno.'

the show was a financial disaster and London was knocked out in round three. When he returned to Blackpool, there was no official welcome, no clamorous gathering of fans – just one teenaged girl with an autograph book. In recent years Brian, who is a very successful businessman, has taken the occasional after-dinner speech and question-and-answer session. In one, a know-all punter stood and asked him:

'How can you stand there talking about boxing when your most famous opponent, Muhammad Ali, is in such poor health, which most people directly attribute to his years in the ring?'

London looked him in the eye and without a flicker of a smile, said: 'Well don't blame me, pal. I never laid a glove on him.'

A month after that ridiculous mismatch, Ali defended against Karl Mildenberger, a solid German southpaw, in Frankfurt and we were back as his promoter. People have asked if dealing with German people and going to Germany to help promote the fight gave me any personal problems because of the holocaust and what had happened to so many of my family. But it didn't worry me. When the war was on, I was a child. I was 10 years old when it started, 16 when it finished. By the 1960s it was all in the past and I had travelled to Germany before.

Officially, Ali's contract with the Louisville syndicate of businessmen who had backed him from the start of his career ran out after the Mildenberger fight, but by then they were in the background and he was represented by the Nation Of Islam. I met Herbert Muhammad, who would become his official manager, and spoke to him a few times. Although he accompanied Ali as spiritual adviser and public relations officer for the Cooper fight, he did not present himself as Muhammad's mentor or boss, and to give credit to Elijah

Muhammad – Herbert's father and the leader of the movement until his death in 1975 – he chose not to capitalise on his position. When we did business with Ali, I dealt mainly with Chris Dundee, the Miami promoter who was the elder brother of Ali's trainer, Angelo. The promotional deal was done by Jarvis and the German promoter, Joachim Gottert, and it broke another broadcasting barrier – it was the first colour satellite transmission of a sporting event.

Mildenberger wasn't a great fighter, but he was capable. He was 28 years old and hadn't lost since the big Welshman Dick Richardson had knocked him out in a round in 1962. He had beaten Eddie Machen and Joe Erskine and drawn with Zora Folley, as well as holding the European title for two years. We didn't expect him to give Ali much trouble but the fight could be sold, which was what mattered. As a result, a crowd of 45,000 watched Mildenberger make his challenge on a rainy night in the Wald Stadium. To the world beyond Germany, of course, Mildenberger was incidental. The story was Ali. He collected a purse of around $300,000, with the promotion grossing more than double that.

Contrary to what has been written from time to time, I do not believe Ali had any trouble with Mildenberger's southpaw style. It took him a couple of rounds to work it out and then he decided to rough him up. It wasn't pretty, but he walked out and mauled him over because he realised it was the best way to do it. Ali's biggest strength was that he never worried about taking a few punches to accomplish victory, if that was the way to accomplish it. There was an amusing moment during the fight when, as Ali toyed with Mildenberger, cuffing him with an open glove and messing him around, he was cautioned by British referee Teddy Waltham. 'Close your glove,' instructed Waltham.

Ali nodded and let fly with a terrific right hand that sent Mildenberger tumbling on to the seat of his trunks.

Ali looked at Waltham. 'Like that?' he said, mockingly.

Mildenberger was floored twice more before Waltham, who was also the secretary of the British Boxing Board of Control, stopped the fight halfway through round 12.

Another incident involving Waltham occurred when we arranged an exhibition for Ali in Italy. Waltham refereed a European title fight on the show, was paid his £3,000 fee in cash and then had his pocket dipped. On the plane back to London, I was speaking about it to Jarvis when Ali tapped me on the shoulder and asked if I was talking about the referee. I explained what had happened. 'That's a shame,' said Ali. 'He did a good job.'

On the way down from the plane, Waltham looked a lot happier and I said:

'Have you found your money, then Teddy?'

'No,' he said. 'But somebody must have told Ali. He's just given it to me again.'

That was typical of Muhammad. He was the most generous of men.

A month after beating Mildenberger, Ali left the Louisville Sponsoring Group and opinion hardened even further against him. He had severed his links with the white businessmen who had backed his career since he was 18 years old and alligned himself with a movement which many Americans felt was subversive, revolutionary and possibly even violent. Ali tried to explain that this was an unfair criticism and again defended his opposition to active participation in the Vietnam War. 'How can I kill somebody when I pray five times a day for peace?' he pleaded.

However, it was seven years before we did promotional business again. He defended his titles in America against Cleveland Williams – which some still consider his peak performance – Ernie Terrell and Zora Folley, and then had his licence withdrawn.

It's hard for youngsters now to realise how big Ali was when he was young. Jarvis told a story of a ride in a limousine along Broadway when Ali claimed – on a bet – that his popularity was so great that he could get out of the car and walk a few blocks without saying a word and gather a crowd. Jarvis took him up on it, and Ali jumped out and began walking. Within minutes there were people everywhere, chanting his name. During his exile from boxing, he spoke at colleges across America, preaching the Black Muslim message and attempting to raise public awareness of the black issues of the time. Many of those people who, at first, despised him and all that he stood for, ended up admiring him for his sincerity and faith.

He was out of the ring from 1967 until 1970, and then after two comeback wins against Jerry Quarry and Oscar Bonavena, he lost the first, classic fight with Joe Frazier in Madison Square Garden.

We put on Ali's first fight with Joe Bugner at the Convention Center, Las Vegas, in a show staged at Caesars Palace in 1973, when Joe took Ali the full 12 rounds. It was a non-title fight and we took 1,500 people out through the Anglo-American Sporting Club. Bugner was very much an underestimated fighter – he was much better than people gave him credit for. He was very hard to hit, had good stamina, speed and a fairly good big-time temperament. The only thing he couldn't do was punch his weight. Whatever Bugner lacked in aggression and power, he was effective. His style was to make people miss often enough to make them easier to hit. The first fight was a learning experience for him. He was only 22 at the time, which in heavyweight terms made him a boxing baby, yet he gave Ali a good fight.

Ali went on to lose to Ken Norton, in the fight when his jaw was broken, beat Norton in a rematch and then outpoint

Frazier at Madison Square Garden in January 1974. Frankly, I wish he had retired then. I don't believe his reputation was enhanced particularly by what he did after that, even though people have celebrated his victory over George Foreman in the 'Rumble in the Jungle' and his win in that dreadfully gruelling third fight with Frazier in Manila in 1975.

I think Foreman did more damage to Ali than is appreciated. There is a real possibility that if he had retired before that fight, he might have all of his faculties today, and his legend would have been practically the same. He picked the silliest possible method of beating Foreman. He let Foreman hit him until George got tired. That was a ridiculous thing to do. When I asked him about it one day, he said: 'Well, only one or two got through.'

Look at the fight on tape. Believe me, more than one or two of Foreman's big, whacking blows got through to his head and body. Fighting is dangerous enough without doing that kind of thing.

It doesn't take an Einstein to work out that Ali went on for far too long. His personal doctor, Ferdie Pacheco, left him in 1977 after he had outpointed Earnie Shavers in the Garden. Pacheco felt he should have retired after the third Frazier fight. 'When Ali was young,' he once said, 'he was the best physical specimen I've ever seen. If God sat down to create the perfect body for a fighter, he'd have created Ali. Every test I did on him was a fine line of perfect.'

Now, many years on, Pacheco saw what was happening and was honest enough to say so. He had also earned the right to expect to be listened to. Ferdie could not live with being a part of the process of prolonging Ali's career once he had assessed the laboratory reports on Ali's physical condition after his win over Shavers. Pacheco said the report, given to him by the New York State Athletic Commission, showed that Ali's kidneys were falling apart. 'Instead of filtering out blood and turning it into urine, pure blood was getting through,' he said.

He explained this in greater detail a few years ago in *A View from the Corner*. He wrote: 'The urine exam had not only revealed blood in the urine, but entire sections of cells from tubules. These cells filter the blood and make urine. They are not replaceable. They scar and impair kidney function.'

Pacheco said he and the doctor from the commission, Frank Guardino, discussed Ali's condition and both agreed there was also evidence of neurological deterioration. Guardino made it clear Ali would never be allowed to box in New York again and suggested that Ferdie recommend the champion retire. Pacheco wrote to Ali, enclosing the findings of the medical report, and sent copies to Herbert Muhammad, Herbert's brother, Wallace, Angelo Dundee and Ali's wife of the time, Veronica. None of them replied, at which point he quit. Why the hell didn't Dundee write back or at least call Pacheco?

Incidentally, some years later Pacheco was acting as an advisor for NBC when he refused to accept Maurice Hope, whom we promoted, on one of their shows. I wasn't best pleased, but Pacheco felt at the time it was wrong for a fighter to box on following surgery for a hole in a retina. 'If that was your son,' he said, as I protested in my customary, forthright manner, 'would you let him fight after a retina operation?'

I took his point. I have always respected Pacheco because he stood up to be counted. He could have stayed on to take Ali's money but he knew what was happening and wanted no part of it. Angelo could have done that too but he has always argued that he did not judge Ali or tell him what to do. I don't accept that as a valid argument, although to be fair to him he did what his brother, Chris, said. In fact, he was totally dominated by Chris. If he walked into a gym on Monday morning and Chris told him it was Sunday he would have believed him. Chris is gone now, and Angelo is 79, I think. Angelo and I generally got on and he never did anything bad to me, but he lost my respect because of the way he behaved in the later stages of Ali's career. He didn't walk out and, whatever he says to the contrary, he should have. By staying he became a party to Ali's terrible physical deterioration and in my view that was shameful.

Before Pacheco left, I was involved in two more Ali fights – the rematch with Joe Bugner in the Merdeka Stadium, Kuala Lumpur, in July 1975 and his comfortable win over Richard Dunn in Munich in May 1976. Bugner had ability but not enough will power. However, if you ask me if he could have found the willpower, could he have whipped Ali in 1975, the answer would still be 'no'. Bugner looked great, trained hard and talked big, but lacked the ability to finish the job.

'I'll break his neck if he tries to break mine,' he said to the media. 'I'm talking about the fight because you asked me to, but if I started worrying about it I'd leave all my energy in the hotel room . . . I'm so fit and mentally prepared and so proud of representing Britain that I'm bubbling all day.'

It was an incredible occasion, of course, as it was every time Ali took his show on the road. When the fight was on, Kuala Lumpur more or less stopped for an hour. The streets were deserted and some businesses rearranged their working hours to fit in with the fight, which was held at 9.30 in the morning to suit American TV peak times. The stadium was only about a quarter-full, but the local television figures were huge.

Bugner went 15 rounds in the sweltering, muggy heat but couldn't apply any real pressure on Ali and lost by a mile.

He was over-cautious and Ali showed him respect by dancing and working behind his left jab, keeping the fight at a distance. Although he cut Ali in the 13th round, Bugner didn't really get started, which was obviously a disappointment to us. Ali, who threw his gloves from the ring to the King of Malaysia, was generous afterwards to his opponent, as he usually was: 'Joe is going to be the next champ as soon as I retire. He's good. I couldn't hurt him until the last few rounds.'

But Joe shrugged off the defeat far too easily for my liking. 'Well, gents,' he said to the British press. 'We tried, but he had too much. The heat was unbearable. When I tried to force things in the late rounds the humidity hit me. I'd have killed myself if I'd have forced the fight too early.'

Even in that heat, most fighters I knew would have fought until they dropped. But not Joe. An hour later, he let himself down badly by going for a dip in his hotel pool. He splashed about happily, waving to his friends, then stopping for a drink of champagne. He looked extremely pleased with his day's work . . . He was heavily criticised by the journalists and rightly so. He should have locked himself in a room and cried his eyes out.

I was so downcast that Joe eventually noticed. He was still bubbling and said: 'You're very quiet, Mickey. What did you think?'

I was tired and depressed and didn't feel like arguing with him.

'I suppose, Joe, at the end of the day, the name of the game is money.'

'Yes,' he said. 'And being able to count it.'

I'm afraid that comment said a lot about Bugner's attitude to the sport.

We could not have promoted the Ali-Dunn fight in England, but in Germany it was just about viable, because, only weeks before the Ali fight, Dunn had stopped German fighter, Bernt August in three rounds to win the European title. The fact that August was German helped us sell Dunn as a reasonable opponent for Ali in Munich. Dunn's manager, George Biddles, an old timer from Leicester, was as good as gold. He was one of the easiest managers to deal with because he was never quite up to the job. He was a booking agent, not a manager. You asked him about a fight and he said 'How much?' We paid Dunn $175,000. He was to be paid $100,000 in advance but when I reached Munich I found that Bob Arum – Ali's promoter – had put Richard and his people in a shocking hotel. I moved them out into the Hilton.

By this time I still hadn't received the $100,000 that was due from Arum and the Hilton wanted to be paid, so I took a cab to the hotel where he and Ali were staying – the Bayerischer Hof, one of the best in Europe. It was really luxurious – a world away from the fleapit he'd put Richard in. When I arrived I saw Arum coming down a grand staircase. I walked straight up to him and we had a furious argument. I suggested if he didn't want to pay the advance he could turn over the British TV rights and closed circuit to us and I would pay Richard. He didn't like that and Ali's biographer, Richard Durham, heard me end the conversation by shouting: 'You don't have a fight. I am taking Dunn home.'

I went back to the Hilton, and an hour later a message came for me to go to Ali's suite. At that time he was feeding a huge entourage, some of whom were no doubt taking liberties with his generosity. I went in, and Ali asked me to explain what had happened. I told him of the trouble I was having with Arum and he pleaded: 'Don't leave, whatever you do. The show has to go on. I have people here who are depending on me for their money. I am being paid $3.3 million. So what if I get $3.2 million. I will give you the

$100,000 out of my purse. I would fight Dunn for nothing anyway.'

We knew that even against a 34-year-old Ali, who had been lucky to beat Jimmy Young in his previous fight, Dunn's chance was minimal, but it was a payday for him, he had paid his dues as a professional and in boxing weird things can happen. So the show did go on.

Dunn was a big, honest 31-year-old Yorkshireman, whose chin wasn't great, but who was persistent, game and a southpaw. He had suddenly come good after years of splitting his time between boxing and labouring on building sites, and the Ali fight capped a marvellous eight months for him. In September 1975 he outpointed Bunny Johnson, a clever boxer who was too small to be a heavyweight, to win the British and Commonwealth titles. As well as a part-time builder, Richard was also a former paratrooper, and when somebody raised the subject at a press conference, Ali interrupted: 'A paratrooper?' said the champion, 'then he should know how to fall.'

Dunn's wife Janet had already said Richard would win because Ali couldn't handle southpaws and Ali enjoyed that. 'I don't like disappointing a lady,' he said, 'but I'm afraid southpaw, northpaw, eastpaw or westpaw, I ain't worried. I'm just looking forward to helping Richard make his final drop.'

Dunn said Ali could talk all he wanted. 'I've never been scientific but I've got a few ideas that will work. I guarantee I'll give him a better fight than Joe Bugner did. I'd be a right berk to come all this way and throw it away.'

In spite of the banter, tickets sold slowly and 2,000 were handed out to United States soldiers and airmen stationed in Germany. Ali did his best to sell it by saying that he had paid for the tickets himself by taking a pay cut of $100,000.

An astonishing example of Ali's generosity came a few

days before the fight. We were waiting to go on a TV show to push the fight and while we were sitting in a room outside the studio we were watching the local television news. They showed a little old lady crying because the old people's home which she ran was being closed down. Apparently, it owed $30,000. She was distraught. After the TV show, we were in Ali's limousine and he said: 'Let's go to that old lady's home.'

Somehow we found it and Ali knocked on the door. The old woman answered it, was scared stiff at the sight of this huge, young black man and tried to shut the door, but Ali stuck his foot in it. 'I'm not going anywhere until you come out here and tell me your story,' he said.

The woman came out, suspiciously at first and then gradually relaxed and told Ali what had happened. When she had finished, he simply wrote her a cheque for $30,000. She was absolutely astonished and so grateful.

'What did you do that for?' I said as we drove away. 'In another year, she'll be broke again and will have to close down.'

'Oh no,' said Ali. 'Once the rich folk around here realise that a nigger has saved their old people's home, they'll make sure it has enough money to stay open.'

When I thought about it, years later, during another trip to Germany, I made a point of checking what had happened. Ali was right. The place was still open.

Before the fight George Biddles gave a strange speech to the press. 'I see myself touring luncheon clubs in southern California. I see a big parade group forming at London Heathrow Airport. I see lovely motorcars heading into the countryside and at every village I see crowds cheering and people throwing flowers. Richard Dunn is world heavyweight champion. His manager is at his side. England cannot contain its joy.'

I'm not sure what the world's media thought of it – and I'm not sure even now whether he believed it or whether he was joking! When a reporter asked if Dunn might fear Ali, Biddles smiled graciously and replied: 'Richard is no more afraid of Ali than he would be of a squirrel.'

Quite where squirrels came into the equation I've never been able to understand, but it was an interesting diversion.

We had Dunn accompanied to the ring by members of the First Parachute Regiment, who were stationed in Berlin, and he sang the national anthem and blew kisses to the crowd. Meanwhile, Ali looked bored.

Dunn tried to make a fight as best he could, but Ali stopped him more or less as he pleased in five rounds. In the dressing room Dunn, who had been knocked down five times, was in tears as he sat on a bench in nothing but his jock strap. He has wanted to win so very much.

'I had a go, like I promised,' Dunn said in his flat Yorkshire accent. 'I couldn't get out of the way of those right hands, but I don't think I disgraced anyone. It were right hard in there. I honestly wouldn't mind another go at him. I'm no fancy dan, I'm a fighter. I had a go, but it weren't good enough.'

Old George Biddles, who was notoriously careful with his money, was white with shock, not because his man had lost, but because somebody in the jostling crowd had picked his pocket. Sadly, Richard is now disabled after badly damaging his legs in an accident when he worked on an oil rig in the North Sea.

Before the fight Ali had agreed to give me his gloves for us to auction at the Anglo-American Sporting Club when we held a benefit for Chris Finnegan, who had retired because of a detached retina. He was a worthy cause. Apparently, Angelo Dundee wanted the gloves as well but I got them when Ali was still in the ring. I had them in my hands when

Ali tapped my shoulder. 'Look inside the gloves,' he said.

I did and found a piece of paper. In his own handwriting was the message: 'Ali wins, round five.'

The man had so much class!

By 1976 Ali was supposed to be having easy fights. Some were, some were not. Probably the easiest was when he fought the Belgian they called the Lion of Flanders, Jean Pierre Coopman, in San Juan, Puerto Rico. Coopman was really bad. He couldn't fight at all. Some said he was even drinking champagne in the dressing room before the fight. After four very tame rounds, Ali had clowned and generally put on a show. Then in the interval he learned over the ropes and said to the fellows from ABC TV: 'You guys had better get all the commercials in now. I can't hold this bum up any longer.'

Eventually he lost his world title to Leon Spinks, who was a seven fight novice at the time. The World Boxing Council number one contender was Ken Norton, who was promoted by Don King. Ali had distanced himself from King after working with him earlier, primarily in the George Foreman fight in Zaire. Ali said he wanted to fight Spinks in a return. Rematches were banned but the WBC rulebook allowed for a rematch under exceptional circumstances and if approved by 75 per cent of the voting members. The issue was debated at the WBC convention and I was one of several people who spoke. I said: 'I am not in favour of return matches but you do have this regulation whereby you can make exceptions. If there is anybody in the world who is worthy of an exception being made it is Muhammad Ali.'

The discussion ended with Ali getting 96 per cent backing. As we were leaving the room, King and Norton were standing by the door and looking at everyone as they passed. King, who always calls me 'Duffer' because he likes the joke, saw me and said to Norton, loud enough for me to hear: 'He don't like black people. You would think Ali was white.'

I could not accept that. I said: 'Don, you are a professional nigger. You are the worst exploiter of black people who ever lived.'

King had played the 'black' card for years in order to use his colour to appeal to black fighters. He would attempt to persuade them that black people should stick together, that they should allow him to guide them and not put their faith in white managers and promoters. All too often it worked. Instead of contracting themselves to the person who had the best deal to offer, whatever their colour, the black fighters King wanted were persuaded to believe in Don, even though what he was saying was essentially racist and not necessarily borne out by the facts. It was an argument he was to use time and again from those days in the 1970s through to the time when he lured Mike Tyson away from Bill Cayton.

Somehow the WBC convention ruling made no difference. Spinks was stripped of the title when he agreed to fight Ali again, leaving that fight for the WBA title only. The WBC gave the title to Norton by default, which was unprecedented, and he lost it to Ali's old sparring partner, Larry Holmes, in June 1978. Three months later Ali regained the WBA championship – and as far as the public were concerned the only one that mattered – by dancing his way to victory over Spinks. Ali retired after that but was still not content.

He was already a sick man when he came back to challenge Holmes for the WBC belt in Las Vegas in October 1980. Muhammad was 38 years old and had to dye the grey out of his hair. He had apparently been given thyroid hormones – a drug named Thyrolar, which was potentially lethal when misapplied – and diuretics to help him lose weight before the fight, something which Ferdie Pacheco would not have allowed. Angelo Dundee, who was almost on the outside looking in by that stage, at least had the say in the corner during the fight. He pulled Ali out after the 10th round. Even then Bundini Brown, Ali's long-time friend and cheerleader, was pleading for him to be sent out one more time. I watched the fight on TV – if you can call it a fight. It was very sad, he was hit from pillar to post.

Ali was in hospital afterwards due to the battering he'd suffered, and Don King short-changed him by more than a million dollars. Ali sucd King in an Illinois court in June 1982 but then dropped the case after King sent a man with $50,000 in cash. Muhammad was in hospital in Los Angeles when he signed King's contract agreeing to drop the lawsuit in return for the money. That fitted perfectly with King's way of doing business. He was always street-sharp, he pays well, and he understands that many of even the most successful boxers are more impressed by cash than contracts.

It disgusts me that those around Ali could even contemplate one more fight after Holmes, when he lost to Trevor Berbick in the Bahamas in December 1981. Even then, in what must have been his darkest despair, Ali had the guts to last the 10-round distance. He was beaten on points, not knocked out.

King was badly beaten up on that trip. He had tried to claim a valid contract for promoting the fight but the local promoter, James Cornelius, objected to what he felt was King's attempt to muscle in on his show. Thugs with brass knuckles administered a battering in a hotel room that left King with a broken nose and minus a few teeth. He flew out of the Bahamas the same night to Florida and went to hospital.

Now, as the world knows, Ali has Parkinson's Disease which I have no doubt is a legacy of all those punches he took in the latter part of a career that eventually went on for 21 years. Don't forget a career is much more than fights. Towards the end Ali used to have some terribly hard sparring sessions as well. He would be insulted if sparring partners were asked to go easy on him. All of this took its toll, even though it's true, of course, that many people who have Parkinson's Disease have never taken so much as a tap on the head. Parkinson's is a disease which can be deceptive. Ali gets extremely tired but when he is not his mind is still as playful and sharp as ever and his eyes twinkle behind a face that seems expressionless.

A few years ago I arranged for Ali to come to an event at the Planet Hollywood restaurant in London. Naturally, he was well paid. We were dining at the function and inevitably we began to talk boxing. The name of Floyd Patterson came up and somebody said he was not really a heavyweight, that he didn't weigh more than 13st, to which I replied: 'No, he was *bigger*.'

Ali didn't seem to have been paying much attention, but, with that, his eyes flashed and he interrupted the conversation. Slowly, he said: 'Did you just call me a nigger?'

It's a good job I knew him well enough to realise he was play-acting!

CHAPTER 10

Taking Control

O ur success, the fruits of our labours, came with our
involvement with Muhammad Ali and the men who
became our world champions in the 1970s and
1980s but the groundwork was done as we learned our jobs
over long, hard years where the rewards were modest and
precarious. The lessons I learned were sometimes hard.

At one time I was invited by the British Board of Control's
Central Area Council to promote at Liverpool. They wanted
somebody with youth and enthusiasm to put some life back
into the city, where they had that great old arena, Liverpool
Stadium, which was known as 'The Graveyard Of Champions'. Partly the nickname came from the tradition of bad
luck suffered by champions who either defended their titles
or simply boxed there. Somehow they lost, looked bad or
picked up an injury. However, few know that the nickname
had a more literal meaning: the Stadium was built on a
medieval cemetery.

I promoted my first show at Liverpool, in February 1960,

and made a profit and eventually spent four years trying my luck in small towns such as Blackburn, Newtown and Corwen in Wales, and cities like Leeds and Newcastle. After four years, I had made nothing – and had picked up a £10 fine for flyposting in Corwen for a show topped by the marvellous Liverpool bantamweight, Alan Rudkin, who would go on to box for the world title three times. The local magistrates even ordered me to take the posters down.

My enemies predicted I would lose a fortune but while that wasn't the case, I didn't make anything either. Once I came back to London from Newcastle and told Harry Levene I had lost £900. He shrugged and said: 'More fool you.'

It was good experience. I wasn't putting anyone out of work because there were no local promoters anyway and it kept me busy. In 1961 alone I worked on 66 shows. My biggest profile was as a matchmaker for Levene at Wembley and Belle Vue, but I also had my own company – Mickey Duff Promotions Limited – which operated on the small shows.

I was extremely proud of the matchmaking standards I set myself. They used to say I made Cupid look like an amateur and I used to say most of my rivals couldn't match the cheeks of their arse. Once I was in America with one of their top matchmakers when a boxer had almost died and the press had attacked him savagely. All he did was laugh. I said: 'If that happened to me, I would sue and clear my name or get out of the business.'

My enthusiasm was absolute. In the 1962 *Boxing News Annual* I put my name to an article entitled 'Making Matches'. In it I said:

'I love boxing ... Making matches occupies almost the whole of my thinking day. I am always conjuring up pairings, no matter where I am. In the bath, eating, looking at television, even when I'm talking, my mind is wondering what fight could top such-and-such a bill; what boy could be put in against so-and-so for a box-office draw somewhere else.

'My desk is a mass of disorder. My filing system doesn't exist. I never know where to find anything, but I rarely forget a result.'

By the mid-1960s we had Levene in the front line and had a deal with Mike Barrett for the Royal Albert Hall. I wanted to promote there and before long I received a phone call from Barrett, saying he had an exclusive contract for the venue and suggesting we work together. What criteria the Albert Hall used when they made their decision to work with a promoter, I don't know. He had promoted only a few small-time shows at places like Manor Place Baths in Walworth and he had made little impact. However, it was true that the contract was his and so we began to do business together. Eventually, Jarvis Astaire, Mike Barrett and I became partners, sharing our profits or losses. Harry Levene was always a separate entity. Later, when I was based more in America, we included Terry Lawless as well.

I loved those years. They were wonderful. I thought I was in a dreamland. I was young, enthusiastic and filled with energy. I was never methodical, more instinctive, working from what I saw and remembered. I carried a black pocket book with me everywhere which contained just about every significant phone number in the boxing world, but I rarely consulted it. Most of the numbers were in my head. Enthusiasm was my biggest asset. I was always looking forward to my next show – and the two after that. The World Association of Boxing Managers once proposed me as matchmaker for Madison Square Garden but I declined. 'As much as I love New York,' I said, 'even Rockefeller couldn't give me enough money to live there instead of London.'

It was our youth and energy which eventually beat Solomons, who will be remembered as the greatest promoter this country has ever had. His power was hurt significantly when his major venue, Harringay Arena, was closed in 1958. Two years later he lost command of the Southern Area Council of the British Board of Control. Jarvis and I supported a move to allow only people without a financial interest in the game on to the council, which destroyed his influence. He resisted it bitterly but lost. In 1967, *Boxing News* ran a front page headline 'Battle For Power In British Boxing'. Underneath it were the faces of Jarvis Astaire, Mike Barrett, myself, Harry Levene and Jack Solomons. By then we knew the 'battle', if that's what it was, was almost won.

In his last years, Solomons more or less retreated to his dinner-boxing venue, the World Sporting Club at the Grosvenor House Hotel, and only rarely attempted anything more ambitious. He died in December 1979, a day short of his 79th birthday. At his peak he was a great showman. He staged 24 world championship fights when that term actually meant something – and he left behind a benevolent fund for old boxers who had fallen on hard times.

The bitter rivalry between Solomons and Levene got if anything more extreme as the years passed. I remember being in Harry's office in Soho, on the day it was announced his great rival had died, when a *Daily Mail* journalist, Peter Moss, phoned to get Harry's reaction. 'Harry, I know you didn't get on,' Moss began, 'but I thought you might like to say something about Jack now after today's sad news.'

There was a lengthy pause while Harry considered his response. Eventually he simply announced coldly the date and venue of his next show and hung up.

One day Harry was ill and took to his bed at home. I went to see him and he looked up at me and said in his hoarse voice:

'Mickey, I'm leaving it all to you.'

I didn't know what to say. He wasn't the sentimental sort. I brushed it aside.

'Don't be silly, Harry. You'll get better soon.'

He looked at me as if I was stupid.

'Of course I'll get better,' he said. 'I mean the show next week. I'm leaving all the work to you.'

Levene outlived Solomons by a little over eight years. Nobody seemed to know exactly how old he was. 'No matter if you're rich or poor,' he used to say. 'As long as you've got money.'

The Anglo-American Sporting Club ran for 19 years from 1964–83. During that time we had a wonderful range of guests, including as I have said, former heavyweight champions Jack Dempsey and Joe Louis. In 1968 the Duke of Edinburgh accepted our invitation and we had every single reigning British champion of the time presented to him.

On another occasion we had world heavyweight champion Joe Frazier, who was in London appearing on stage with his group 'The Knockouts'. They were terrible, but Frazier was a great success at the club. Willie Pep, one of the greatest featherweights in history, was also a guest in 1967. Pep was a brilliant boxer who had more than 240 fights in a career which spanned a quarter of a century. He was world champion in two spells from 1942 until 1950 and had four terrific battles with another wonderful champion, Sandy Saddler. Once he demonstrated to a friend that it was possible to win a round without throwing a punch. He avoided everything his opponent could throw at him, feinted him this way and that, didn't take a shot and demoralised the man to the point where he didn't know what to do next. The judges gave it to Willie because he had indeed dominated the round. Sadly, when Pep was our guest he was snubbed by the British Boxing Board of Control, which was embarrassing. Pep was 44 years old but had only retired from boxing the previous year and we thought it would be a good idea to ask Pep to box an exhibition with the reigning British and European champion

Howard Winstone, who was probably our most skilful boxer of the decade. It wouldn't be too serious – both men would have worn headguards – but would have provided a few great memories of the occasion. We applied for permission to run the exhibition and were absolutely amazed to be given a letter in reply saying our application had been refused. They gave no reason. Privately we heard someone in a position of power felt the idea was in bad taste. What cheek! Pep, who had boxed exhibitions all over the world, saw the decision as an insult. At least the Anglo-American club members gave him a standing ovation when we presented him with an inscribed silver salver to mark the occasion.

Pep was a fine story-teller and remained very popular after his ring career was over. He also had a great fund of one-liners. Once, his death was reported and a local newspaperman phoned the house to ask for details. Pep himself answered:

'No, I'm not dead,' he assured him. 'I ain't even been out of the house.'

He was also married several times.

'I've got it made,' he would say. 'I've got a wife and a TV set – and they're both working.'

And again:

'My wives were very good housekeepers. When we got divorced, they kept the house.'

Pep remained unaffected by his incredible ring career – I haven't counted but he must have fought thousands of rounds – and is in his late 70s and still living in Connecticut.

Two of our other guests at the Anglo were Raymond Glendenning and W. Barrington Dalby, the famous BBC radio commentary team.

With Wembley and the Albert Hall, we had the two best arenas in London. We also had a contract with the BBC to televise our shows, which put us ahead of the rest of the field because we could generate more revenue than anyone else. As Terry Lawless's East End stable improved in the mid-1970s, we also had a bank of top class fighters to choose from who would go on to become major champions.

Naturally, it all took time but my influence and contacts increased steadily year by year and our partnership eventually became so powerful people began to speak jealously of the monopolistic stranglehold we were exercising over the rest of British boxing. They did have a point, but we were good for the game. We were a benevolent monopoly, if that's what we constituted. People worked with us because it was generally better for their own businesses if they did so. Before Lawless became such an influential manager, we worked with whoever happened to be the manager of the boxer we wanted to promote. With Joe Bugner, it was Andy Smith; with John Conteh, it was George Francis; with Chris and Kevin Finnegan, it was Sam Burns; and with Alan Minter, it was Doug Bidwell.

Of course it was our dream to guide one of our boxers to the world heavyweight title. We had Billy Walker, promoted Henry Cooper's fight with Muhammad Ali, and were involved in the challenges to Ali of Joe Bugner and Richard Dunn in the 1970s. Then in the 1980s there was Frank Bruno.

Against anyone but Ali, Bugner might have been the man to break the mould. He had been born in Hungary and I felt something for him because like me he had come here as a refugee. He never knew his father, and his mother took him, his sister and two brothers out to Yugoslavia, travelling the first part of the journey by bus and then walking through woods to freedom. For 18 months they lived in a refugee camp before coming to England, in St Ives, where he became a very successful junior athlete. He was a British schools discus champion.

Athletics did not afford him the openings he wanted, however, and he took up boxing with local manager Andy Smith, whom we knew well. In the early days Joe was so young he called his manager 'Mr Smith'. In return, Smith called him 'Joseph'. We promoted him for the first nine years of his career, until he left to live in Hollywood to try an easier way of earning a living: acting. He didn't make it. Since then, he has made several comebacks and although they were promoted by others, we did use him as an opponent for Frank Bruno in 1987.

Bugner was a big, muscular kid. In fact he struck quite a pose. Billy Walker, shortly before he retired in 1969 looked at Bugner's 6ft 3in, 15st frame and said to him: 'I'm glad I'll be out of the game when you've grown into a really big boy.'

However, despite Bugner's physical presence, when he made his debut at the Anglo-American Sporting Club in December 1967, it was disaster. An ordinary heavyweight from Birmingham, Paul Brown, knocked him out in the third round. I felt very sorry for him and rang Smith at 3 a.m. to sympathise and check the boy was all right. I make no apology for matching him carefully for the next couple of years because it was a terrible start and could have put Joe off the sport completely. He was a teenager and heavyweights don't traditionally mature until they are about 25. He beat Brown easily twice in rematches and had to overcome a very difficult psychological situation when he outpointed a fighter named Ulric Regis at Shoreditch in 1969. Regis collapsed later that night and, although he underwent a brain operation, it was unsuccessful and he died. There were doubtful circumstances that suggested the eight-round bout with Bugner might not have been solely responsible, but Joe was very young – only a couple of days short of his 19th birthday – and had to show a lot of maturity to go on.

Bugner outpointed a giant American, Jack O'Halloran,

who later went into acting and dabbled in boxing management. Then he lost an eight-round decision to an American named Dick Hall but kept progressing. In 1970 he ended the careers of Johnny Prescott and Brian London and stopped the American known as the 'Bayonne Bleeder', Chuck Wepner on a third round cut.

Wepner was one of the great characters of the day. He needed something ridiculous like 50 stitches in his face after he lost to Sonny Liston – it was Liston's last fight – and went on to become the role model for Sylvester Stallone's 'Rocky'. Wepner made most of his living as a beer salesman but dreamed of winning the heavyweight title. There is a legendary story about his fight with Ali in 1975 which went into the 15th round before getting stopped. Before he left his hotel room, he paused at the doorway and threw a sexy negligee on to the bed where his wife was sitting.

'Tonight,' he said gallantly. 'You will be sleeping with the heavyweight champion of the world.'

Hours later he opened the door and trudged wearily in, his face a mass of cuts and bruises. His wife, who was wearing the negligee, said:

'Well, honey, is Muhammad coming here or am I going to his place?'

Boxing would not be the crazy sport it is without the Chuck Wepners of the world.

Bugner's progress continued. He beat clever fighters like the Argentine, Eduardo Corletti, who was very popular here in the 1960s, and the Welshman Carl Gizzi.

He was three days past his 21st birthday when he outpointed Henry Cooper over 15 rounds at the Empire Pool, Wembley, to become British, Commonwealth and European heavyweight champion. Henry and his manager Jim Wicks made a lot of noise about the decision of referee Harry Gibbs. I didn't see a lot wrong with it. If anything Gibbs, who gave it to Bugner by a quarter of a point or one round, had it too close. Strictly on ability, Bugner was as good as anybody.

When he beat Cooper he boxed well but he wasn't experienced enough to deal with Jack Bodell's awkward style six months later. Bodell, a southpaw who had won hard fights with Billy Walker, Johnny Prescott and Brian London, was a real handful if you couldn't hurt him. Bugner just couldn't work him out and lost 14 rounds out of 15, which was a major setback.

It put Bodell in the limelight for a while – he was from Swadlincote in Derbyshire, dressed as if the 1950s hadn't ended yet, and combed what was left of his hair into a Brylcreemed quiff. He was supposed to be a pig farmer but I suspect his crafty old manager, George Biddles, was being economical with the truth. The last I heard of Bodell he had a fish and chip shop. He was a triple champion after he beat Bugner and well-worth promoting. But he was already in his 30s. There was no point in hanging about and so we made a match with the best white heavyweight in the world, Jerry Quarry, for Wembley in 1971. There was just an outside chance that Quarry might be confused, as Bugner had been, by Bodell's southpaw, rushing, trampling style. He wasn't. Jack lasted little more than a minute. One reporter, more or less at a loss as to what to ask Quarry, said:

'Jerry, did you find Bodell awkward at all?'

'Well,' said Quarry, trying to be reasonable. 'He sure fell awkward.'

So much for Bodell. After the Quarry fight he lost the European title to Jose Urtain of Spain, the British and Commonwealth championships to Danny McAlinden, and retired.

Bugner picked up the pieces slowly and regained the European title by knocking out Jurgen Blin from Germany. He was still only 22 when we took him to Caesars Palace, Las

Vegas, where he coped with an early cut eye and lasted 12 good rounds with Muhammad Ali in a non-title fight.

On the back of that I almost made a world championship bout with George Foreman, but it fell through. However, Joe Frazier was a more than capable alternative and I persuaded Frazier to come to Earls Court to fight Bugner in July 1973. Lou Viscusi, an Italian-American who had brought Bob Foster to Britain to fight Chris Finnegan at Wembley the previous November, vouched for the fact that I did a straight deal and I clinched it on a fishing trip with Frazier's manager, Yank Durham. In hindsight that 12 rounds with Frazier was Bugner's finest hour. He fought hard, survived a knockdown and pushed the former world champion the full distance.

Joe kept winning, but then it all came to nothing when it mattered most. He staged that terribly disappointing display with Ali in Malaysia and announced his first retirement. I was asked for my opinion and gave it.

'I'm delighted Joe is in such a strong financial position at 25. If it's true that he's lost his love for boxing, he's right to get out now. It's tough enough when you love it. He's done everything asked of him, except win a world title.'

The retirement was a false dawn. It lasted nine months before he came back and knocked out Richard Dunn in one round at Wembley to regain the British, Commonwealth and European titles. He retired again, divorced and moved to Los Angeles. In 1977 he boxed Ron Lyle in Las Vegas and I had a small role as a radio inter-rounds summariser with the BBC, as well as my overall job as boxing consultant with Caesars Palace. At the time the Nevada State Athletic Commission were experimenting with announcing the scores of the judges to a TV audience only at the end of each round. From where I was sitting, Bugner was losing clearly after eight rounds, but suddenly I saw a TV monitor which showed the judges had him level. I went to the corner to tell them and desperately tried to inspire Bugner to pull out a big effort over the closing rounds. He didn't respond and lost on points. Joe was, as always, honest enough after the event and showed once again that he was far from in love with fighting for a living.

'I have to wonder if all this is worth the money?' he said. 'I have to consider how much my health is worth. I shouldn't have been marked against a man like Lyle, but he's busted me up worse than Joe Frazier did and it wasn't even that much of a fight.'

I knew he had gone as far as he was going in terms of titles, though if anyone had told me Joe would still have been fighting in 1999 I would have laughed.

'Whatever Joe wants to do now is entirely his business,' I said. 'Nobody forces him to do anything and whatever he decides is OK by me. He happens to be a mate more than a boxer I promote.'

He went off on holiday to Fiji and didn't return to England until he agreed to fight for Frank Warren and helped him establish himself with ITV. That lasted a while and then he drifted away again. We did promote one more of his fights, in 1987 when, through Barry Hearn, he came to White Hart Lane, the home of Tottenham Hotspur football club – and fought Frank Bruno. Bugner was 37 and didn't have much left. We knew it was an easy fight for Bruno and we also knew it would sell and at the time we had no objection to Hearn being a part of it. Good money was made. Of course, Bugner lost and then returned to Australia where he lived with his second wife, Marlene. Every so often he would make a comeback and finally seemed to have retired in 1999, by which time he was nearly 50.

Britain has had only three Olympic boxing gold medallists since World War Two. Of those, only one, Dick McTaggart, didn't turn pro. We promoted the other two, Terry Spinks

– who won the British featherweight title – and Chris Finnegan, the 1968 middleweight gold medal winner.

Spinks was a chirpy, baby-faced youngster from the East End, who boxed for West Ham. He was only 18 when he won the flyweight gold medal in Melbourne in 1956. He beat Bobby Neil, who later trained Alan Minter and Lloyd Honeyghan, for the British featherweight title. At one time it looked as if he might be champion for a long time but he lost it to Howard Winstone, who was probably the most talented British boxer pound for pound in the 1960s. Terry was still only 24 when he announced his retirement in December 1962, following a torrid fight which he won against a Battersea fighter named Johnny Mantle on one of our shows at the Royal Albert Hall. Terry is still around and I often see him at meetings of the London Ex-Boxers Association.

Finnegan was a counter-punching southpaw as an amateur but had a rugged charm. He won the hearts of the sporting nation when he joked after his Olympic final victory: 'Now I'm not just a silly old bricklayer.'

We had to make Finnegan very colourful, because when he turned professional, all he really had going for him was the Olympic gold medal. He was a capable boxer but uninteresting, which meant that his amateur career would fairly soon have been pushed into the background. Chris fought more often than not at the Anglo-American Sporting Club, but his first title challenge was at middleweight in Copenhagen against the Danish ticket seller, Tom Bogs. He lost on points. In 1971 Chris became British and Commonwealth light-heavyweight champ by stopping Welshman Eddie Avoth in the 15th round at Jack Solomons' World Sporting Club – Jack won the purse bids – and then we went to Berlin for a bizarre European title fight with Conny Velensek.

At press conferences Velensek, who was short and stocky,

wore a toupee. We got used to him wearing it and it was a momentary shock when this bald little fellow came out of the corner. As the rounds passed Finnegan was winning by a mile. In fact, Chris boxed Velensek's head off and left him with a grotesque lump on his right eye. But the fight lasted the distance and was declared a draw. It was outrageous. Throughout the fight a German reporter near our corner had been routinely prodding me in the back for reasons best known to himself. I had ignored him mostly because Chris was doing so well, but when the scorecards were read out he gave me one prod too many and grinned broadly. Quite what he wanted or was trying to say I don't know but my temper snapped and I flattened him.

Finnegan was highly delighted with that. In the dressing room he merrily declared it the best right hand he'd ever seen. Not even that could mask our disappointment, however. Finnegan, true to form, took himself off on the town and sank his disappointment with a beer or six. Out of training or after a fight Chris liked what is euphemistically known in the East End as a nice drink. That is, he could drink most normal human beings under the table while he was still warming up. In training he was as dedicated as anybody.

In a rematch in Nottingham in February 1972 Finnegan gave Velensek another 15-round boxing lesson and this time received the verdict. He defended the European title once, but was 28 when his chance came against that great world champion Bob Foster. Although we persuaded Foster to come to Wembley, it coincided with the beginning of the end for Chris. As an athlete I think he had run his route. Unfortunately, boxers reach that stage more quickly than footballers, and although he tried hard against a man who will be remembered as one of the best of all the light-heavyweight titleholders, Finnegan was knocked out in the 14th round.

He did box on for three more years and was British champion when he retired because of a detached retina in 1975, but defeats by Rudiger Schmidtke of Germany and two by John Conteh had knocked him out of world class.

It might surprise many but I don't rate Chris Finnegan as highly as I do his brother, Kevin, who would be on my list of unlucky British boxers, who had the talent to win a world title but not the breaks. On his day Kevin was brilliant although he was something of an eccentric and, like his brother, was also fond of a drink. He made his first impression at the 1967 ABA finals when, no doubt the worse for wear, he climbed into the ring to protest at a bad decision given against Chris. He stormed around in cricket trousers and a wig (don't ask me why!), which he unceremoniously dumped in a bucket near the officials. They banned him for life, which was the ABA's loss and the professional game's gain.

In 1974 Kevin travelled to Paris and won the European title when he outboxed one of the best fighters of the time, Jean Claude Bouttier, who had twice given world middleweight champion, Carlos Monzon, all the trouble he needed. This was a hugely successful night for British boxing – on the same show at the Roland Garros Stadium John H. Stracey also won a European title at welterweight by stopping the Frenchman, Roger Menetrey.

We had Finnegan lined up for a world title fight but his luck ran out – he broke his jaw against a German named Frank Reiche at Wembley. He was so brave he stuck the job out for 10 rounds and refused to quit, but never quite came close enough again. He lost a 15-round decision to Gratien Tonna in Monte Carlo, which cost him the European championship, and he was beaten three times by Alan Minter because he wasn't as good against southpaws as he was orthodox boxers. All were tremendous fights. In 1978, Kevin twice fought Marvin Hagler. This was before Hagler was champion. The first fight was a war from start to finish and at one point I thought Hagler might be ready to go but eventually, Kevin picked up a horrible gash on his face. I called in the doctor, which was the rule at the time and waited for him to stop the fight. There was no other sensible choice but the doctor had other ideas. 'Get out there, son, and give this son of a bitch a whipping!' he said.

It was crazy. I pulled Kevin out myself. His cheek was nearly falling off. In the return he lost on cuts again but was still good enough in his 30s to beat Tony Sibson and regain the European title. Unlike his brother, Kevin also had a sensitive side – he was an extremely talented painter – but as far as I know spent the money he earned from the ring within a few years. Chris still appears at boxing functions from time to time.

The Finnegan brothers were undoubtedly gifted, but, let me tell you, John Conteh was the most talented fighter I was ever involved with. If he had stayed with our promotional team he would have dominated the light-heavyweight division for many years. His decision to go his own way was a great disappointment to us, after the years of hard work we had put into building him up, but it did Conteh no favours either. It cost him a lot of money and in the end he returned to us after about three years, by which time he was more or less finished.

Conteh was from a big, poor Liverpool family. He was a brilliant amateur, although he had flopped in his final bout when he lost a fight in the European championships which he should have won easily. John said he had offers from America, but eventually signed for north London manager George Francis. I understand the original £10,000 signing-on fee came from a guy who didn't even have a Board of Control licence named Lenny Martin. Conteh actually had his first couple of fights for Jack Solomons at the World Sporting Club before we took over, and featured him at Wembley. We insisted, however, on dealing with Francis, not Martin. We made it plain we had no interest in discussing Conteh, or any other fighter for that matter, with anyone who was acting without a licence. If Martin hovered in the background that was Conteh's problem not ours, but he did not deal with us.

Francis was a fine conditioner, a disciplinarian whose boxers were always in top shape. He used to take them out over Hampstead Heath at the crack of dawn and end the runs with a dive into the icy lake. I think George was a far better trainer than he was a manager. He would always want an all-in deal and was never prepared to take a chance on a percentage. There were times when this worked for him, but times when it didn't.

I was cautious and deliberate with Conteh's matches. He boxed at heavyweight at the start of his career, when as a 20-year-old it looked as if he might grow. I didn't rush him because I believed he needed time. He was an extremely valuable property and we moved him forward only when he was ready.

We took him to Dublin to box on the Muhammad Ali-Al 'Blue' Lewis bill in 1972 (not our promotion) and to Las Vegas on the undercard of Ali-Bugner. However, by then it was clear he was not going to fill out into a heavyweight and he trained down to make light-heavy, where, of course, he made such a dramatic impact. He won the European title by stopping the courageous German, Rudiger Schmidtke, in the 12th round and twice beat Chris Finnegan. There was no point in rushing him into a fight with Bob Foster before he was ready but he learned and improved and, by 1974, when Foster gave up the title John was 23 with a solid grounding behind him. He had lost only once, on a terrible decision to an American, Eddie Duncan.

Jorge Ahumada, a tough Argentine, was the No.1 contender because he had drawn with Foster in Bob's home town of Albuquerque. We made the match between Ahumada and Conteh for Wembley in October 1974. John showed that night what an exceptional fighter he was, picking his punches beautifully most of the way to win clearly. Although I didn't manage him, I felt proud. However, something happened to Conteh during that fight. Fifteen rounds against a man like Ahumada is a hard struggle and although he won clearly, the depths to which he had to dig to find the strength to win seemed to exhaust him mentally more than physically. Francis later told me that Conteh had described the experience as like being in a long, dark tunnel when you don't know if you will see the other side. Clearly something had disturbed him because, the following day, he stormed into Harry Levene's office in Soho, leaned over the desk and shouted at him: 'You don't know what it's like in there!'

We had Conteh on a two-fight option deal, which was not especially restrictive. In the first of these, he earned £33,000 for fighting Lonnie Bennett and won in round five on a cut eye. Eddie Futch, one of the biggest names among trainers in the last 30 years, was in Bennett's corner. Angelo Dundee tipped the American to win, which probably put the kiss of death on him. Bennett was a typical ghetto tough-nut who had served time for a shooting and then moved from Chicago to Los Angeles and sorted out his life. Conteh wanted to win far more than him.

Then we offered Conteh a non-title fight, an easy job, for £15,000. Even though he was world champion we didn't want to burn him out and we wanted to guide him well. In our view, big money fights would happen – but only when the time was right. Conteh, like many young men, wanted everything quickly and disagreed with us. People were talking to him about a fight with his rival WBA champion Victor

Galindez and with the great middleweight champion of the time, Carlos Monzon. He listened to all the talk and felt he was being short-changed. It happens to fighters when they enjoy some success. They acquire friends they never knew they had. Conteh began to ask questions in public: 'Why should I take all the punches in the ring and the promoters take the biggest slice of the profits?' he asked once.

I think we were doing a fine job with him and I have never forgotten that boxers are the men taking the shots. Sometimes our shows made a profit and sometimes they didn't, but fighters who worked for us always got paid.

In 1975 he sacked Francis, refused the second fight and said he would no longer work with us. It was a straightforward breach of contract and I took it to the Board of Control. Conteh did not attend the hearing and the Board suspended his licence until he did. Conteh's lawyers eventually had that restraint lifted – but the World Boxing Council ruled that he had to pay us compensation.

What happened to him after that was very sad. He got it all horribly wrong. In his first fight without Francis, a non-title job in Scranton, Pennsylvania, he broke his hand. Francis had always taken special care in the wrapping of Conteh's hands, which were quite slender, and I suspect whoever did the job for him this time didn't do it as meticulously. He was out of the ring for more than a year – I remember he had some kind of crackpot scheme to fight in Uganda before Idi Amin, which to nobody's surprise came to nothing – and then his brother Tony negotiated him a deal to defend his world title, 15 rounds against Alvaro 'Yaqui' Lopez in Copenhagen. I understand he was supposed to earn £100,000 – and got £2,000! John was always influenced by how much he had to pay anybody and his brother came cheap, I suppose. He left us because he felt the grass was greener elsewhere. It must have been a hard lesson.

I met Conteh for three hours in 1976 to discuss our fall-out. Conteh acknowledged I had been honest with him and payments had always been made and received by him in an orderly manner. I left hoping that one day we could do business again.

He did earn good money for a defence in Liverpool, when Bob Arum brought American TV money into the equation, and a full house at the old stadium saw him beat an American named Lenny Hutchins in three rounds. But, following that he was badly advised again, refusing to go through with a contracted defence against Miguel Angel Cuello of Argentina in Monte Carlo. The WBC, who had been more than fair in the past, stripped him. Even then they allowed him to sort out his problems and challenge the new champion, Mate Parlov, in 1978. He lost and had nowhere to go but back to us.

I went to see him at his house in Bushey Heath, Hertfordshire, and we signed a contract for him to fight Leonardo Rogers of the Dominican Republic for £25,000. It was a fair deal but the public did not buy it. Afterwards I told the press: 'The show was no good financially. If Harry Levene wants to do business with Conteh he will do so, but I'm reluctant to because I feel everybody in the game is entitled to their share of the profit.'

In other words I didn't think Conteh was still the market force he thought he was. With Francis training him, he fought for us at the Anglo-American Sporting Club and a 33-year-old American, Jesse Burnett, showed us how far Conteh's powers had waned. John was on the floor twice and got a draw. He wasn't quite 28 but had been living the wrong kind of life for some time and preferred night clubs to boxing. Basically, he blew his money on bad living. He has admitted his errors many times and I don't want to rub them in but they do illustrate just how far off the rails this extremely talented man went and show the extent to which he seemed determined to go to waste his talent. I wasn't around John when he went out at night, but in his own autobiography he admitted he once spent £4,500 on a round of drinks in a West End club. He also admitted using cocaine. On another occasion he crashed his Rolls Royce into six parked cars in the early hours somewhere in Mayfair. In the accident he smashed his already suspect right hand so badly that he could never make a proper fist again.

He did stage one more magnificent battle when he almost beat Matthew Saad Muhammad over 15 rounds for his old WBC belt in Atlantic City. Only some late knockdowns foiled him – and an illegal substance that Saad's trainers jammed into a bad cut over his eye, which allowed the champion to see the fight out. It was dreadful stuff, almost like cement, and those responsible were banned from boxing for life. John was also awarded a rematch. As brilliant as he was in the first fight, he was dreadful second time around. All the tension had gone out of him and he folded tamely in round four. He wasn't knocked out. He just kept getting knocked down. Afterwards he admitted thinking as he knelt on the canvas: 'What am I doing here? I should be in Tramps enjoying myself.'

That night he went berserk in his hotel. It was a terrible time for him and no doubt somewhere deep in his mind he had realised what he had thrown away, but I am happy to say he's all right today. He works well as an after-dinner speaker. Recently he said to me at one function, half-joking: 'Mickey, are you still doing those all-in deals?'

I reminded him the all-in deals were at the insistence of his manager, not me. He was a very talented fighter and in spite of all that happened, I couldn't help liking him. I wish him well.

CHAPTER 11

Lawless Men

Terry Lawless ran a gym at the Royal Oak pub on the Barking Road in Canning Town, training and managing fighters. We worked together steadily from the early 1970s, building up our respective businesses until towards the end of the decade when I began to spend more and more time in America and had hopes of a successful career there. Lawless had been relying on my matchmaking abilities and was nervous that his business might suffer if I left for the States, so the possibility arose of his signing an income-sharing agreement with us. Jarvis was reluctant at first but the contract was drawn up, under which either party could terminate by giving six months' notice. We did not have control of his fighters and he didn't have any control over our promotions. That is why, years later, the British Boxing Board of Control found we had done nothing wrong and we were commended as to the way we ran our business.

We don't talk now for reasons I'll mention later, but I have to acknowledge the enormous input Terry had. We used to have the most terrible arguments over a match during the day, shouting at each other, and then go to dinner at night as if nothing had happened. That's my way. Terry was always the most cautious of managers and every time one of his fighters was beaten, he would always say:

'I didn't fancy that match.'

And I used to ask him: 'And how many matches didn't you fancy that you won?'

When you suggested a fight to him, his immediate reaction was 'no'. Then you would have to do a number on him to persuade him. It was his way of negotiating.

John H. Stracey was Terry's first major success. When he was 17 he was knocked out in the ABA semi-finals by Jim Watt but he boxed in the Mexico Olympics, won the ABA title the following year and turned professional just before his 19th birthday. When John was an amateur, Terry had helped him sort out a leg injury by contacting the West Ham United physio, Rob Jenkins, and they became friends. Stracey was the original East End kid. His mum and dad had a council flat off the Whitechapel Road, overlooking the Blind Beggar, and his father Dave was his biggest fan. He always had fantastic home support, in fact he was very tied to his roots. After he won the world title, a job offer came up that would have meant him living in Las Vegas. I remember him saying: 'Leave Britain? I wouldn't ever leave Bethnal Green. It's where I belong.'

John – the H was for Henry – lost his first British title fight when he was disqualified for a low punch against Bobby Arthur of Coventry at the Albert Hall in 1972. It was a harsh decision and he put it right in style with a fourth round, one punch knockout of Arthur the following year. In 1974 he travelled to Paris and stopped European champion Roger Menetrey in a wonderful performance.

The world champion was the great Jose Napoles, one

of the classiest fighters in the history of the welterweight division. He had been born in Cuba and had fought there in the 1950s but like so many of his compatriots had left the country when Fidel Castro's government banned professional boxing in the early sixties. He had settled in Mexico and made a new life for himself. He was probably the best welterweight in the world for some time before he had his chance against the Texan, Curtis Cokes, in 1969. He beat Cokes twice and apart from an interruption caused by an unlucky cut eye defeat against an ordinary fighter named Billy Backus, had been champion since then. Napoles had been very popular when he had come to London in 1972 and knocked out Ralph Charles, one of the early Lawless fighters, in seven rounds at Wembley. John H. sparred with him briefly at the time for a little bit of experience. They called Napoles 'Mantequilla', which I am told means 'smooth as butter'. That said everything about his style – he had the easy, relaxed way of doing things that great fighters have. He was a consummate boxer who could punch.

However, by 1975 Napoles was fading. How much I wasn't sure and so I travelled to watch him fight Armando Muniz in Mexico City. He won but looked ready for the taking. I found a phone, rang Terry and said:

'Now is the time. He's gone. The next man he meets who can fight will lick him.'

'Are you sure?' said Terry.

'I'm sure.'

I had already pressed for John to be accepted as the WBC's No.1 contender and, unknown to Terry, agreed the fight in principle with George Parnassus, who was the biggest promoter in Los Angeles.

'Where are we fighting?' he said. 'At Wembley?'

'No,' I replied. 'In Mexico City.'

It took two weeks to persuade Terry but we took it. We

argued and negotiated but blended well. It was a great partnership. I was sure Napoles was ready to go but we didn't
know for sure whether or not Stracey could do the job. We
had more than one dispute with the local promoter in the
weeks building up to the fight but kept them from John and
one by one they were resolved.

The scar tissue was visible over Napoles' eyes at the weigh-in
but the champion was relaxed. When somebody asked him
whether his age would be a factor – he was officially 35 but
rumoured to be older – he smiled. 'Age doesn't matter,' he
said. 'I have a grandfather who is 92 years old and he is still
making love to all the pretty girls he can undress!'

I watched him on the scales, was unhappy with what I
saw and made him come back a second time. He made the
weight but it was my job to make sure in my own mind that
he had done so – and I wanted to make the point that we
weren't just there for the ride. It was important that the
officials – the referee, judges and supervisor – took us seriously. There was also the chance that any fuss I made might
just get under Napoles' skin if he was having trouble making
147lbs. Basically, we were fighting our corner as fiercely as
we could. Stracey had his father and fiancee in Mexico City
but missed home and we didn't know how he would respond
once the bell rang. After all, the last British welterweight to
win a world title away from home was Ted Kid Lewis – and
that was 60 years ago.

'I was homesick right up to the moment I got into the
ring,' said Stracey later.

The fight had hardly started when he was knocked down.
He was too tense and got caught. I was behind Terry in the
corner and he was crouched on the steps to the ring with
his hands together as if he were praying. I heard him say:
'Please God, not the first round.'

But Stracey got up, fought back, put Napoles down, shut

his eye and by round six was pummelling him against the ropes. A Mexican referee, Octavio Meyran, stopped the fight. John H. was the welterweight champion of the world! John and Terry were in tears and I admit that for once I shed one or two.

Napoles never fought again and a few years ago was reportedly a sad, Mr. Bojangles kind of character, singing for his supper in the bars of Mexico City.

I think we did a wonderful job with Stracey. He turned out to be a far better fighter than he looked in the early days of his career. His first defence was against Hedgemon Lewis, a fighter managed by the actor, Ryan O'Neal. We wanted a showcase occasion for Stracey at Wembley and he rose to it very well. Lewis was over the hill by then and had twice lost to Napoles. In fact, I got him accepted as challenger even though he had won only two of his previous six fights. Stracey stopped him in the 10th round and Lewis, like Napoles, never fought again.

In June 1976 Stracey made a second defence against Carlos Palomino, an intelligent Mexican who lived in Los Angeles. We knew he would be tougher than Lewis but still believed Stracey would win. In hindsight, John was nearer the end of his career than we had imagined. He had been an amateur a long time and had nearly 50 professional fights. Nevertheless, when Palomino arrived in London with his manager, Jackie McCoy, he looked nothing. The British champion of the day, Henry Rhiney of Luton, made him look terrible in sparring at the Duke of Wellington gym in Highgate. I remember telling McCoy that I thought his fighter was very ordinary.

Before the fight McCoy came over to me and was full of himself, which was unusual for him. Of course they were only getting challenger's money and he said to me: 'We didn't come here for the payday. We came here to take the title and that's what we're going to do.'

That wasn't in McCoy's character. He was a Los Angeles trainer in his 50s who worked with half a dozen world champions and knew his business. His extraordinarily positive attitude worried me.

As it turned out, Palomino beat Stracey systematically and stopped him with body punches in the 12th round. Palomino's left hook, to head or body, was his pet punch. Outside the ring he was a classy, well-spoken, educated guy who went on to become an actor and eventually worked with the California Commission. He held the world title until Wilfred Benitez took it from him and he retired after losing on points to Roberto Duran.

In 1977 John H. lost to Dave Green at Wembley, which was his last fight for us. I don't think Palomino or Green would have beaten him in his prime. Certainly not Green. After Stracey walked away from us he had one more fight in 1978, won it and retired. His time had run out. Like John Conteh, he now does very well working on the after-dinner circuit and with a cabaret act.

Dave Green, whom we called 'The Fen Tiger', was very exciting, especially as a very young fighter. The problem was that he never improved. Fighters get better in stages. They come through pressure fights at different levels and go on from them. Green came through contests but was no better. After he beat Stracey, we brought Palomino back to defend the WBC welterweight title against him at Wembley in June 1977. It was a wonderful fight and Green fought well but Palomino had a little more. Green had strength and power, ambition and dedication, but was 10 per cent short on skills and natural ability and that was the difference between winning and losing. Palomino knocked him out with a left hook in the eleventh round.

In 1980 Green was also knocked out by Ray Leonard in four rounds of a second WBC title fight in Maryland. We took that fight because we knew it was close to packing-up time for Dave – and at that stage in his career it was an offer you couldn't refuse.

I had a very good relationship with Andy Smith, who managed Green and Joe Bugner. It wasn't as warm and as powerful as the one we had with Lawless but it was close. We had no financial interest in the management of his fighters and he was nothing to do with our promotions, but we got on well.

When people criticise us for creating home-made fighters, they should look at how many titles our boxers won away from home. Stracey won in Mexico City, Alan Minter won in Las Vegas, Maurice Hope won in San Remo and later Lloyd Honeyghan won in Atlantic City.

It would be wrong of me to say I saw Mo Hope as a world champion in his early days but then I didn't see Lloyd Honeyghan in those terms either. In almost every case anybody who sees future world champions in novice professionals is either naive, a dreamer or a liar. What you usually think is 'This guy has talent, now how far can he go?' You need to find out what he's like, whether or not he has the temperament, attitude of mind – which are not quite the same things – and the dedication. However much foresight you have and however good a judge you are, you never know for sure, until it happens, how the guy will stand up under big fight pressure.

I saw potential in Hope, in that I thought he would become much better than he was when he started. Terry Lawless was an extremely patient trainer and, largely, a great motivator. I like to think that unlike a lot of managers we were firstly motivated by success rather than by money. We were both great believers that you get successful first and money will invariably follow. Sometimes a world champion is colourless and just doesn't draw. Building him takes time and thought.

Hope was a typical example. When he first came to prominence he couldn't fill a telephone booth and in fact his drawing power never came close to matching his true ability. He was always a good fighter but never a big attraction. Look at Hope's record, though, and you will see a tough, competent professional who worked hard for his breaks and had some excellent wins.

He won the British light-middleweight title early in his career and became European champion with a fine 15th round stoppage of Vito Antuofermo in Rome. In 1977 he was robbed in a world title fight in Berlin when the officials gave him a draw against the German, Eckhard Dagge. I thought he won by a street and had no trouble whatsoever, apart from when he got a thumb in the eye in the 10th round. Harry Gibbs was the British judge and he had Maurice winning clearly. We pushed for a rematch but had to wait for two years before he challenged Rocky Mattioli in San Remo in March 1979. Maurice knocked the Italian down in the first round and stopped him in eight. Mattioli's people complained that their fighter had broken his wrist when his hand took his body weight in the first round knockdown, but I couldn't see their point. 'There's no argument,' I said. 'If he hadn't been knocked down, he wouldn't have broken it.'

Afterwards Hope's long-time partner Pat was so overcome with emotion that she fainted. After she had recovered Maurice, who had a dry sense of humour, said: 'I didn't know she was chinny.'

They were eventually married in the Imperial Palace, Las Vegas, in 1981 when Maurice was over there for his world title fight with Wilfred Benitez. Terry was best man.

After beating Mattioli, Maurice had a straightforward first defence against the safest challenger I could find, Mike Baker from Washington DC. Maurice won in the seventh. Baker's appearance at No.7 in the WBC ratings was strange but I knew he was the obvious option. Later investigation by a New York writer, Peter Heller, revealed that his manager was a Washington attorney named Edward Bennett Williams, whose clients included Don King. This 'convenience' was nothing to do with us but did provide us with an opportunity for Maurice to defend his championship against an opponent that, on paper, wasn't at all dangerous. But don't forget this is boxing – Baker could easily have been much better than he seemed.

Because Mattioli's people had made such a noise about the broken hand a rematch wasn't a bad idea and Mo stopped him again, in 11. Later he admitted the energy began to go out of him at this time and although he outpointed a tough Argentine named Carlos Herrera at Wembley in November 1980, it was unnecessarily hard. That night, after the live bouts, we drew down six huge screens and played out the Ray Leonard-Roberto Duran rematch, which Jarvis's company also played to closed circuit audiences around the country.

While it was true Hope didn't sell a huge amount of tickets at home, he was increasing in popularity and had the World Boxing Council belt, which made him a commodity in America. Unfortunately, he needed time out while he underwent laser beam surgery at Moorfields Eye Hospital under David McLeod, a leading eye surgeon who we used regularly, to repair a hole in the retina of his left eye.

I tried to make a fight between Hope and Ray Leonard. Terry put the price at $1 million and Mike Trainer, for Leonard, offered $700,000. They also wanted Bob Arum on board with Top Rank but, as far as I was concerned, Arum still owed us a lot of money from the Leonard-Duran fight. I didn't want to do business with him. I asked for the world TV rights outside the USA on top of the $700,000, which would bring us up to what Terry wanted, and Trainer agreed.

Then he came back and wanted to add a 30-day buy-back clause which in effect meant that if it was a lousy fight that wouldn't sell he would allow us to have the rights, but if it was a blockbuster he wanted it. You can't have it both ways, so I declined that, and asked for no overseas rights but a $500,000 increase in the purse. In effect, I was selling them back to him. That would have taken us to $1.2 million but at that point the deal went cold. No progress could be made.

Instead we agreed a fight with Wilfred Benitez, who had been only 17 years old when he had won the WBA light-welterweight title. After that he had moved up to beat Carlos Palomino for the WBC welterweight championship and now wanted to be a three-weight champion. Benitez was managed by the late Jim Jacobs, with whom I could deal. We made the fight for Las Vegas in May 1981 but Maurice was badly knocked out in the 12th round. It was a worry for a while. He was on the floor for ten minutes and although he recovered he was advised to spend the night in hospital under observation. On the way to the ambulance they wanted to put him on a stretcher but he insisted on walking. He wanted to go out of the building with dignity. 'Let me walk,' he said. 'Don't do that to me, man.'

Benitez was very callous. He didn't care at all about the man he had just beaten. Even while Mo was on the floor, Benitez was noisily celebrating. When the press asked if he was concerned for Hope, he was totally insensitive.

'I feel the punch right through my body,' he said. 'It was the best knockout of my life.'

Somebody pointed out that Hope had, in fact, lost two front teeth, but that cut no ice with Benitez.

'Maybe the tooth fairy will make a wish for him come true,' he said.

Jim Jacobs was a decent, compassionate man. He went to the hospital and said to us: 'I felt I ought to be here.'

It was almost the end of Mo's career. He lost a close decision in a European title fight with a brawling Italian, Luigi Minchillo, in 1982 and retired. There was no happy ending. In 1987 he admitted debts of more than £63,000 and no assets in a bankruptcy court. He had bought a big house for his family and sent the children to private schools but could not build his ring earnings into anything worthwhile. A business went into liquidation and eventually he returned to Antigua, where he had been born in a wooden shack all those years before.

Jim Watt, another of the Lawless stable, was a seasoned professional when he came to us. He had stayed in Glasgow with a local manager, Jim Murray, but they had eventually fallen out. He had been British champion, but had lost decisions away from home in Commonwealth and European title fights and was considering retirement. Terry and I discussed him and we both felt that that would be a waste of talent. Terry rang him and Jim couldn't believe he was interested in his career. Fortunately, we began a relationship that brought Jim a world title and was fruitful for all of us. Jim was blessed with commonsense and understood what we were trying to do. We brought him to London, where he fought most of the time and, in 1977, he became European champion with a first round cuts win over a Frenchman, Andre Holyk. The fight took place in the St Andrews Sporting Club, Glasgow, where a Yorkshireman, Les Roberts, made the matches. Roberts was really hard work. Sometimes I thought he should have been prosecuted for impersonating a human being! We did a deal based on gate money but most of Roberts' club members were away on holiday and didn't want tickets and the venue was half-empty. Jim earned virtually nothing above his training expenses.

We lost the purse bids for his second defence against the former WBC light-welterweight champion, Perico Fernandez, and had to go to Madrid. Jim earned more than £12,000 but I would have preferred him to have fought at home where the risk was less. He was floored in the first round, but dictated the rest of the fight and won very easily. By the closing stages the fickle Spanish fans had turned on Fernandez and were chanting 'cobarde' (coward) at him. They cheered Jim all the way to his dressing room.

I was reluctant to stage fights in Glasgow, where promoters had lost money for years. Lawless thought Watt could sell there but I really didn't think so and could not justify a high purse bid for a European title defence against another Spaniard, Antonio Guinaldo, in 1978. I happened to be on holiday with Terry and his family in the Adriatic when the purse deadline was looming and all through the week, Terry kept chipping away at me to take the fight. Wherever we were, he wouldn't let the subject rest. Finally I shouted at him: 'Stop it! You're ruining my holiday.'

Eventually, just to get Terry off my back, I telephoned the leading Italian promoter, Rodolfo Sabatini, in Rome and asked him to make an offer for the fight of just over £15,000. To my horror it turned out to be the winning bid. I took the phone call from Sabatini with the news and went over to Terry. 'Terrible news,' I said and saw his face drop. 'I got the fight.'

We staged it in the Kelvin Hall, in partnership with Peter Keenan with whom we promoted all of Jim's Scottish fights, and managed to sell it in spite of clashing with a Rangers European Cup tie the same night. Jim forced Guinaldo to quit in the fifth round and the British Board of Control took such a dim view of his surrender that they withheld part of his purse. I thought they were very harsh.

There was a postscript to this story when the late Johnny Owen fought in Spain shortly afterwards, in a European title fight in Almeria against Juan Francisco Rodriguez. The

Spaniards were using some kind of wintergreen type of oil on their man which got into Owen's eyes and made the whites pink. The British Boxing Board of Control representative, Harry Vines, went around to protest and he was kicked in the groin by a security man. Owen was robbed of the decision and then short-changed. Apparently the Spanish Federation had decided to deduct from his purse the exact amount which had been taken from Guinaldo. The incident caused a fall-out between the British Board and the Spanish Federation which lasted some years.

Once we had proved Watt could sell tickets in his home city, we set about bringing a world title fight there. Roberto Duran had dominated the lightweight division since he beat Ken Buchanan in 1972 but had now relinquished it to move up in weight. The WBC had Watt at No.2 and therefore in line to box for the vacant title. I heard they wanted to match the No.1, Alfredo Pitalua of Colombia, with Andy Ganigan from Hawaii, and were prepared to relegate Watt in order to make the fight. I lobbied very hard at the WBC Convention in Las Vegas, with backing from the British Board of Control, and our man stayed at No.2. Don King had Pitalua under contract but at the time wasn't particularly bothered about him. In Miami, I paid King $20,000 to allow Pitalua to box for us. Before I came home I saw Pitalua's people in Mexico City and talked about a television deal in New York. When we managed to increase the seating capacity at the larger arena in the Kelvin Hall to 10,000, we felt we could make it pay. It was a wonderful occasion, one of the high points of the decade, and Watt won the WBC belt by stopping Pitalua in the 12th round. I made him pay a fierce price for his new status – as we all rushed into the ring at the end, I kissed him on the cheek. I hope he's forgiven me!

The biggest promotion we staged in Scotland was Jim's defence against Howard Davis, the 1976 Olympic gold medallist, at Ibrox Stadium in June 1980. Davis had won the Best Stylist award in Montreal ahead of Ray Leonard and had been built up by CBS. I didn't want the fight to go to the States because we knew what bringing the American to Glasgow might do to him. After a lot of hard work, I did a deal with ABC which would cut out CBS – and allow us to put it on at Ibrox, the home of Jim's beloved Rangers. I went to the purse opening in Mexico City, where Davis's managers Dennis Rappaport and Mike Jones were not even contemplating losing the bid. You could almost hear the thud as their faces hit the floor when Jose Sulaiman announced we had the fight. We won it by a whisker.

Watt trained in his usual professional manner and was given an extra edge by the arrogance of Davis, Rappaport and Jones, who labelled him 'Jim Who'. They argued about everything, from the size of the gloves to appearing at press conferences. They were actually quite capable in their way. I can't really knock them – except they simply wanted to run roughshod over the whole promotion which, of course, we weren't prepared to accept.

Heavy rain and the early hours start to fit ABC's schedules kept the crowd down to 12,000 but everything went beautifully. Watt outboxed and outfought Davis to win a unanimous decision after 15 rounds.

If that was a chaotic deal, Watt's defence against Sean O'Grady from Oklahoma was ridiculous. To get the services of Sean, you had to talk to his father Pat . . . and his mother Jean. When they arrived it was with sisters, brothers and even Grandma O'Grady and they argued and complained all the way. At one point they threatened to go home. They objected to all three of the WBC officials – Arthur Mercante, Harry Gibbs and Raymond Baldeyrou of France – and just before the weigh-in they claimed they had received a death threat.

Somewhere along the way O'Grady had posed for a photograph in a Celtic shirt. The line was that a Rangers fan had taken exception to it and sent a letter to them. I was far from convinced. I saw them at their hotel, called in the police, who offered them protection and they finally relented. In my opinion it was a ridiculous charade. Fortunately, Watt took full retribution, surviving a bad gash over his right eye to cut O'Grady horribly on the forehead. Watt won in the 12th round. We were extremely glad to see the back of the whole O'Grady bunch. Predictably, they lobbied the WBC for a rematch the moment they arrived home, and claimed they had been shafted, but were told to wait.

Instead, we negotiated a best ever payday for Watt to defend against Alexis Arguello at Wembley in June 1981. It took a while. When purse bids were opened at the WBC headquarters in Mexico City, a 34-year-old Mexican named Rogelio Robles stunned everyone by bidding $1 million. Don King, Bob Arum and I all put together independent offers of more than $800,000 but none of us could match Robles. I had worked with Robles in Los Angeles, where I had been promoting with Don Chargin, and knew him well. All I could say was: 'The bid is fantastic and it's a hell of an achievement for him to pull it off. I'm sorry in a way that Jim has to travel but I'm delighted for him that he will be getting so well paid.'

Privately, I knew nothing was certain in boxing. Robles had ten days to lodge 10 per cent of the bid with the WBC and still had to find the rest. Eventually, we came to an arrangement. Robles was smart. He worked out that he could earn more money by promoting the fight in England. Jim and Arguello fought at Wembley under the promotional mouthful of 'Harry Levene and Mickey Duff on behalf of Azteca Promotions together with Rogelio Robles'. Watt fought a determined fight, survived a knockdown and went down on points against one of the greatest fighters of the modern era. Both are gentlemen. After he lost, I went to see Jim at his hotel to make sure he was all right. 'Don't worry about me,' he said. 'You and Terry have changed the course of my life. I can do all the things I've always wanted. I owe you that.'

There is one thought that Terry Lawless and I always had in common – we were great believers in the saying that there was no place like home. We would avoid going away if we possibly could and with Jim we built him up into a big story in Glasgow. We knew what an advantage it was for him to fight in front of his own people. I'm not saying that Jim wouldn't have won those fights if they had been abroad, but the money was never good enough to tempt us to go. If the offer is only 25 or 30 per cent more than you would earn at home, the difference is soon swallowed up in expenditure and cancels out the plus points. We did go away when we had to, and the record of our fighters away from home was a very good one, but we preferred to keep all risks to a minimum. Jim was very successful, came out of it in good physical condition and has gone on to be a great success as a television analyst.

Charlie Magri was the fourth of the Lawless world champions. Born in Tunisia to French parents, he was raised in the East End and boxed for Britain in the 1976 Olympics. He was a very colourful little fighter. He could fight but there weren't a lot of good flyweights around at the time and I don't rate him as one of our better world champions. He wasn't as good as Duke McKenzie, for instance, who won three world titles with me later on. Nevertheless, Magri was game enough to ride a couple of setbacks – he was knocked out twice by Mexicans, Juan 'Monito' Diaz and Jose Torres – and won the WBC flyweight title in 1983. He stopped a little guy from the Dominican Republic, Eleoncio Mercedes, in the seventh round. Mercedes was later shot dead while standing on a street corner in his home town of La Romana, but that made no difference to one of the world authorities, who continued to rate him in their top ten! People have accused me of importing stiffs from time to time but that was ridiculous. Magri couldn't hold on to the title. A Filipino farmer named Frank Cedeno stopped him in his first defence. It was a shame but he can always say he was a world champion. He is still in the game, managing and training fighters, and has a sports shop in the East End.

They were wonderful times. Lawless had other fighters in the gym like Jimmy Batten and John L. Gardner, who both won European titles. Batten gave Roberto Duran a hard 10 rounds. Gardner was in the shake-up for a world title fight at one time but it didn't quite happen.

As I said, Lawless and I no longer speak. We fell out only a couple of years ago over a question of loyalty. I had a confrontation with a London matchmaker who worked for us, Terry Toole, in our Wardour Street office. Toole was extremely upset and Lawless did not give me the support I expected after our years of working together. Terry tried to stick up for Toole by attempting to make me understand why he was offended. Instead of backing me, he said: 'Mickey, you've got to understand that he's a very proud man.'

I was very angry – and from that moment we have not spoken. It wasn't exactly what he said – it was his attitude at a time when he was called on to take sides. He decided to take the other side when I needed help and I felt very badly let down. I did send his wife a card when I heard she was ill. I didn't expect a reply, and didn't receive one, but I felt it was the proper thing to do. We are still business partners because of the deal that was in place at the time but we no longer communicate.

No matter. At our peak we had a system which worked and we used it well. Of course, we had our enemies and there were those who were jealous of our success, but I think we can look back at our track record and say the 1970s was a golden era for British boxing – and largely thanks to the success we had. Terry Lawless and I, Jarvis Astaire, Mike Barrett and Harry Levene were a formidable team who understood enough of the way boxing worked on an international level for us, and our boxers, to prosper.

CHAPTER 12

The Middleweights

The middleweight division is special: its fighters are big enough to be powerful and small enough to need plenty of skill to survive. Britain produced Randolph Turpin in the 1950s, Terry Downes in the sixties and Alan Minter at the turn of the eighties.

Minter was a spectacular middleweight. I think our development of him was one of our best achievements but he could fight and he did beat good opponents. It takes a special breed of fighter to win a world title against an American champion in Las Vegas, but Minter did it when he outboxed Vito Antuofermo on a split decision at Caesars Palace in March 1980. Split decision? In my opinion Minter won by a long, long way. British judge Roland Dakin took some terrible stick in America for a lop-sided scorecard in favour of Alan but more should have been made of the guy who scored for Antuofermo. In my opinion, he should never have been allowed to judge again. People often ask if judges are crooked. No, not in the conventional sense. They may occasionally get leaned on and be weak enough to allow themselves to become biased but 90 per cent of the time they give what they see. And I have always said that sometimes a stupid judge will do what you can never pay a bent one to do. I've no reason to suppose the guy who scored for Antuofermo didn't give what he saw, but in my opinion his view was badly wrong.

Minter was robbed in the semi-finals of the 1972 Olympic Games and his luck wasn't much better in the early days of his professional career. He lost four fights because of cut eyes and we wondered if that weakness might prevent him reaching the top. It certainly delayed him but it made his success all the sweeter when it happened. His three wins over Kevin Finnegan, whom I rate very highly, prove his quality. He won two of the three fights without much argument and got the decision in the second fight which some felt Finnegan won. He also stopped a middleweight I managed named Billy Knight, who was a brilliant amateur and had plenty of skill but didn't have the temperament for the big time. Minter stopped him in two rounds.

One match I didn't make for Minter – and which I was furious about – was when he was put in with an American named Ronnie Harris, who was the 1968 Olympic light-weight gold medallist. By 1977, he was in the 'Who needs him club?' with 21 consecutive professional victories. His nickname was 'Mazel' and he was suddenly claiming to be Jewish, even though he was a black American from Ohio. I was in California at the time, when I heard Mike Barrett had made the match for Minter. I knew Harris and rang them up in London and kicked up hell about it. I was shouting at them – went completely potty. They had already contracted the fight and were too far down the road with it. Predictably, Harris was too cute for Minter, busted up his lip and stopped him in the eighth round. Later that year when Alan lost his

European title to Gratien Tonna of France on a cut eye in Milan, again it looked as if he would fall short of the very top.

In 1978 he also had to overcome the psychological problems caused by the death of an opponent, Angelo Jacopucci, when he regained the European title in Bellaria, Italy. Jacopucci was stopped in the 12th round, went out to a club afterwards and collapsed with a brain injury. He died a few days later. Minter was understandably upset but managed to overcome it, stopped Tonna in a terrific performance at Wembley and then waited for his chance at the middleweight title. We had a piece of luck when Marvin Hagler was given only a draw with Antuofermo in Las Vegas when most thought he had romped it. That let us in with a challenge from Minter before Hagler was given the rematch he deserved. Antuofermo probably looked at Minter's relatively ordinary record and took what he thought would be a safer payday.

Minter beat Antuofermo, then because of the controversy of the split decision, we staged a rematch at Wembley in June 1980. By then Alan was attracting a mob that was hard to keep out. They were raucous and looked a little bit dangerous but stayed within the limits of reasonable behaviour. It was a night when Minter flaunted his patriotism and the crowd went crazy for him as he cut Antuofermo to defeat in eight rounds.

The mob let him down when Alan lost his title in his second defence, against Hagler at Wembley in September 1980. He was outpunched from the start and sliced to ribbons in three rounds. The fight had to be stopped because of his cuts. Hagler couldn't miss him. Before he could be crowned as champion and receive his championship belt in the ring, the plastic bottles of beer and general debris began flying in – all of it apparently aimed at Hagler and his cornermen, the Petronelli brothers. They shielded him from the worst of it and then we managed to get them out under police escort. It was a depressing, terribly disappointing moment which has rightly gone down as one of the low points in British boxing history. The mob which Minter had attracted showed their real colours, showed exactly what kind of people they were. It had never happened before and as far as we were concerned it was totally unanticipated.

Of course we asked ourselves if we had been responsible in any way. Looking back, there was an atmosphere before the fight which may have been fuelled partly by the quote often attributed to Minter: 'I'm not going to allow a black man to take away my title.'

Even if he had believed it, it would have been a very stupid thing to say. Alan said he had been badly misquoted, or at least misconstrued and what he had intended to say was not meant to be racist. The damage was done, of course. Given the circumstances, should we have allowed Alan to wear Union flag trunks, should we have allowed him to be accompanied to the ring by a person carrying the flags of England and the United Kingdom, and should we have had a section of the band of Royal Marines fanfaring both men into the ring? Maybe, maybe not. I don't really know why the violence happened on that night. Crowd disturbances do occur at boxing shows from time to time, with no easily identifiable common cause, but the vast majority, probably 99.5 per cent, of promotions in Britain provoke no crowd trouble whatsoever.

Minter was almost at the end. He won a 10-round work-out at Wembley against a journeyman named Ernie Singletary, lost a disputed decision to Mustafa Hamsho in Las Vegas and was then knocked out by Tony Sibson. Recently he came up to me at a London Ex-Boxers Association meeting and said his son was a good boxer, who might eventually turn professional. And he paid me a nice compliment. 'If he does,' he said, 'I want you to manage him.'

Incidentally, Minter was managed by his father-in-law, Doug Bidwell. I never got on with Bidwell and, it has to be said, he was not the most competent of men. I remember being with Minter once when someone asked if I acted for Alan.

'Do you manage this fighter?' they said.

'No,' I said. 'I manage the manager.'

Typical of Bidwell was the stroke he pulled on us when Minter fought Sibson at Wembley in 1981, in what proved to be his last fight. The show, as usual, was on BBC television where, as everyone in Britain knows, no advertising is allowed on a boxer's clothing. Everything was checked in the dressing room, but then, in the ring, when he took his gown off, Minter's shorts had 'DAF Trucks' written all over them. There was nothing we could do. Bidwell had turned us over for some extra cash. He was a spiv. In fact, it didn't work because the BBC refused to screen the fight as we had broken our contract. It was a shambles. It also happened to rob Sibson of public acclaim of his finest win because he knocked out Minter in three rounds to become European champion. And Minter, whose nose was broken, never boxed again.

Sibson was a boy from Leicester who also had a big following that could sometimes get out of hand. He was a nice lad who was managed at first by a local man named Carl Gunns, who made a mistake in putting him in with one of my fighters, a world class light-heavyweight named Lottie Mwale. Sibson eventually won a British title by stopping another middleweight I managed, Frankie Lucas, but then lost it to Kevin Finnegan and left Gunns to sign for Sam Burns. With us promoting and Sam managing, Sibson went all the way to a world title shot, when he grossed half a million dollars to fight Hagler on a snowbound night in Worcester, Massachusetts, in 1983. Sibson was a good puncher, but his preparations went badly in Leicester and he just wasn't mentally ready for a night as big as that. He did try, but everything went wrong for him and Hagler won easily in six rounds. While we were inside the arena, a blizzard came down outside and a lot of people were stranded and had to walk through deep snow to reach their hotels or some kind of shelter. Eventually, Sibson left us and was promoted by Frank Warren. He boxed twice more for world titles but lost both.

Hagler was proving to be a thorn in our side, but I thought I had found a fighter to beat him in the Ugandan, John 'The Beast' Mugabi, who was trained by George Francis and managed by me. Bill Caplan, a publicity man who did a spot of ring announcing, gave him his nickname. Mugabi was boxing on a show promoted by Don Chargin on the West Coast somewhere. Before the fight Caplan was with us when another manager came up and said to me: 'That fighter of yours – man, he's a beast.'

Caplan heard it, liked it and promptly introduced him as John 'The Beast' Mugabi. It stuck for the rest of his career.

Mugabi used to drive me crazy. At times he could be very arrogant and stubborn. He loved spending his money and always promised me he would start saving soon. It was always 'soon' with him, never 'now'. He would just go out and buy anything but then would forget to pay his bills. He couldn't read and could barely write anything more than his name, and when the bills came to his house he would just throw them out with the garbage.

Once, in a fight with James 'Hard Rock' Green in 1984, Mugabi took a thumb in the eye. He said his vision was blurred and he wanted to quit. I told him to stay calm and the vision would clear. At the end of the next round the doctor came in to see him. John was sulking, very cross indeed and the doctor said: 'Where are you?'

I could tell Mugabi wasn't interested in him – and he just stared straight ahead. The doctor would have stopped the fight, so in desperation I said: 'Doc, he doesn't understand a word of English.'

I don't know whether he believed me or not but he let the fight go on, Mugabi's vision cleared and he went on to win on a 10th round stoppage.

I was convinced he had a good chance to beat Hagler because as George Francis put it you could see opponents' faces drain of colour when Mugabi hit them. The one nagging doubt in my mind was that I could not get him to work 15 rounds in a gym. I thought he needed to do that, so that he knew he could do it in the ring. I knew he could, but he didn't. Every time he got to nine or ten rounds, he would break off and say: 'That's it. No more. Finished.'

And there was nothing you could do to persuade him to carry on. Hagler, who in the end held the middleweight title for nearly seven years, had just a little too much all-round ability and mental tenacity when they fought in Las Vegas in 1986, and knocked him out in round 11. At the end of the sixth round Mugabi came back to the corner and said:

'My hand is very bad.'

'You can't give up just because of a bad hand,' I told him.

He took a deep breath, carried on and didn't mention it again, but the right hand was badly swollen when we took off his glove at the end. I wonder what might have happened if his hand had held out. Mugabi did exceptionally well with Hagler when you consider that afterwards he won the light-middleweight title. Really, he was conceding natural weight. Don Curry, the world welterweight champion of the time, was working ringside as a television analyst and said:

'I've never seen better motivation in a corner than that Mickey Duff is giving to Mugabi.'

All I can say now is that it wasn't good enough, was it!

I brought him back and he went on to win the WBC light-middleweight title. During the build up to the fight we were strolling around and Mugabi stopped to admire a Rolex watch in a shop.

'If you win the title,' I said, 'I will buy you one as a gift.'

He won and, true to my word, I bought him a Rolex, which at the time was worth about £1,500. Later, I found out he had sold it for $100.

Mugabi got a very good pay day for the Hagler fight but, as I've said, the man just couldn't stop spending, and true to form he had spent the lot in a matter of weeks. Long after both the fighters had retired, I was at a function and Hagler came up to me and asked me very coldly:

'Did you steal John Mugabi's money?'

'You must be joking,' I said.

'You know, he had half a million dollars to fight me,' continued Hagler. 'How can a guy like that end up broke?'

The next time I saw him I half-ignored him for what I saw as an unnecessary slur. He said something, and then I told him I was very upset at what he had said about Mugabi's money. I had looked back at the books and found that, after deductions and income tax, Mugabi had received $320,000 from fighting Marvin. Six weeks later he had mailed me to ask me to pay for an air ticket. In that time he had bought five cars, given some money away, and paid for all kinds of other nonsense. He was broke. In six weeks. There are some people you simply cannot help.

At my induction into the Hall of Fame, Hagler was there. He must have taken in what I had said, gone away and done some checking of his own because he got up and spoke: 'I said something to Mickey Duff once. He knows what it was and I know. And I want to make a public apology.'

We shook hands and that was that.

I rate Hagler as the best middleweight in history. He would have beaten Ray Robinson as a middleweight – and Carlos Monzon. At the end he wasn't quite as good, but at his best he would have beaten everybody. His victory over Thomas Hearns in 1985 was breathtaking, one of the finest fights you could ever wish to see. He was cut on the forehead – a deep gash – and the blood was running into his eyes. They had traded ferocious punches for two rounds and it was obvious it couldn't go on like that for much longer. Referee Richard Steele went to Hagler's corner and said to him:

'Can you see?'

As the corner worked on the cut, Hagler looked at Steele with those cold eyes and said:

'I ain't missin' him, am I?'

He knocked out Hearns in the next round. It was a fabulous fight between two great fighters.

CHAPTER 13

Outside Boxing

Over the years I have been passionate about gambling. Boxing has been my consuming interest and my business but having a bet has been great fun. I have a favourite saying for gamblers. There are two kinds of casino players – losers and liars. You can have winning nights and a winning run of three or four nights but you won't have a winning year or even a winning six months.

I won the biggest bet of my life on the Marvin Hagler-Sugar Ray Leonard fight in April 1987. I put on $200,000 to win $275,000. I felt Hagler had gone back enough and Leonard's style would always give him problems. Once I knew how well Leonard had prepared, I was convinced he would win. The decision went narrowly against Hagler – it was only the third time he had lost in his career – and he felt very bitter about it. I had no doubts Leonard had won and I had $275,000. I did quake just a little bit when I heard the words 'split decision', but it came out right.

If you sum up all the gambling I have done, combining

casinos, boxing and an occasional football match, I am certainly not behind and probably a little ahead. That's because I mainly gambled on the one thing I knew about more than anything else – boxing. I was always brave with my money when I believed a boxer would win. Sure, it's not always worked out and you never squeal about it when you lose but when it has, it's more than made up for my losses. And even though I have been a massive gambler at times, money has never been my god.

Of course, from time to time I have been asked about crooked fights and boxing people are always talking about bent judges and fighters taking dives. Let me state quite categorically, I have never been involved in one. I have heard of them but I have never known of one for sure. I'm not saying I haven't arranged fights that were one-sided – ones that you were pretty sure there was only going to be one winner, but then I've been wrong about that a few times.

I did try to fix a fight once – one of my own! I knew before I fought a guy named Neil McCearn of Glasgow at West Ham on 7 December 1948 that I was going to retire afterwards and I thought it would be handy to get a few quid to lose. I saw a bookmaker and told him: 'I am fighting tonight. For a good offer, I will go crooked.'

He looked at me as if I had gone mad. Don't forget I was only 19 and trying to be wise.

'No son,' he said. 'You try to win. I still want to bet the other side!'

He was right, of course. I tried – and lost on points.

At one time in the early 1970s I had a credit line at Caesars Palace in Las Vegas of $50,000 and I was very friendly with Bill Weinberger, who was Caesars' vice president. We used to call him Uncle Bill. One day when he was away I got too involved in the casino playing baccarat. I lost $50,000 – the extent of my credit line. To cut a long story short, at my request they kept extending . . . and I lost another $175,000. I lost $225,000 in one day. I went back to my room absolutely horrified at what I had done. I didn't sleep at all. I just tossed and turned until my phone rang at 9 a.m. It was Bill, who had just returned. 'Have you gone out of your fucking mind?' he said. 'Come and have breakfast with me.'

I got dressed and went down to the coffee shop, which is where I always ate in Caesars. You could get anything you wanted there. I sat down with Bill and he said:

'If I had been here, there is no way you'd have had that kind of credit.'

'Bill,' I pleaded. 'I'm over 21. The only thing I need is time.'

Fortunately, he agreed. He knew I would pay. As soon as I got home I sent him $50,000 to cover my credit line, which I felt was my obligation. He rang me to say he had received it, but there was a large amount still outstanding of course.

'Sorry Bill,' I said. 'I will need a bit of time with the rest.'

'Take as long as you like. I know you're all right.'

As we got talking the conversation came around to boxing and, with that, a possible solution to my debt arose. 'Why can't we do one of your fights here? Bill said

I said I was sure we could.

'What can you offer?'

'Well, how about Ali and Bugner,' I said. 'I think I could do that.'

He offered to pay my flight over to discuss it but I didn't want to be under any further obligation. I flew to Vegas after making preliminary enquiries. I explained to Bill that I had partners and anything that came off my debt at the end of it must not affect their share. He came straight to the point.

He knew I would bring in casino players through my contacts at the Anglo-American Sporting Club. We ran a trip for 600 people and filled it. In return, Bill gave us rooms and complimentary food for us and them. We had about 200 couples, although the wives didn't gamble and about 200 single men, who were gamblers. My luck was in and theirs was out. They all did their cobblers and the show did well. It didn't sell out but it drew a good house.

Uncle Bill had a meeting with one of his directors, explained that I should never have been given credit because I was over my credit line, that we had worked together well on the boxing show and might be able to do further business. They agreed to wipe off my debt. If he were alive, I wouldn't tell the story because it would have embarrassed him, but it was an act of kindness I will never forget. It was an example of how a dire situation can be turned around to your benefit. Sure, I was very lucky, but it was because I was a player that Weinberger gave me the chance to put on that show, and we went on to work together again, but not always at Caesars and obviously not always with fights as famous as Ali and Bugner. For the future shows, I would bring in a plane load of players and he always found a way for me to make money. It was a great relationship.

As a casino gambler I could win $2,000 and walk away. But if I lost I would stay chasing it and might keep on losing. You do get desperate. I was always brave and daring, especially when I was losing! Weinberger said to me once: 'You know your trouble, Mickey? You eat like a bird and shit like an elephant.' What he meant of course was that when I was ahead I was cautious and 'ate', or won, small. And when I was behind I played big – and messed up big.

Boxing was naturally my strong point. Another of my big coups was when I won $50,000 on the Larry Holmes-Gerry Cooney fight in 1982. I put a lot on Holmes when he was 1–2 on as I thought they were the best odds I would get, but as the fight neared, a lot of daft money – sentimental money from the heart not the head – went on Cooney. I couldn't believe it when the price on Holmes went out to even money and so I put even more on. Cooney fought well but Holmes was the better man most of the way and won in the 13th round.

The most I lost, I think, was $25,000 when I backed Wilfred Benitez to beat Thomas Hearns in a WBC light-middleweight title fight in December 1982. Benitez was one of my fighters at the time and I really believed he would have too much ability for Hearns, but he lost on points.

I have also had the odd side bet along the way. Way back in the 1950s when gambling was illegal I was once fined for having a £2 bet at ringside. More recently, I remember a guy named Sam Norman, who managed a middleweight named Art Serwano, being totally convinced his man would beat Richie Woodhall, one of my fighters, in a Commonwealth title fight here. I thought there was no way Serwano would win, so I told Norman to put his money where his mouth was. He did, Woodhall stopped Serwano in the 10th round – and I had a £500 bonus. It's not usually that easy, but it's very nice when it is.

One venture that did go wrong was in the 1960s, just after high street betting shops were legalised. A promoter I had worked with, Harry Grossmith, and I opened a bookmakers in Clapton but somehow we managed to do our money. It only lasted a few months. After that I stuck to gambling. I'm safer at it!

Some years ago I took my late uncle, a very orthodox Jew who lived in Antwerp, to Knocke-le-Zoute, which is a Belgian coastal resort where they have a large casino. My uncle was a very good businessman who dealt in raw diamonds. His biggest worry when I suggested we go inside a casino was that he would have to remove his hat. He watched the proceedings for about 45 minutes, staring mainly at the roulette wheel. I could see he wanted to leave, so I said:

'Come on, let's go. I only wanted to have a look.'

'You have got to be mad to come into these places,' he replied.

'Uncle, you're quite right,' I said, 'but how can you make a comment like that when you don't even understand the rules.'

'You don't have to understand the rules,' he said. 'You only have to watch. When you win, they pay you with their hand. When they win, they need rakes to get the money in.'

My uncle's assessment was absolutely accurate. Over the years, however, all I can say in my defence is that losing and winning money, by hand or rake, has been fun! This way of life is a long way from the codes I was taught in my childhood and the strict, religious habits of my father, but it has never affected anyone else. My brother is very comfortable. My son, with only the amount of help from me that a father would naturally give, is successful. He has a petrol station and convenience store in Florida and does very nicely, and I have two granddaughters, Natalie and Danielle, who are adorable.

Apart from that one crazy day at Caesars, gambling has never got me into trouble. It has given me a social life, without costing me any real money. I may have used up money by gambling but that money was created by opportunities which have occurred through gambling.

And to some extent I did not choose my way of life. I was thrown into it by the complete disregard of my father. My mother would always feed me at her restaurant, so that as a boy I was never hungry, but she never gave me money. She simply told me to go out and earn it, which I have done.

My son didn't show any interest in becoming a boxer at all. If he had, I might have tried to talk him out of it because financially he had no need to do it. But if he had really been that way inclined there would have been nothing I could have done to prevent him – just as there was nothing my parents could have done to prevent me nearly 60 years ago. He never asked 'Can I box?' I always explained to him the dangers and told him it wasn't financially worthwhile unless you were at the very top.

He did love to watch fights, however, and at one time he had five people working for him when he ran the British arm of the Big Fights Inc. company, which was owned by Bill Cayton and Jim Jacobs in New York. Jacobs, who was one of my greatest friends, would scour the country to find old films, and I helped him on several occasions. The way they operated was to check if there was a registered owner and if not register themselves as owners. In this way Jacobs and Cayton bought a library worth an absolute fortune and preserved it for posterity. It was a good business – and a service to fight fans, boxing historians and the old champions themselves.

Sometimes I wonder whether or not the films exposed the myths a little too much. For example, there is no film of the great middleweight Harry Greb, who fought more than 300 battles before his premature death in 1926. Greb's talents and style are the stuff of legend. If we had film of him, would he be as great? Certainly, when Jacobs first showed us film of old-timers like Bob Fitzsimmons and Jim Corbett we couldn't believe our eyes: they looked terrible! Nevertheless, Jacobs and Cayton made a lot of money together and Gary did very well here for some time. He ran film shows of famous fights at clubs all over the country. He did well until, after Jacobs' death, Cayton sold the library rights in Britain and, without warning, put a block on Gary's business. He was perfectly entitled to act as he did but it was hard as Gary had just paid out thousands of pounds to increase the quality of his equipment. Cayton, who can be a cold man, was unsympathetic.

Now Gary is 46, is married with two daughters of ten and 14, and is successful to the point where, when he wakes in the morning he is not faced by problems he can't solve.

Even though I was apart from him for long stretches during his childhood, I always did my best to maintain a good relationship and we have always been close. I can't remember the last time we went a week without speaking on the phone.

Apart from gambling and my family, I have had very few interests beyond boxing. I did enjoy football – a photograph still exists of me playing in goal in a charity game in the mid-1960s. The caption said, as in my boxing career, I stopped everything. It was inaccurate but a good joke.

I used to watch Tottenham Hotspur but stopped going a few years ago. After fights I would have a meal, perhaps, or go to the casino, just to wind down for a few hours, but I am serious when I say that my consuming interest for almost 60 years has been the business which made me – boxing. I've been so devoted to it that there has been little or no time for anything else. If that seems strange, so be it. It's the way I've lived and, when everything is balanced out, I wouldn't have changed a thing.

The day after a show I would be in the office as usual. A business doesn't wind down, it moves forward. There are fighters to be paid, managers to talk to. You have to discuss the effects of the results of the show – where to go with the winners and what to do if you've had losers. For there are times when a fighter who has been an asset becomes a liability and you have to work out the best way of handling the situation. Until very recently I was a workaholic. At one time I averaged half a million miles a year in travel. My passport and air tickets proved it.

When my son was young of course I paid him as much attention as I could and I had responsibilities to my home life as a whole. As I said earlier, however, my wife and I very quickly realised we were incompatible. It didn't take a lot of time for the relationship to die off, and I spent less and less time at home, which is why our marriage lasted more than 40 years.

However, I wasn't a womaniser. Boxing was my life. Winning a European title meant more to me than going to bed with the best looking bird who ever lived. You can imagine what winning a *world* title meant!

CHAPTER 14

The Fighting Business

I have my friends in boxing, and of course there are those I deal with but don't like and those with whom I do not speak. Over the years I have worked with and dealt with all of the major promoters in the world.

Bob Arum, who along with Don King is the most powerful promoter in the world, was a Harvard-educated lawyer, who had been on the staff of the late Robert Kennedy. Arum came into the business without paying any dues, and didn't love the game in any way, shape or form. He saw a deal to promote a Muhammad Ali fight with George Chuvalo in Toronto and became involved.

Arum is not one of my best friends, but we talk. In fact we are dealing with the situation regarding the World Boxing Council lightweight title now. He has the champion, Stevie Johnston, and I manage the No.1 contender, Billy Schwer. We will do the necessary business and that's it. We know where we stand. My attitude to him was cemented by an experience in the early 1980s. I made a deal over a particular fight and we agreed that I would be paid $125,000 for my services. When the fight was over, I approached Bob.

'We need to sort out the $125,000,' I said.

'Where's your contract?' he replied.

'Contract? What are you talking about, "where's my contract?" We have a gentlemen's agreement.'

He looked at me and said:

'Who says I'm a gentleman?'

He didn't pay. After that experience, I have had absolutely everything in writing with him.

Another instance of his slippery conduct was in 1994 in a show promoted by Top Rank, his company, with Barry Hearn, which went belly-up in Hong Kong. Arum had agreed to pay $75,000 for us to release the promotional rights for Frank Bruno to fight Ray Mercer on that show and it took us three years to get paid. Fortunately, the contracts were signed in London and so court proceedings were started here.

There was also the incident when the American writer, Bob Waters, from *Newsday*, listened to him talking at a press conference and called out:

'But Bob, that's the exact opposite of what you told us yesterday.'

Arum barely hesitated.

'I know,' he said. 'Yesterday I was lying. Today I am telling the truth.'

Arum now says that story was the product of a conversation in a bar during a snowstorm and that it has been twisted out of context in an attempt to sum up, totally inaccurately, his general philosophy. But is he lying or telling the truth?

Cus D'Amato, who worked with Jacobs in the formative years of Mike Tyson's life and who trained world champions Floyd Patterson and Ingemar Johansson, once called Arum 'the worst person in the Western hemisphere', then added: 'I don't know the Eastern hemisphere very well but I suspect he'd be one of the worst people there, too. When Arum pats you on the back, he's just looking for a spot to stick the knife.'

Arum probably takes these insults as compliments, which is what most boxing promoters do, but there is no disputing the fact that he is one of the leading figures in boxing over the past 30 years. I respect his success.

Arum was involved with Muhammad Ali's career, which got him started and he has gone on to big things in recent years with Oscar De La Hoya, who most people consider the best pound for pound fighter in the world.

It has often been said that the only difference between Arum and Don King is that one is black and the other is white. Arum and I never went out socially. In fact, I spent more time with King in that way because he is a more social type of person, but I was never disillusioned as to the kind of man I was dealing with. The emergence of King was the arrival of a new way of doing business in boxing in America. For example, you would always meet Teddy Brenner, the matchmaker for Madison Square Garden, for lunch. But King was a night animal. You didn't have lunch with him. He liked to do his business over dinner late at night. The people King had working for him were expected to be available to him at all hours of the night as well as day time. Brenner was a family man and understood the needs of people he employed who had families. I don't think it occurs to King to be so considerate.

I may have trodden on a few toes over the years but I have never knowingly kicked anybody when they are down. I don't think we misused our powers. I never said to a manager: 'If you don't do this you won't work for us again.' But I've heard Don King say that.

I first met King when he originally came on the scene in

New York. I treated him with indifference because I thought he was just another lunatic. He was a numbers runner from Cleveland who had done time for stamping a man to death on a sidewalk. When I met him I was with Al Braverman, who was an agent at the time, and who ended up working for King. Braverman wasn't a pleasant man, either. He was the epitomy of the boxing underworld in New York and he never achieved anything. He was always tenth in command wherever he was, even though he always made the most noise. This was all well before the Rumble in the Jungle in Zaire, when Don really got his claws into Muhammad Ali. He had a couple of heavyweights, Earnie Shavers and Jeff Merritt, but generally people had little time for him.

Once he became an influence with Ali, he just marched through to the top. He was a powerful personality of course, and now will be remembered as one of the biggest promoters boxing has ever seen. He will also be remembered as a villain who got away with it.

You can't work with him. You do what he tells you – and that's not my style. That's the way he works, whether you agree with him or not.

Someone came up with a good line, which summed King up perfectly, at the International Hall of Fame the year before I was inducted. King posed for a picture with the heavyweight Carl 'The Truth' Williams, who fought Mike Tyson and Frank Bruno a few years back. As they stood side by side smiling, somebody shouted: 'That's the nearest Don King has ever been to The Truth.'

What King did to Tim Witherspoon over his fight with Frank Bruno at Wembley Stadium in 1986 was disgraceful. Bruno, the challenger and loser, came out with ten times more than the champion and winner. We dealt with Dynamic Duo, the business name used for that brief period by Don King and Ronald 'Butch' Lewis, who had moved into the heavyweight picture as the manager of Michael Spinks. We paid them $1 million to deliver Witherspoon. It wasn't our business how they carved up the money but Witherspoon said later he received only $90,000. Eventually, Witherspoon sued over this and other issues, citing fraud and conflict of interest, and they settled out of court. It was believed to have cost King $1 million.

Now King is under pressure again from the authorities after the controversial draw between Evander Holyfield and Lennox Lewis in Madison Square Garden in March 1999. The verdict has caused a tremendous storm in New York and King, as the major promoter of the show, is getting the blame for it. He is perceived as a man who is not to be trusted, who is likely to attempt to corrupt people around him in order to get the result he wants. I am not saying he has done that, but it's nobody's fault but his own that this is the way people perceive him.

I don't think he approached the judges in the Holyfield-Lewis fight, but I do think that one judge, Eugenia Williams, was stupid. Her scoring of round five, when Lewis almost stopped Holyfield and yet she gave it to Holyfield, leaves absolutely no doubt that something was wrong. She was clearly incompetent. She said in her defence that she couldn't see how many of Lewis's punches were landing, or how hurt Holyfield was, because Lewis's body was in the way. She also blamed photographers for blocking her line of vision, but that's rubbish. If she was unable to see, she should have scored the round even.

I know the flaws of the judging system and I have been privy to a lot of what goes on. The governing bodies, the most powerful of which are the World Boxing Council, World Boxing Association and the International Boxing Federation, each have lists of officials from which they appoint referees and judges for particular contests. It doesn't go by rota. Some perfectly good officials can be ignored and earn nothing while others – who are no better than they are – might have several jobs. And you are not talking about prestige here. On a big show, an official might earn $7,500. Multiply that by, say, six for a year, and you've got a person who earns $45,000 from officiating major contests in a year. That's respectable money, and money not to be jeopardised. It only takes a representative from the organisation to point out how much a certain boxer has achieved or how valuable they are, for the possibility to creep in that a weak judge might be worried about the way a fight might go. It's possible then, even if only on an unconscious level, that if they can make that favourite fighter win, they will. Nobody hands over huge sums of money to judges – there are too many honest judges for that to happen – and the vulnerability of the system is much more subtle than that.

There has always been competition in this business and there always will be. Times change, younger people try to take over and the older ones resist the change. It's the way of the world. When Barry Hearn came into boxing in 1987 on the Frank Bruno-Joe Bugner fight at White Hart Lane, he had the attitude that he would take over boxing. He was brash and egotistical. A few years later he said he had lost nearly £2 million in sport. Maybe he could afford to, I don't know, but it must have been a lesson for him. He had walked into boxing as if he was Jack The Lad, ready to take it over, without understanding what he was really up against. Maybe he knows more now. Certainly, he has honoured the agreements we have had, but at times he seemed to be under the illusion that when God issued brains he was the only one around.

Early in the 1980s I think Frank Warren thought he could blow me away like a cobweb. Well, we're still here. Sure, we have wound down over the last few years, but I am 70 years of age. I have done what I wanted to do. Warren entered boxing by defying the British Boxing Board of Control and the Board gave in. His form of promoting was to be aggressive. No doubt he felt it was the best way to challenge us. I do understand him, though. He's in boxing because he wants to make a profit. I do not, however, agree with some of his methods.

Frank Maloney is another manager of more recent times with whom I've had frequent dealings. Maloney, of course, shot to fame on the back of Britain's Lennox Lewis. He was ridiculed at first but over time I think he has done a good job with Lewis. We used to joke about him all the time – as I'm sure he did, probably still does, about me. My favourite was: 'Maloney's so superstitious he won't walk under a black cat.'

All boxing promoters say things about each other which people in more conventional walks of life would consider insults of the highest order. We generally accept them and get on with the job, even if that includes dealing with that person the following week. I remember the late Dan Duva, the brains behind the Main Events organisation, slaughtering Don King in public: 'Don King is a damn sleazebag,' he said. 'King is nothing but a strong-arm man. He has taken gangsterism and put it into boxing.'

This was in the *New York Daily News* in 1986. King probably laughed. He certainly didn't bother suing. And I'd lay money that they would have been working together as soon as the need arose.

Promoters come and go and the better ones usually remain. One that came and went in a blaze of publicity was Harold J. Smith – real name Ross Eugene Fields – who made a name for himself by throwing money around in the early 1980s as if it grew in his back garden. Smith set up an organisation called Muhammad Ali Professional Sports, with Muhammad's blessing, in May 1979 and contacted me because he wanted to do business. Smith wanted the European heavyweight champion, John L. Gardner – whom we managed and promoted – to fight Muhammad Ali in, he said, either Honolulu or Puerto Rico. Furthermore, he was prepared to offer Jim Watt $1 million to fight Arguello. I went to see him in Los Angeles in January 1981.

We talked and he said quite happily that he would give me $350,000 as a downpayment for the services of Gardner and Watt. There was no guarantee of either fight materialising – and to be frank, I didn't particularly want to be involved in an Ali fight at that stage. The Watt-Arguello fight made sense – and in fact, did happen, but without Smith's input. When he mentioned the downpayment I was of course expecting a banker's draft but, right in front of me, he just opened up a case and handed me $350,000 in cash. I was taken aback but he explained he had $5 million in cash 'floating around' after winning some huge bets on the rematch between Ray Leonard and Roberto Duran, which was staged the previous November. He claimed to have been banned from several Las Vegas casinos because of his success. I took the $350,000 away in a bag to a hotel where Jarvis Astaire happened to be staying while on movie business. Jarvis put it in the hotel safe. We went out and bought two large holdall bags, put the money into them and flew to New York to put it in a deposit box.

Three weeks later, I heard Smith had gone missing and was believed to have taken part in a huge theft case. I rang Jarvis in the middle of the night to tell him and he advised me to find out whether the money we had was stolen. I flew to Los Angeles to meet with Jarvis's lawyer and reported all that I knew to the District Attorney. Smith was later arrested and convicted of stealing $21.3 million from the Wells Fargo Bank. He was sentenced to ten years in jail. I think he served five. The District Attorney was not interested in our $350,000 because there was no reason to believe it had been stolen and no way to prove it one way or another. 'Money's got no eyes,' he said. 'It doesn't know where it's been and it doesn't know where it's going.'

That was fine by me. I was called to give evidence at his trial by Dean Allison, the chief of the Special Prosecutions Unit, along with Ferdie Pacheco, New York promoter Sam Glass, and two leading American boxing writers, Mike Marley and Jack Fiske. As well as the incident I had described, Smith had paid me $100,000 for the services of Lottie Mwale – for whom I held the promotional contract – against WBC light-heavyweight champion Matthew Saad Muhammad, who was already promoted by Smith, in November 1980. The fight was not especially attractive and Smith had raised eyebrows by putting it on in San Diego, where there was no obvious interest in a Philadelphia fighter boxing a Zambian. The promotion lost more than $200,000.

I was furious when two years after the incident the *Sunday Times* published a story which said I had 'formed an alliance' with Smith, 'who was funding promotions with money stolen from the Wells Fargo Bank'. The implication was obvious – that I had known exactly what kind of a man I was dealing with and where his money had come from. I sued and was awarded £10,000 in damages. The money didn't matter, but the principle did. A lawyer is an expense that you have to expect in this business.

As this book was being written I won a libel case against the *Daily Mirror*. The article, by John Dillon, was on Frank Warren and was very complimentary to him about all of the things he had accomplished, but ended with a defamatory remark about me. I am not going to dignify what he said by repeating it, but the quote was underlined and placed in inverted commas to give it particular emphasis. I sued the

Daily Mirror and the case was heard in the Law Courts in the Strand. At one point the *Mirror* actually wrote to our lawyers saying Dillon, who is or was on the committee of the Boxing Writers' Club, was unaware that Warren and I did not get on. For a boxing writer not to have known that was ridiculous – like saying he didn't remember who won the 'Rumble In the Jungle'.

The hearing lasted two days, at the end of which the judge gave the jury a guide as to the amount they could award, were they to find for me. He said the maximum they could award was £25,000. I had no worry about winning the case and proving my point but I had been put in a position where I was forced to gamble. The newspaper lodged £5,000 with the court, which I could have accepted as a settlement. Once I had chosen for the case to be heard, even if I won, if the judgement was £5,000 or less I would have to pay my own costs. Naturally, if I had lost I would have had to pay the costs for both sides, which would have been in the region of £100,000. That was a lot of money and frankly, after the jury had gone out, it was between me and my laundry how I felt. The jury were out for less than an hour. They came back and the foreman announced that they had found in my favour and the award would be £25,000. I was so pleased – and very relieved.

Some years ago I also won a case against *The Sun* when Chris Eubank called me a skinflint and a cheapskate. He told them that I took him out to talk business and only forked out for a £2 plate of fish and chips. My secretary, Eileen Allen, who has been with me for 20 years, was absolutely furious when she read the article and said to me: 'I think I have got the bill somewhere from that lunch.'

It turned out that the bill was for Graham's restaurant in Poland Street and was for £67 for three of us, including his trainer. As a result I sued and they settled with me out of court for £25,000, including costs. It was the best lunch I have ever paid for.

To date I have lost only one case, when Michael Watson was released from his contract with us. I lost because the judge, Mr. Justice Scott, ruled that there was no evidence of wrongdoing by me, but in his opinion a promoter who acts as a manager negotiates with himself. It cost us £150,000 in legal costs and I didn't appeal because our lawyers advised me not to. The case went against us because the Board of Control boxer-manager contract in force at the time did not provide a boxer with the right to negotiate. Afterwards, a new clause was added, on the recommendation of our counsel, to give boxers this right and, ironically, it was my failure to stick to this rule which allowed another boxer, Joe Calzaghe, to break away from the contract he had with us.

I do understand the argument against managers being allowed to promote, and vice versa, but know in my heart I have always tried to do the best I can for a boxer. I suppose it depends who the promoter and manager is.

For instance, I took no commission from Michael Watson in the early part of his career. I brought him along slowly and he was learning all the time. I don't take a penny from a fighter until they're earning a reasonable amount of money. Until then I am backing my judgement of them as a boxer with potential. When Watson challenged Nigel Benn for the Commonwealth middleweight title on that hyped-up show in Finsbury Park in 1989 I was so sure Michael would win I backed him heavily. I could see exactly what was going to happen: Benn would come in swinging and Watson would drill him down the middle with straight punches. He broke Benn up in six rounds, counter-punched him as he liked. The negotiations for that fight were interesting. Benn's business advisor was Ambrose Mendy but I would not entertain the idea of entering discussions with him as he did not hold a

Board licence. In the end Frank Maloney spoke for them and negotiations went on until 10 p.m. in the offices of Benn's lawyer, Henri Brandman, and then for another five hours in a local restaurant. We got the deal we wanted. I remember shouting a lot!

I didn't want Watson to fight Mike McCallum for the WBA middleweight title on a Barry Hearn promotion at the Albert Hall in April 1990. I pleaded with him not to take the fight. Certainly, I never told him he couldn't win – you don't tell fighters things like that – but I kept saying it would be very, very difficult against a man like McCallum, even though the Jamaican they called 'The Body Snatcher' was in his 30s.

McCallum was a cunning, hard punching ring general who knew the business inside out. He had held the light-middleweight title for years before beating one of the clever-est boxers Britain produced in the 1980s, Herol Graham, to become WBA middleweight champ. Nobody in their right minds should have gone looking for McCallum. As it happens, Watson got what I call a scientific hiding. It was a slow, systematic boxing lesson and he was knocked out badly in round 11. For him, it was hard-earned money. The truth is I didn't make money out of Watson. I might have broken even, but no better. That's the chance we take. It's that kind of a game.

The following year Watson was offered the first of his fights with Chris Eubank on a Barry Hearn promotion. I didn't want him to take it and advised him to have two or three easier, small-hall workouts, but after I had fixed up an American, named Troy Wortham, for the York Hall for £6,000 and he had agreed both the opponent and the money, he backed out of it. He said he wanted another manager – but I wasn't Father Christmas. I had made my investment in Watson and why should I just let him give somebody else the financial return? I lost the court case, which freed him from all obligation to us, and yet a couple of years later the Office of Fair Trading ruled that a promoter could be a manager and that to deny one the opportunity to act as the other was in itself a restraint of trade.

After our contractual dispute, Watson went on to lose a majority decision to Eubank in their first fight at Earls Court and then, when on the brink of victory in the return at White Hart Lane, was stopped in the last round and suffered brain damage. I felt deeply sorry for him because whatever the arguments between us there had been good times and I admired his talent. He showed his character by fighting back as well as he could and, given the nature of his injuries, has done remarkably well to be as fit as he is. In September 1999 Watson won his case for compensation for his injuries from the British Boxing Board of Control.

One court case which is outstanding as I write this book is with the German promoter, Wilfried Sauerland, whom I have known for more than 20 years. He was a partner with me from the start of John Mugabi's career and on the same basis I became his partner in the handling of the former Olympic gold medallist Henry Maske. In the days before the Berlin Wall was torn down and Germany was unified, Sauerland was a West German – actually, he lived in Switzerland – and Maske was the great hero of East German boxing. Maske wanted to turn professional in 1990 but it was difficult for Sauerland to sign him. I took Maske to Safety Harbor, Florida, where Mugabi was training and based Henry there.

We started his professional career at Wembley Conference Centre in May 1990. He was a tall, well organised southpaw whose style didn't make much impression in England, but once Germany opened up he became enormously popular. I okayed all of his early opponents and we used to go to the fights and discuss tactics beforehand. Sauerland used to introduce me to people as his teacher. I also got them Maske's regular cutman, Dennie Mancini, who worked with him to the end of his career. We had an agreement and Sauerland was the last man I believed would question it, but all of a sudden he tried to suggest that he had no legal obligation to pay me. This was rubbish. Of course he did. We had received money from him all the way through Maske's career on an organised, well understood basis. Henry won the International Boxing Federation light-heavyweight title in 1993, made 10 successful defences and then lost it in a unification fight with the World Boxing Association champion Virgil Hill. Maske was a huge star in Germany – always immaculately turned out, handsome and articulate – and his fights were fantastic productions that drew big gates every time. He generated a lot of money.

When Sauerland bought a property in Headley, in the Surrey countryside, he invited me to the house-warming. I wrote to him to thank him for the invitation but said I felt I could not attend in view of the business dispute we were in. Then, as we knew precisely where he would be that evening, we served the first writ on him at his house-warming. The preliminary hearings have taken place in the High Court.

The biggest, most significant out-of-the-ring controversy which involved me was the public revelation of the contracted income-sharing agreement I had with Jarvis, Mike Barrett and Terry Lawless.

The document was stolen from my house by my brother-in-law and was later sold to the *News of the World*, who ran it together with the *Sunday Times*. The general inference was that we had been operating a monopoly against the interests of the sport and had been exploiting our fighters. There was an outcry with words like 'syndicate' and 'cartel' being bandied about but we had done nothing wrong. Jack

Solomons had used those words years before when we had begun to challenge his authority. If people get together and combine to run a business, the power they hold is not automatically destructive. The Board of Control took swift action, arranging a preliminary meeting within a week, the Office of Fair Trading asked for copies of the relevant documents and a question was at one point scheduled to be tabled in the House of Commons to the Minister of Sport. John H. Stracey told the *News of the World* that he believed he had been badly paid, citing his defence against Hedgemon Lewis, when he said he netted £20,000. Charlie Magri made complaints in the *Sunday Times* which he quickly retracted. While other boxers, including Frank Bruno, came out publicly in our defence, the allegations were, nonetheless, painful. I know Terry Lawless said he felt like standing on the street with his accounts books in his hands and showing everyone and anyone that he had done nothing wrong. I would gladly have done the same. Terry called his boxers to a meeting and explained his position and told them they were free to walk away from him if they felt he was exploiting them. None did. People have argued that fighters did not understand what was happening but I think it was obvious that Lawless worked with me and I think boxers went to him because of it.

The argument against us was that we had not operated a free and open market because, principally, of the conflict between Terry's position as a manager and representative of his boxer's interests and his position as a sharer in the profits, or losses, which our business incurred. The trade paper, *Boxing News*, ran a front page editorial, which included the following assessment of the situation:

'As a manager Lawless has a responsibility to keep his boxers winning: from this agreement, it follows that in effect he also has an interest in ensuring that the overheads of the promotions at the Albert Hall and Wembley be kept as low as possible.

'The fusion of those interests has resulted in his boxers and those managed by Barrett and Duff, being matched with vastly inferior – and therefore cheap – imported opponents.

'Since 1979, the year the contract was signed, a total of 167 foreign boxers have appeared in non-title fights on shows staged by the parties concerned (110 of them against boxers managed or guided by Lawless, Duff or Barrett).

'Only 18 of them have gone home as winners (nine against boxers managed by those three) and an amazing 108 have failed to go the distance.

'Of the 110 Lawless, Duff and Barrett opponents, 78 failed to finish. Twenty-seven of those were beaten on clean countout.

'This cannot be in the best interests of the sport . . .'

These were obviously extremely serious allegations. Yes, it was true we wanted to keep our boxers winning. Yes, it was true we wanted to keep the public entertained and had to find a balance between protecting our fighters and so developing them properly and running a balanced show. And in spite of the statistics and the growing competition from Frank Warren, the public did still support our shows.

We opened our books completely to the Board and they investigated every aspect of the case very thoroughly. It all lasted for months and the Board's findings at the end of the final six-hour hearing were that we had not broken their rules, and nor had we acted against the laws of the country. The statement which they issued through chairman David, later Sir David, Hopkin also said: 'Furthermore, but for the input of these people, British boxing would not be in the healthy state it is in today.'

We were totally exonerated. The boxers had been well paid, there was no misuse of managerial position and as promoters we had been good for the sport. We were obviously extremely pleased at the outcome. As a follow-up to that investigation, the Office of Fair Trading looked at the case and decided it was not worthy of their interest.

As for the mismatches alleged by *Boxing News*, yes we were careful with our boxers but we did try to make meaningful matches for them. We took a long-term view. It's true that Terry Lawless was even more cautious than I was and we argued long and loud about it, but we both wanted the same thing: for our boxers to succeed at the highest level possible. To burn them out too soon would have been folly – and if we had done that then we would have been open to accusations of mis-management and poor promotion of their interests. The one thing I can never claim is that I was a brave promoter.

Occasionally, things did go badly and we left ourselves open to mismatch allegations. There was the case of the four Mexicans who were sent over by our Los Angeles agent, Don Chargin, in 1980. All of them were knocked out inside two rounds by Cornelius Boza-Edwards, Charlie Magri, Dave Green and a heavy punching featherweight of the time, Jimmy Flint. We didn't pull wool over anyone's eyes. These fights were not eliminators or championship contests and our boxers could all punch hard. They were all very good that night. However, it was true that on the night the Mexicans we employed were not good enough and we held up our hands.

The job of an agent is to bring over the right type of opponent to help your fighter get the type of bout he needs at that stage of his career. We were in the business of building up boxers not knocking them down. Our agents were not expected to provide winners but while there were times when we needed an opponent who would give our man a serious test, there were times when we needed his confidence boosting or perhaps, following a hard fight, we wanted him to have an easier workout.

Agents are useful because they save you time – and because if a major matchmaker rings a small-town manager for the services of one of his boxers, that manager immediately thinks he's in the big time and doubles his price. If an agent rings, he thinks he is just another player in the market.

Over the years we made regular use of an American agent named Johnny Bos. He was a colourful character with long fair hair and fur coats. He hasn't changed, except he's had to dye his hair blond now because he's going grey. In his youthful enthusiasm and encylopedic knowledge of boxing, he reminded me of myself when I was a kid and I began asking his opinions of fighters I hadn't seen. He knew everybody, the good fighters and the bad.

Eventually he became an agent for us and brought in many boxers. The opponents were very carefully selected but nobody was paid to lose. I have never done that in my life. Bos was absolutely excellent – a one-off – who was invaluable in the early stages of Frank Bruno's career. He was young, but had old-school ideas. For him, a handshake or my word on the phone was as good as a written contract. He still gets business from us and has also worked with other promoters in Europe like Michel and Louis Acaries in France and Wilfried Sauerland in Germany. Bos also helped with the early career of Gerry Cooney and managed a world champion of his own, Joey Gamache.

Bos was different to the guy we used at first, Dewey Fragetta, whom we found we couldn't trust. If Bos got something extra, he would tell you about it and I respected that.

I had a wonderful relationship with Ray Clarke, who was secretary of the Board of Control from 1972 until his retirement in 1986. Whenever we were making a fight he would look at an opponent's record and say to me:

'This guy looks awful.'

I would argue with him and he would always ask me the same thing: 'Have you seen him?'

I never lied. If I had, I would say so. If I hadn't, I would never tell him I had, but I would say who I had spoken to, who had seen him. Remember these were the days before it was possible to view prospective opponents on video. Obviously, I did not take opponents unless I had seen them, or someone I trusted had seen them. If he was satisfied by my answer, he trusted me that the opponent was reasonable.

Clarke was a great help because he agreed with my policy of protecting our boxers and he, like me, took the view that when you announce an opponent for a boxer like Frank Bruno, the public has to be told of the full qualifications of that boxer by the press. Whether or not they agree to pay to go and watch is up to them. Occasionally, the public were let down, but they are in other sports. There is such a thing as a bad football or rugby match, after all. Boxing fans know this is a business where there are no guarantees. To a large extent that's the beauty of it.

Apart from that long-ago £2 bet when gambling was prohibited, I have never been found guilty of improper conduct in nearly 50 years. As a manager you are vulnerable and the more successful you are, the more people like to knock you down. That's OK. I'm still standing!

CHAPTER 15

Ragamuffin and the Gifted One

Fighters are not always the easiest sportsmen to manage and two of the more difficult boxers I have had to deal with during my career were Lloyd Honeyghan and Kirkland Laing. Honeyghan won a world title with one of the great displays by a British boxer, when in 1986 he beat Don Curry in Atlantic City. Laing should have at least fought for a world title. He had the talent but was a law unto himself.

Laing was originally from Nottingham but had Jamaican roots. He was flashy, very clever and precocious. As a 17-year-old featherweight he won the ABA title – and promptly fell over in shock. Some said he even fainted! He was one of the most natural talents I have ever seen, but he was so unpredictable that he could make you grow old overnight if you let him. He was with Terry Lawless at the start, and I think Terry, who worried about his fighters even if there was nothing to worry about, aged several years in a few months trying to keep some kind of grip on Kirk. He won the British welterweight title when he floored Henry Rhiney of Luton six times for a 10th round stoppage in Birmingham, at a sporting club we used to run there. But Colin Jones beat him twice, when he got careless after dominating the fights. Laing could either be brilliant or awful and you never really knew which you were going to get. In his later career, when he was managing himself, he called himself 'The Gifted One'. Despite his earlier failings, he wasn't wrong.

Laing's greatest moment was in 1982 when he outboxed the great Roberto Duran over 10 rounds in Detroit. Duran needed a comeback outing before a projected fight with Tony Ayala, a bull-like Texan who was an unbeaten sensation. Circumstances were such that I worked with Don King for the fight. We matched Duran with Laing but with the Ayala fight in the wings, King said to me: 'If this guy Laing's tough, take him out.'

I said it would be ok, mainly because I didn't want Laing to lose the opportunity. He won and neither King, nor Shelly Finkel – who was also involved – forgave me for a long time.

Laing was absolutely brilliant that night. He licked Duran out of sight, beat him easily, and don't forget Duran went on to win two more world titles after that. He wasn't an old man then, he was only 31. It was one of the few occasions that Kirk got himself mentally and physically in shape – and he already knew he could box. In the dressing room before the fight he had absolutely no doubt that he was going to win. He had so much natural ability. You can't teach anybody to fight the way Laing did, on instinct, using his reflexes, but with the basic skills schooled into him from when he was a boy. Fighters of that calibre are born, not made. If you put the gloves on him now, Laing could probably fight, even though he's in his mid-40s. He would instinctively know what to do.

Everybody wanted to know him after that success. We came home and the phone began to ring with offers. Ray Leonard still held the World Boxing Council welterweight title, but he had serious eye problems and would eventually retire. We all knew it was going to happen and there was an offer on the table for Laing to box for the vacant title. There were other fights, big paydays, there for him and he was poised to make it in the big time. But then, one day, he just disappeared! I couldn't get hold of him. He was nowhere to be found. For six months I kept trying. Eventually he surfaced and it turned out he had got himself involved with a woman. I know boxers are not rocket scientists, but this was ridiculous. Unbelievable. He had thrown away hundreds of thousands of dollars. In the end I gave up on him. It was the only thing to do.

It was 12 months before he boxed again and then it was at light-middleweight against a big puncher, Fred Hutchings, in Atlantic City. Laing was knocked out in the 10th round and went to hospital. Hutchings went on to a world title fight and Kirk disappeared again. It was 14 months before he came back on a show at Wembley. He regained the British welterweight title and put on a masterclass when he stopped George Collins, one of Frank Warren's proteges, at Reading in 1989. He won the European title, too, but lost it in Italy to the former Olympic gold medallist Patrizio Oliva, who held the WBA title at light-welterweight. And when he lost the British title to Del Bryan, another Nottingham fighter – in a fight he should have won at the Albert Hall in 1991 – I just shrugged. 'You win some, you lose some . . .'

He finished his career on his own and was 40 years old when he finally retired.

Like Laing, Lloyd Honeyghan was a difficult man, but his attitude was right almost all of the time, which is why he was such a successful fighter. He believed in himself. If you had matched him with Larry Holmes he would have said: 'They are mad. I'm much too fast for him.'

He couldn't see himself losing to anybody. He was

supremely confident and very brash with it. I remember once after one of his fights I called him a cab. He was most put out.

'I'm not getting in one of those,' he said. 'I want a limo.'

I had to get him a limousine – for which, I hardly need to say, he paid.

As an amateur he was nothing special. He was just another 20-year-old kid in Terry Lawless's gym at the start. We were cautious with him, which he didn't appreciate, and we brought him through at the pace we felt was right. He won the Southern Area title and then twice beat Cliff Gilpin of Telford in good, 12-round British title fights. I waited with him because I wasn't quite as convinced as Honeyghan as to how good he actually was.

But it was when he went to Perugia in Italy in early January 1985 that we realised what a good prospect we had. He took the talented Italian Gianfranco Rosi apart in three rounds to win the European welterweight championship. Rosi was one of the cleverest old ring generals of the day who would hold versions of the world light-middleweight for several years but Honeyghan just took him out.

Shortly afterwards Lawless and he parted company, but he didn't leave Lawless. Terry slung him out of the gym because they just couldn't get on. I was amazed.

'You must be crazy,' I told him.

'Well, you sign him then,' Lawless replied.

So I did. The next thing I knew I was taking a call from Honeyghan. He came over to see me and we signed there and then.

We got him an easy final eliminator at Wembley and he stopped an American, Horace Shufford, in eight. Then we were in a position to fight Don Curry, who was the undisputed world champion and the only rival to Marvin Hagler as the best pound for pound fighter in the world. There was

Below: John H. Stracey wins the world welterweight title against the great Jose Napoles in Mexico City in 1975. His win moved me to tears.

Above: A proud Englishman. A young Stracey wears his Lonsdale belt.

Left: Celebrating with the one and only Lloyd Honeyghan in Atlantic City. He's just trounced Don Curry for the undisputed welterweight title.

Right: Honeyghan wins again. Managing Lloyd was never dull and he could be troublesome. 'There is nothing in our contract that says we have to like each other,' I once said.

Above: World heavyweight champion, Sonny Liston, rides like a conquering hero through the streets of Newcastle in 1963. I liked Sonny, but his appetite for women knew no bounds.

The Hurricane. Ruben Carter turned me into an unwitting gun smuggler.

John Conteh.
The most talented
world champion
I've ever worked
with … and the
most frustrating.

he Gifted One.
ccentric Kirkland
aing beat the
gendary Roberto
uran and had the
oxing world at his
et – and then he
isappeared for
early a year!

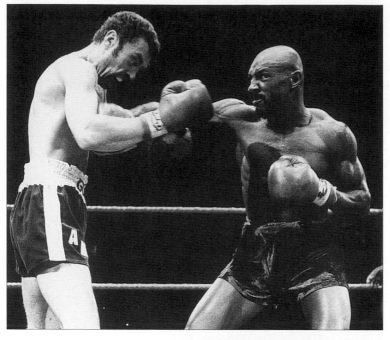

Marvin Hagler, the best middleweight of them all, batters our Alan Minter to become world champion on that riotous night at Wembley in 1980.

Right: The Irish duo. Barry McGuigan was as accomplished as anyone in the eighties.
I worked behind the scenes with his manager, Barney Eastwood, from the start of his career.

Left: One of the nice guys of the ring. Duke McKenzie was the first British boxer this century to win world titles at three weights.

Above: Iron Mike Tyson destroys Frank Bruno's world title dream in Las Vegas. Bruno could have won, but he didn't believe in himself.

Left: There were good times with Big Frank, but it ended sourly. When he finally won the world heavyweight title, at his fourth attempt, I didn't bother watching.

Terry Lawless and I worked side by side for a quarter of a century. Together we produced a string of world champions. Nobody can take that away from us.

Jim Jacobs with the young, impressionable, Mike Tyson. If Jacobs had not died in 1988, I believe Tyson's life might have turned out differently.

With Tyson and actress, Robin Givens, during their disastrous marriage. Givens and her mother wanted control of Mike's career after Jacobs' death, but Don King won the battle.

above: Surely not! Me shouting at a referee, in this case Larry O'Connell. It may surprise people to know that I don't go looking for confrontations…

above: I can't look! I spent 40 years working corners for six-round kids and world champions alike. There's nothing better than the buzz of fight night.

right: Michael Watson beat Nigel Benn with me, then left over a contractual dispute – it's still the only case I've ever lost.

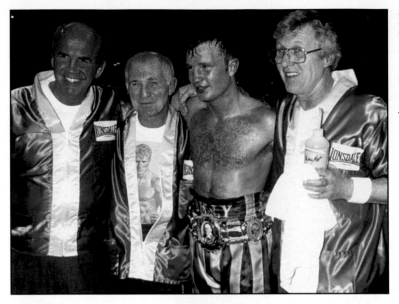

Left: My last world champ? Billy Schwer with his father Billy senior (second from left) and trainer Jack Lindsay. They are a wonderful team.

My induction to the International Boxing Hall of Fame at Canastota New York, in June 1999 was one of the highlights of m career. I shall retur to the summer convention for every year that Go gives me.

Right: A few old faces. With Sugar Ray Leonard and Marvin Hagler at the Hall of Fame. They were just two of the many old fighters with whom I renewed my acquaintance, during a memorable weekend.

no other way to go. If it had been today, we might have had the luxury of selecting the easiest target but if we wanted the world title, it was Curry or nobody. Not that it worried me. With a fighter like Honeyghan, you didn't cast aside world title chances.

When we arrived in Atlantic City, we were considered no-hopers. All the talk was of Curry leaving the welterweights behind after taking care of Honeyghan and earning $10 million for a fight with Hagler for the middleweight title. Curry, a slick, beautifully skilled Texan, had won the WBA title in 1983 and in three years had beaten everybody who was put in front of him: Marlon Starling, Milton McCrory and in Birmingham, the heavy-handed Welshman Colin Jones. He had won 25 consecutive fights and was at his peak at just turned 25. Honeyghan was a year older.

I worked Lloyd's corner along with his trainer, the former British featherweight champion from the early 1960s, Bobby Neill. Incidentally, Bobby did a great job modifying Alan Minter's style 10 years before he worked with Honeyghan.

When I rang Las Vegas for the odds on the Honeyghan-Curry fight – at the time you couldn't bet on fights anywhere in America apart from Vegas – I found that Lloyd was seven and a half to one against. Even against Curry, that was crazy. I knew that Lloyd was capable of an upset if he got it right and there were also stories that Curry was having trouble with the 147lb weight limit. There was the distinct possibility that we had caught him at the right time. I laid down $5,000 to win $37,500. I went into our hotel and told Lloyd what I'd done.

'We'll split it down the middle,' he said.

'We won't,' I said. 'You put your own bets on.'

He asked me to put $5,000 down for him and I made him sign a piece of paper to the effect that he had authorised me to do so. When I went back, the price had come in to 6–1.

I put the bet down, $5,000 to win $30,000, and told him the price change.

'That's OK,' he said. 'We'll split the difference.'

'No, we won't.'

He could not contemplate defeat. It just wasn't in his nature. He told the world's press: 'I ain't scared of nobody. I'm going out there to bash him up.'

He was insulted by Curry's attitude and complained the champion had spoken as if he wasn't even in the room. One of the American's wise-guys named Akbar Muhammad was chanting the nursery rhyme 'London Bridge is Falling Down', but in the dressing room Lloyd was so cool he might have been getting ready for an eight rounder at York Hall, instead of a world title fight at Caesars on the Boardwalk at Atlantic City.

At the start of the fight, he walked straight out and landed a big right hand on Curry's jaw and for six rounds he kicked the crap out of him. Curry made a big effort in round three but Lloyd didn't flinch and kept throwing punches back. By the sixth, Curry's face looked as if it had been ripped apart. His bottom lip was torn, his nose was broken and he had a cut over his left eye that would need 20 stitches. They pulled him out at the end of the round. Bobby Neill and I leapt on Honeyghan and the photograph of me sprawled on top of him on the canvas is probably the most undignified I have ever seen of me in a ring. Not that I care. Days like that make life special.

Lloyd won $30,000 on the bet. I got $37,500, and I did split the difference with him. I gave him $3,750 which was only fair. He had gone out and won the fight. Bob Arum, who promoted Curry, couldn't believe it. Mike Tyson, who was 20 years old and not yet heavyweight champion, was very impressed. 'Lloyd doesn't fight like a British guy,' Tyson said. 'He's mean and nasty, a great boxer.'

Of course, Honeyghan returned to south London to a marvellous welcome from the people around Bermondsey and the Elephant and Castle, where his parents had a council maisonette. I think his dad worked at Sainsbury's and his mother was a nurse.

Unfortunately the hero's welcome was short-lived. We had an immediate problem when the WBA ordered him to defend the title against a South African, Harold Volbrecht. Lloyd took an anti-apartheid stance and refused to meet Volbrecht, who has since become an extremely successful trainer. We respected his view as a black man. There was nothing we would have done to interfere with his views and he handed back the WBA belt. The publicity didn't help his image when he agreed to photographers' requests to be pictured dumping the belt in a dustbin. It showed a lack of respect.

His decision to relinquish the WBA championship was a shame only in that it meant the title was no longer unified but there was no serious dispute that Honeyghan was the No.1 welterweight in the world. He was always truculent and outspoken but we just let him talk, even when he said before he outpointed Maurice Blocker, a top class American, at the Albert Hall: 'Managers and promoters treat you like meat. They have no love in their hearts. They don't care what happens to you. They just pretend.'

Not true at all. We were absolutely straight in our dealings with him and we have always cared about what happens to fighters. That's why I've spent a lifetime being careful about matching them.

Honeyghan was ruthless in those days. I'll never forget the way he took out the IBF No.1 contender, Johnny Bumphus, in two rounds at Wembley Grand Hall in February 1987. He put Bumphus down and almost stopped him in the first and was up out of his stool and halfway across the ring before the bell rang to start round two. The American was only just straightening up when Lloyd bounded over and knocked him down with a left hook. Bumphus's trainer, Lou Duva, was still getting out of the ring! Lou charged back in screaming and yelling and succeeded in buying Bumphus some time and getting a point deducted from Honeyghan's score. But the damage was done – Bumphus had nothing left and the referee, Sam Williams from Detroit, pulled him out about half a minute later. Duva complained but I said: 'Lou's a licenced squealer. I've never known him lose a fight without making a commotion.'

The contoversy soon died down. Honeyghan's 45-second win over Gene Hatcher in a Marbella bullring in August 1987 showed exactly what he was all about. Heavy rain had delayed the fight for 24 hours and Honeyghan couldn't wait to get the job over. He tore out from the corner and overwhelmed Hatcher, who had held the WBC light-welterweight title and wasn't a bad fighter. Hatcher had gone completely when the referee stopped it. I said afterwards: 'The best fighter I have been involved with was John Conteh, even though he never reached his full potential. Lloyd is catching him up fast. I've never known a more dedicated fighter.'

And he was. He ran miles before breakfast every day and worked tremendously hard in the gym, despite having been a pain with Terry. I suppose things began to slide when he lost the title to Jorge Vaca, a very ordinary Mexican, on a low-key show at Wembley Conference Centre. Lloyd was having hand trouble by then but was generally flat, not his usual, pumped-up self. People said he had personal problems and, with five children by three women, that's possible.

The fight with Vaca was close when a crack of heads in the eighth round left the Mexican with an S-shaped cut over an eye and he couldn't go on. It was nobody's fault and in the old days Lloyd would have retained his title. But the WBC had been implementing the technical decision rule for some time. The referee ruled it an accidental butt but, as Lloyd had not been cut, he had a point deducted. It was ridiculous as it was nobody's fault anyway. To make things worse, the one point deduction which occurred in round eight counted, despite the fact that the round had not been completed. The ruling that Vaca had won the title on a technical split decision – two of the three judges had him just in front, but only because of the point penalty – did none of our tempers any good. If the scores had simply been totalled after the seven completed rounds, Lloyd would have retained the title. It was especially disastrous as American cable TV giants Home Box Office had been ready to sign Honeyghan to a contract once that fight was out of the way.

We handed Honeyghan a chance to regain the title by paying Vaca £100,000 to defend at Wembley in March 1988. Vaca must have thought he had won the lottery. Meanwhile, Honeyghan came up with a bizarre story that he had found a cure for his hand in the Blue Mountains outside Kingston, Jamaica.

'Legend has it,' he said with a straight face, 'that a slave was beaten up by his master and was miraculously healed by taking a dip in a water spa in the mountains. Local people go there to cure their arthritis and rheumatism. An old man told me to do it and gave me some herbs and roots to take.'

Well, at least it was original.

Honeyghan steamed straight into Vaca with the kind of all-or-nothing attack that would have probably meant he would have blown up in half a dozen rounds. As it was, by round three Vaca had been knocked out.

As I've said, Lloyd was always very brash and opinionated and, at a press conference afterwards, Lloyd let rip at me.

'Mickey and I don't mix outside boxing,' he said. 'He looks at me as a pawn, a commodity. I don't like him.'

I think it was Colin Hart of *The Sun* who called me to ask what I had to say in response.

'Fortunately,' I said, 'there is nothing in our contract that says we have to like each other. I will continue to do the best job I can for him.'

And I did. He kept earning well in title fights, then lost his title in Las Vegas to Marlon Starling. I felt sorry for him. His hands were getting worse (despite the Jamaican water!) and a left hook from Starling landed on a nerve in the third round, leaving him with a horribly swollen face. 'The pain was so terrible,' he said, after being stopped in round nine. 'It was like someone drilling my head all the time. After a while I didn't try to win. I was just trying to avoid getting hit in the face.'

He wanted to carry on, but he put on a shocking performance when he lost in three rounds to Mark Breland in a WBA title fight at Wembley in 1990. For all his injury problems and his sometimes brash 'Ragamuffin Man' exterior, I liked him, and we stayed together. In 1993 he fought at light-middleweight against Vinny Pazienza, a cunning, tough brawler from Rhode Island, in one last trip to Atlantic City. It was stopped in the 10th round. Lloyd didn't have the physical strength to handle Pazienza, who would eventually go up to super-middleweight. I should have stopped it after the ninth round, but I asked him if he was all right and like all boxers he said he was. I doubted it but let him get off his stool and I shouldn't have. I should have pulled him out. I threw in the towel with less than a minute gone. He eventually retired in 1995.

We are not the best of friends – we never have been – but we still talk to each other from time to time. He manages fighters these days and so may be beginning to learn a new side to the boxing story. I hope he is as tolerant of his fighters as I was with him.

CHAPTER 16

Little Big Men

Barry McGuigan was an exceptionally accomplished fighter – and of course one of the sporting heroes of the 1980s. His fights commanded substantial television audiences as well as fanatical support from his Irish fans, and with his polite demeanour and success in crossing the sectarian divide in Northern Ireland he became – briefly at least – a symbol of peace. I was involved in his career from day one right up to his world featherweight title defence against Danilo Cabrera in Dublin in February 1986.

Like everyone else in Britain, I had seen him as a tearful 17-year-old on the gold medal rostrum at the Commonwealth Games in Edmonton, Alberta. I thought he was a wonderful prospect and I took the rare step of sending a letter to him, inviting him to talk to us if he ever decided to turn professional. He considered several options and one day Barney Eastwood – whom I had known for some years – rang me, said he was going to sign McGuigan and asked if I might help him with advice. I did, and we developed into a very successful team. All the money that came to me from Eastwood went into our income sharing agreement. He used to say I'd taught him well.

Barry's second fight was on the undercard of the Jim Watt-Alexis Arguello promotion at Wembley in June 1981 and two years later I promoted a fight for him in Chicago with Cedric Kushner, a South African who was a rock music promoter before making a name for himself in boxing. Frank Bruno and Lloyd Honeyghan also boxed on that show and had wins. McGuigan knocked out his man, Lavon McGowan, in one round.

Mike Barrett and I were the licensed promoters of his European title defence against a Spaniard, Esteban Eguia, at the Albert Hall in 1984, and we also staged another European defence against Farid Gallouze – a very poor Frenchman – at Wembley in March 1985. By that stage at Eastwood's request I was working as his partner and international agent. I brought in the Puerto Rican, Juan LaPorte, for example. I also used my American contacts to persuade CBS to take one of McGuigan's 1984 non-title fights in Belfast against an American, Paul DeVorce. Barry won in five rounds and CBS were happy.

The time was approaching for McGuigan to take a shot at a world title. Eusebio Pedroza of Panama had been the WBA featherweight champion for seven years. A stylish boxer who knew enough dirty tricks for half a dozen men, he had made 19 defences. Men as good as Rocky Lockridge, Ruben Olivares, Jorge Lujan and McGuigan's toughest opponent up to that point, LaPorte, had all been good enough to win world titles in their own right. Pedroza had beaten them all.

I went to Panama three times, twice with Eastwood, to make the world title fight for McGuigan. Luis Spada was the intermediary in the deal with Pedroza's manager, Santiago Del Rio, but we seemed to be getting nowhere. Barney was getting frustrated. He wanted to go home and he told me I was wasting my time. But I insisted: 'Just give it another day.'

I felt there was still a chance. After a final 11-hour meeting we brought the fight to London, to Loftus Road, home of Queen's Park Rangers football team in Shepherds Bush on what was officially a joint promotion between Eastwood and us. It was a magnificent fight that drew huge viewing figures on BBC television here and ABC in America. They witnessed a great night for British boxing. McGuigan beat Pedroza on points after 15 rounds.

Yet Eastwood, in the middle of the euphoric immediate post-fight celebrations, first spoke of dispensing with my services. We had talked about a written contract but I had turned it down. It had not seemed necessary. Eastwood refuted my claims to the possession of a verbal agreement when he told the *Mail on Sunday*:

'Mickey is not my partner and there is no agreement, verbal or otherwise. If he had been offered a verbal agreement by me, wouldn't he have said "Let's make this legal, let's get it down on paper". I'll tell you if Mickey Duff was dealing with his great granny, he'd have it all down in writing – and he'd have two options.'

I answered that easily enough.

'Sure I would, but only if I felt I couldn't trust my great granny.'

However, in the same article Eastwood admitted that in the past that when I had 'delivered the goods', I had been given 'a share of the profits'. Eastwood admitted I played a big part in the negotiations with Pedroza but then tried to minimalise what I had done by saying: 'He must not over-estimate his importance.'

I was annoyed by that. Without me, the fight would not have happened. Without me, McGuigan would not have won the title and Eastwood wouldn't have been managing a world champion. I had a deal and I expected it to be honoured.

I was also involved in McGuigan's defences against Bernard Taylor in Belfast and Danilo Cabrera in Dublin. Eastwood came to me immediately after McGuigan had stopped Cabrera in 14 rounds and said quite bluntly: 'I'm going to have to give you the old heave-ho.'

I told him we'd see about that. I started legal proceedings and eventually he settled with me. Quite frankly, I don't remember the amount but it was between £100,000 and £150,000. It was still the verbal agreement I had always had. The old saying that a verbal agreement isn't worth the paper it's written on was proven wrong in this case because there was a clear precedent.

After stopping Cabrera, Barry looked like going on to being a major worldwide star. I tried to negotiate a fight for him against the great Puerto Rican, Wilfredo Gomez, in New York, which would have been massive, but it didn't happen. I think he would have stopped Gomez, who had been a wonderful champion at super-bantamweight and later super-featherweight but by then he was past his best. In fact, Gomez lost on a stoppage to a Panamanian named Alfredo Layne. It proved to be a lost opportunity.

Instead of fighting Gomez, McGuigan fought Stevie Cruz in the Las Vegas heat and lost the title. From the time I left, Eastwood and McGuigan's relationship deteriorated and they wound up in legal dispute. Barry might have done much better if Eastwood had allowed me to stay in. He eventually made a comeback with Frank Warren, which finished when he lost to Jim McDonnell, one of our former fighters, in Manchester in 1989.

Personally, Barry and I never had any disagreement, although I do remember travelling to Belfast to a meeting with him and Eastwood to discuss a forthcoming fight in which some hard bargaining was done. He wrote in his book that he had no idea I was involved to such an extent in the path of his career but there was not necessarily any reason for him to have been aware of the exact nature of my arrangement with Eastwood.

That was all a long time ago and these days I am happy to say I am on the best of terms with him. He's an able analyst with Sky television and is a valuable asset to the business.

Cornelius Boza-Edwards was the first world champion I managed. Like John Mugabi later, he was brought to me by Jack Edwards, who was a planter in Uganda from the old days, and who brought him to England. He asked me if I could look after him and asked if the boy, whose African name was Cornelius Bosa, could retain his name for the ring as well. I wrote it down and asked Corny if he minded if we changed the 's' to a 'z'. Boza looked like an African nickname. Bosa looked like nothing. He didn't mind.

A clever, combination punching southpaw, he looked sensational as an amateur, although he lost a great fight with Pat Cowdell in the ABA championships. He was 20 years old when he turned professional with me at the Anglo-American Sporting Club in December 1976. Apart from an early cut eye defeat, everything went well, although it wasn't easy to move him forward. He wasn't eligible for either the British or European titles and he also suffered a personal tragedy when his first wife, whom he met in London, died. Eventually, I mixed his fights between Britain and the USA, where he began to make a name. The fight which more than any other made his career was one he lost: an eighth round retirement defeat against Alexis Arguello in Atlantic City in 1980, which was screened live on ABC. This was ten months before Arguello beat Jim Watt at Wembley. The fabulous

Nicaraguan was still the WBC super-featherweight champion at the time. Boza's bout with Arguello wasn't for a title but he made such an impression that Alexis described him as the man to take over when he had moved up to lightweight. Boza was very game and learned a lot, even though he had to pull out. We took it at relatively short notice and although he was in shape, it wasn't the kind of fitness level you needed to handle 'The Explosive Thin Man' from Managua. 'I was surprised he didn't go down,' said Arguello. 'I hit him so hard my hands hurt.'

Boza won the WBC super-featherweight title by out-pointing a tough Mexican southpaw named Rafael 'Bazooka' Limon in Stockton, California, in March 1981. It was a wonderful performance. Then he successfully defended it with a 13th round stoppage of Bobby Chacon in Las Vegas before surprisingly losing to a Filipino, named Rolando Navarette, in five rounds in Italy.

He did come back and win the European title – he had qualified for it on residential grounds by then – but his only other world championship attempt ended in a points defeat by Hector Camacho, who just ran away from him all night in Miami in 1986.

Boza should have boxed Bobby Chacon for the super-featherweight crown in 1983 but boxing politics got in the way of that. Boza was the WBC No.1 contender and Don King had three options on Chacon. King had no deal with Boza or me, but did have a six-fight deal with Camacho. When NBC signed the mandatory fight between Chacon and Boza, King attempted to have Corny replaced by Camacho. When the television people refused, suddenly the WBC withdrew recognition of the fight. It was scandalous but we went ahead anyway. Chacon needed 40 stitches afterwards but got the decision. Incidentally, soon afterwards Chacon was matched with Camacho. When he made it clear he preferred a $1 million offer from Don Chargin, from California, instead of the $450,000 gross on offer from King, he was stripped of the title.

Another fighter I managed, Duke McKenzie, was in awe of Boza. 'To watch Boza train is something special,' he said. 'He seems to have a never-ending supply of energy. One time he took his Doberman for a run in the hills behind his home and came back carrying the dog!'

Boza settled in Las Vegas, where he married again, and still lives there. He's a lovely man – like a son to me. I saw him and Arguello at my induction into the Hall of Fame. He's working with Bob Arum now and trains and handles fighters: mainly losers, but he's in that business. You start by supplying losers and gradually you find a few winners. He helps Justin Juuko, a Ugandan super-featherweight who fought Floyd Mayweather for the WBC title in 1999, and trains the veteran heavyweight Orlin Norris.

I take great pride in the achievements of Duke McKenzie, who won three world title fights with us. He trained hard and had talent, although if we were to be ultra-critical we could say he lacked the finishing instinct. It was also hard selling him to the public because he rarely said anything controversial and certainly lived plainly, without getting involved in scandal of any kind. He was a very nice lad. Outside boxing, he also distinguished himself in the Clapham train disaster a few years ago. It happened on the railway line which ran past the end of the garden of his home and he raced up the embankment to help people from the wreckage. That was typical of him.

Duke was from a boxing family. The best before him was Clinton, his elder brother, who boxed Ray Leonard in the 1976 Olympics and was a British and European champion. He was a good fighter but had trouble selling any tickets. I remember one terrific 15-rounder Clinton had with another

London fighter, Colin Power, in a British title fight. It was so tough it made the hairs on your neck stand on end. Clinton had the capacity to drive himself on, to dig deep when ordinary men would stop themselves from going over the fine line. He put himself on the very edge. One fight I didn't want him to take was a defence of the British light-welterweight title against Terry Marsh on a Frank Warren show. I would have preferred him to give up the belt and move up towards a world title, but he wouldn't have it. Marsh hadn't ever boxed at that level, but fought cleverly and won on points.

Duke was quietly spoken and his style reflected his character. He wasn't much as an amateur but came on slowly and ended the career of Charlie Magri in 1986. I remember we took him to Italy to defend the European title in a little Italian town called Acqui Terme in 1986. The local challenger, Piero Pinna, wasn't in Duke's league, was knocked down and generally outboxed and I thought Duke won very clearly. It turned out he had, but only by a majority decision. It transpired that one judge – a customs officer from Luxembourg – had scored all 12 rounds even for a total of 120–120. He hadn't even registered the knockdown! His explanation? 'I didn't think either man particularly got on top of the other,' he said.

I've selected a few choice words when arguing with an official or three along the way – but this idiot left me speechless! At least Duke came back with the title intact.

In 1988, Duke won the IBF flyweight title with an 11th round knockout of a gritty little Filipino named Rolando Bohol in the small hall at Wembley, with Lloyd Honeyghan shouting encouragement all the way. They couldn't have been more different as people but they thought a lot of each other. I couldn't have been more pleased with the result. McKenzie was delighted and close to tears. I had a problem with my leg at the time and so couldn't work the corner, but wanted to leap up and down. I still managed to shout instructions to him. I was anxious that he settled down because he had a few nerves and I wasn't worried about him losing the early rounds. He really made the fight his in round three when he opened up and Bohol backed off as if he was surprised at the speed and sharpness of McKenzie's punches. The fight was his from that moment and Duke showed a lot of maturity by taking his time and eventually knocking him out.

He was a very tall flyweight at 5ft 7in and the grind of getting down to 112lbs eventually weakened him. He's of West Indian origin, but he looked a pale shade of grey when he climbed into the ring at Wembley against Dave McAuley from Ireland in June 1989 and I wasn't surprised at all when he gave a flat performance and lost on points. We immediately moved him up to bantamweight and in 1991 he gave perhaps his finest performance in easily outboxing Gaby Canizales, a sheriff in the Texan border town of Laredo whose brother Orlando was one of the best fighters of the 1980s, for the World Boxing Organisation belt. Duke also outpointed Cesar Soto, a tough Mexican who would go on to be a world champion at featherweight, before he was caught cold by a challenger from the Dominican Republic, Rafael del Valle. He lost in one round and I don't think either of us will really understand why. He put that behind him and became the first British boxer this century to win a world title at three separate weights when, in October 1992, at Catford in south London he outscored Texan southpaw Jesse Benavides. The Americans were extremely confident but Duke boxed beautifully and deserved his win. I thought he had done enough to retain his title against Daniel Jimenez, a good little fighter from Puerto Rico, in the same ring in 1993 but the judges went against him. So much for home advantage. Duke went up to featherweight and fought well in a WBO title fight with Steve Robinson before a body shot took everything out of him in round nine. He only retired a year or two ago. He was a very good professional all the way through his career and a treat to manage.

CHAPTER 17

Bruno

On Saturday, 2nd September 1995, when thousands of people walked through the turnstiles at Wembley Stadium to watch Frank Bruno beat Oliver McCall, one of the worst heavyweight champions in the history of the sport, I was not among them. I felt so badly let down by Bruno that I just didn't want to go. I didn't even want to watch it on television and I just spent a quiet evening, having a meal and minding my own business. I still haven't seen the fight and have no wish to.

That may seem odd behaviour, given that I had been involved with Bruno from the start of his career and promoted him over a 12-year period, during which he earned a conservative £10 million, and steered him to three lucrative world title fights. But whatever happened to Bruno had long since been of interest to me, since the way he chose to end our relationship was by a curt letter.

I didn't think much of him for leaving Terry Lawless and installing his wife, Laura, as his adviser. She used to call me from time to time but, unofficially, from the time he left Terry I did the work of a manager without getting paid for it.

Then, when he left me, he ended our relationship with a letter, issued on his behalf by his lawyer Henri Brandman, a few weeks before our contract expired. He simply instructed me not to make any more matches for him as he would not be renewing the contract. If he'd had the decency to have gone to dinner with me and explained – even if I had paid! – it might have been more acceptable. He did nothing wrong legally, but morally I thought it was disgusting. In fact, I still get angry when I think about it now and I haven't seen and spoken to him since. He doesn't owe me anything financially because we both earned very well but in the manner of his leaving, in my opinion, he did himself no justice. I simply couldn't bring myself to join the nation in celebrating Britain's favourite sporting son winning a world title. It is no sour grapes to say either, that, after three failed world title attempts when I promoted him, he could hardly fail against a faded man like McCall.

The ironic truth is that we couldn't use him anyway. The BBC had said they didn't want him, but Bruno didn't know that – and I've never told him.

It would be very wrong of me not to acknowledge how vital the input of Terry Lawless was in the making of Bruno, beginning from the time he paid for Frank to travel to Bogota, Colombia, for a pioneering eye operation to cure a problem that would have prevented him from obtaining a Board of Control licence. Indirectly, we all paid for it, because it was a business expense, but Terry's insistence ensured that we made a very heavy investment in Bruno even before he turned professional. He had not done that much as an amateur. He was ABA champion at 18 but had not won a European or Olympic medal and had lost to Joe Christle, from the family of Irish boxing brothers. (Joe's brother Terry was a qualified doctor even while he was fighting as a middleweight and Mel, who was also a heavyweight, is now the head of the Irish Boxing Federation.)

Bruno's early fights were a succession of quick knockouts. I make no apology for that. I didn't go much lower than my normal procedure. I was very careful with him because, apart from his youth, heavyweights are always more likely to get hurt early in their careers. They are trading hard punches.

It was very important not to rush him and even though at times fans, pressmen and once or twice even the British Board of Control became exasperated with us, we stuck to our policy of developing him at our own rate. Sure, some of his opponents were poor, but we had to find out all kinds of things about Bruno in order to be sure of every move when he finally reached world class. As time went on, he developed an affinity with the public and of course became one of the most loved British sportsmen of the modern era. His reaction to the public was not forced, he didn't have to work at it, and the catch phrases he became well known for weren't coached. They just came naturally and, of course, he is still an attraction today.

In private, he was more suspicious. When anyone said anything to him, he would appear to think: 'What has he said? What did he mean?'

Bruno was a good fighter and however much he was to upset me personally, he was never a phoney. He had the equipment to compete in world class. We just brought it out in the best way possible and if we hadn't had him, it's probable that somebody else could have done it. However, I don't think anybody could have done a better job in Bruno's formative stages than Lawless did. It got to the stage where we would argue fiercely and Terry would almost abuse his position as a partner in order to act favourably towards Bruno – as to a lesser extent he did to all of his boxers. Terry's attitude to opponents was simple. He wanted to impose a condition that they could defend themselves but couldn't hit back. And I don't think any British fighter has attracted the consistently high level of TV audiences that Bruno did in the 1980s with BBC. I don't think there has ever been a fighter who has been promoted as cautiously yet as vigorously as Bruno was.

Frank was 6ft 3½in and more than 15st when he turned professional as a 20-year-old in 1982. He was always extremely fit because Terry taught him from the start that it was the only way for him to get the best out of himself. With the help of my American agent Johnny Bos and the co-operation of Ray Clarke, the British Board of Control secretary, Bruno learned how to take out his opponents impressively. Technically, he developed well against the people we brought in for him, even if some were very limited indeed. Every so often we tested him a little harder but we knew we had the luxury of time to play with and so we used it. Of course, I kept defending the quality of the opponents as best I could.

It became obvious fairly early in his career that he had a lot of ability but had a weakness in his temperament. He was never a Lloyd Honeyghan, who was unaffected by occasion or opponent.

Heavyweights can punch hard and nobody's chin was designed for taking the punches of a 220lb athlete. When the first alarm bells rang in public about Bruno's vulnerability – he was almost knocked out on his feet by a recently released convict, Floyd 'Jumbo' Cummings, in 1983 – we patched it up as well as we could. And after all, apart from that moment when he was badly wobbled at the end of round one, Frank boxed well and won on a stoppage in round seven. He had his fitness to thank for the fact that he recovered so quickly in the minute's interval at the end of the opening session and of course his grit and desire brought him through. He received a standing ovation.

Our reaction was to be even more careful with him. Jumbo Cummings had been a bigger test than most, even though he wasn't in top shape, and for his next couple of fights we dropped Frank down a notch. Walter Santemore from New Orleans called himself 'Mad Dog' but behaved more like a puppy and went over in round four. Juan Figueroa, the Argentine champion, was hopeless and Bruno knocked him out efficiently in 67 seconds. The crowd booed. Afterwards, he said the right things about wanting to fight for a world title. He had watched Greg Page and Tim Witherspoon and said he could beat either of them. Talk was fine. It sold tickets.

Then in May 1984 we made a serious mistake: we brought in James 'Bonecrusher' Smith to face Frank at Wembley. For nine rounds I wasn't worried in the slightest. Bruno boxed as well as I had ever seen him and was in complete control against a man who looked heavy-punching but was slow and predictable. Then everything caved in. Bruno stopped boxing and moving and for some reason best known to himself wanted to stand and trade punches. Bonecrusher couldn't believe his luck and knocked him out. I will never forget the sight of Frank falling slowly to the floor to be counted out by Harry Gibbs. Terry was almost beside himself with sorrow, especially as on the same show another of his fighters, Mark Kaylor, had been badly beaten by Buster Drayton, whom coincidentally I later went on to manage to the IBF light-middleweight title. Bruno talked Lawless round to facing the press the next day and we set about the task of building up public faith in him. I was impressed with Bruno for giving Terry a pep-talk. 'If you quit, I'll quit, but we've come too far to give it all up now,' he said.

It's normally trainers who have to talk to boxers like that!

We used even more caution in making his next few fights and then signed a European title fight with a 6ft 6in Swede, Anders Eklund, for Wembley in October 1985. Eklund wasn't awful, but Bruno at his worst would have struggled to lose to him and knocked him out well in round four. We were moving up again. The European title was an irrelevance and Bruno relinquished it without defending it. Terry Lawless was never one for allowing commissions or governing bodies to manage or match his fighters, and wasn't over-keen on letting the European Boxing Union tell us who we should defend their belt against.

Finally, with Bruno at 24 years old, weighing about 16st and nearing the years when we might reasonably expect him to be at his peak, we pulled off a deal that would get him his first world title fight.

Gerrie Coetzee, the No.1 contender for the WBA title, had a track record that on paper was impressive. He had held the WBA title a few years earlier after a good knockout over Michael 'Dynamite' Dokes in Richfield, Ohio, which was Dokes' home town. Incidentally, Dokes observed Don King at his finest that night. Before the fight, King came in with Dokes, applauding and taking up his position as cheerleader-in-chief. As Dokes lay on the canvas, he saw King step over his fallen body in his rush to congratulate Coetzee, the new champion. Don always prided himself on arriving with the winner – and leaving with the winner.

Coetzee had lost the WBA title on a controversial knockout in Sun City, South Africa, in 1984 to Greg Page. The timekeeper messed up and miscounted the minutes of the round. Page won at three minutes 40 seconds of round eight in a fight contracted for 12 three-minute rounds. If Coetzee had been my fighter I would have sued and had the bout ruled a No Contest but the WBA refused to change the result and were allowed to get away with it. They did, however, agree to keep the South African at No.1 in their rankings. After that disaster, he boxed only once, a 10-round win over another great character, James 'Quick' Tillis, in Johannesburg in September 1985. I suspected that at 30, Coetzee's heart might have gone out of the game.

I persuaded the WBA to recognise a fight between Coetzee and Bruno as a final eliminator for their championship, and made it for Wembley on 4 March 1986. It cost us a lot of money but it was worth every penny. It bought us what we needed. Bruno was at his best that night, fired up and ready to let the big shots go from the first bell, and Coetzee looked like a man out of love with the sport. It was all over in one minute 50 seconds.

Bruno, incidentally, had to put up with pressure from the anti-apartheid movement because Coetzee was South African. A little later, Lloyd Honeyghan was to hand back the WBA belt rather than fight a South African, and I respected his views, but I had known Coetzee for some years and was aware of his own opposition to the apartheid laws. He had made his own point when his black sparring partner, Randy Stephens, had been best man at his wedding, and again by publicly adopting a young black boxer who had suddenly been orphaned.

Bruno went away to think about the implications of fighting him and made his own decision to do it. I think it was the right one. As soon as he met the British press, Coetzee spelled out his hatred for apartheid and the situation eventually cooled down.

We had to put up with it again when another white South African, Brian Mitchell, who had more black fans than white in his own country, defended the WBA super-featherweight title against Jim McDonnell. The protesters made their point but Mitchell made his by beating Jim on points. Mitchell, who had fought mostly in the townships in the early stages of his career, was an amazing man the writers nicknamed 'The Road Warrior' because soon after he won the title, the WBA announced they would not sanction fights in South Africa nor allow South Africans to fight for their titles. With that single decision, Mitchell was denied home advantage in his fights and made aware that the moment he lost his title, he would not be allowed another chance. Therefore, he fought every fight as if it were his last and kept the title for five years until after Nelson Mandela was out of jail and the apartheid regime had broken up.

After Bruno had knocked out Coetzee, we negotiated a deal for WBA champion Tim Witherspoon, who was promoted by Don King and managed by his step-son Carl – in other words by Don – to come to London to defend against Bruno at Wembley Stadium in July 1986. Witherspoon was a good fighter but not the most dedicated of trainers. Nicknamed 'Terrible Tim', he was good-natured, fun-loving guy from Philadelphia, who had proved he could fight in 1983 when, as a relative novice, he had given Larry Holmes a hard 12 rounds for the WBC title. When Holmes defected from the WBC to the IBF in 1984, Witherspoon won the vacant WBC title by outpointing Greg Page, but then showed how erratic he could be as he lost in his first defence to Pinklon Thomas. These were the dark days of the heavyweight division when Don King controlled virtually everyone in the ratings and shuffled the pack as he saw fit. Witherspoon had won the WBA title from another King fighter, Tony Tubbs, in January 1986, but then found he had to deal with us because we had the No.1 slot.

It was a wonderful opportunity for Frank. Witherspoon was the same kind of size as him at 6ft 3in but we felt Bruno had the ability and the fitness to become the first British world heavyweight champion since Bob Fitzsimmons in 1897. It was an exciting time for everyone connected to the

promotion and Bruno worked extremely hard to get himself
ready. We had a problem before the fight when the BBC,
who of course worked with us, and ITV, who worked with
King, both claimed rights to the screening of the fight, but
fortunately it ended in a sensible compromise. Both showed
it on delay, with HBO taking it live in the USA from mid-
night. In the minutes before the fight we had Muhammad
Ali and Henry Cooper meet in the ring where they had fought
almost a quarter of a century before. The crowd loved it –
and I think, so did they.

Bruno could and should have beaten Witherspoon. Frank
was hurt in round six, but for nine rounds the fight was
even. Then the tension in Bruno's mind played its part and
he came apart. Witherspoon wasn't worried by anything in
there. He could fight for as long as you wanted him to. He
enjoyed it. Bruno was a more complex human being when
it came to competition. When it came down to it, his temperament was not strong enough at the highest level. That
was the difference between them. At the end Lawless ran
into the ring to hold Bruno in his arms as the referee tried
to pick Frank up. Some of the crowd threw chairs at
Witherspoon as he left the ring and the police made some
arrests as fighting broke out, which was annoying for us as
we had done what we could to make the promotion a good
one. You cannot legislate for a tiny minority in a crowd of
40,000 excited people. Bruno was taken to hospital for
checks – his face was horribly swollen. While he was there,
he said a guy with a broken leg came to see him. The fellow
had broken it by somehow managing to fall down the steps
outside the stadium on the way *into* the building. He hadn't
even seen the fight and said to Bruno: 'At least you got paid
for the state you're in!'

After the fight, George Francis, who had trained John
Conteh, Cornelius Boza-Edwards and John Mugabi, replaced

Jimmy Tibbs in the Bruno training team alongside Terry and Frank Black. Tibbs went to work with Frank Warren.

For Bruno's next fight, we lined up Greg Page, which we felt would be a quick way back to a world title fight, but Page pulled out with a cut in training and I had James Tillis replace him. Tillis was a funny man who once gave a wonderful description of what it was like to be knocked down by the single greatest puncher of the time, Earnie Shavers. 'I was in the land of make-believe,' he said. 'I heard saxophones, trombones . . . I saw little blue rats and they was smokin' cee-gars and drinkin' whisky.'

Some thought Tillis unlucky to lose a WBA title fight with Mike Weaver in 1981, but as time had gone on his career had drifted. When he lost a fight before meeting Bruno he said: 'Maybe God is trying to tell me to do something else.' *Boxing News*, in an acidic preview of the fight, suggested: 'Maybe God should speak a little louder.'

Bruno stopped Tillis in five rounds, which was just what we needed at that stage. We had Mike Tyson at ringside. While he was here, he did an entertaining show for BBC on the great heavyweights of the past with Harry Carpenter.

Then came the farcical match in Cannes in which Bruno knocked out a terrible American, Chuck Gardner, in June 1987. It was a bad one. Gardner had shaved his head, he had a pale, flabby torso and a bandage on his knee. Bruno knocked him out in less than a minute and when the referee took his gumshield out as he lay on the floor, somebody said his dentures came with it! It was embarrassing, although we tried to argue our corner. Terry was indignant with reporters who wanted him to justify the match, but for some reason Mike Barrett decided to hold his hands up. I should point out that the promoter was the Frenchman, Roger Ferrer, and Gardner was sent by Johnny Bos. I wasn't even there. Barrett spoke out, when Terry thought he should have kept out of it because he was benefitting from Bruno as much as the rest of us. They never really got on. 'This was one of the most disgraceful mismatches in boxing history and those involved have to take responsibility,' said Barrett. 'It gives boxing such a bad image.' He went so far as to suggest Gardner could have been killed, which was unnecessary.

It was a time we all needed to stick together and sort out the difficulties in private. It was the result of the general conflict between Lawless and I over the matching of Bruno, which of course Barrett knew all about.

'All you want is for your fighters to win all your fights,' he said.

'Yes, of course I do,' said Terry.

Some time later Barrett was bought out of our partnership for £250,000 – he had said he could not be a part of it any more. I thought his atttitude was laughable. Fighters get hurt. You can't keep making wars and Bruno had been in a very hard fight with Witherspoon. Sure, the Gardner fight was a mistake but if you ask 'did I have a problem with the overall way we were conducting our business?' my answer has been the same from that day to this: 'None whatsoever'. There is only one law. You don't say to a fighter: 'You're getting so much money not to win.' That's crooked. I don't accept the criticism that our shows were too one-sided, but this one wasn't our show anyway.

We all felt the best thing we could do was bring Bruno back as quickly as possible, which we did in Marbella on the same show that Lloyd Honeyghan destroyed Gene Hatcher in defence of his welterweight title. Again, I lined up Greg Page, who was still very competent but not the force he was. Again, he pulled out. Then I brought in Reggie Gross, a decent fighter who had been taken out in one by Mike Tyson, but whose overall credentials were reasonable. Gross's career had been interrupted by a seven month spell in jail on a murder charge, which had been dropped and when he fought Bruno he was clean. The fight should have been stopped long before the referee finally led Gross away in the eighth. Lawless was furious with the ref for letting the fight go on too long and I remember him standing on the ring apron screaming at the guy.

I was still trying to move Bruno up and thought we had a match with Trevor Berbick, the former WBC champion who had lost the title to Tyson, until a back injury forced him out.

It was during this period that Barry Hearn suddenly arrived on the scene. He said he could produce Joe Bugner, who at the time was making one of his comebacks in Australia, where he had apparently given up on trying to grow wine for a living. I didn't want to do business with Hearn. I knew of him from his successes in the snooker world but had no reason to want to work with him in boxing. Terry was very positive about it, though, and I think was ready to consider possible alternatives. I was finding Terry particularly difficult to deal with by then and over-protective even by his standards. Anyway, Lawless was ready to do business with Hearn over Bugner and reluctantly I agreed. Hearn said publicly:

'Terry has never wanted this fight but I don't think he had a lot of choice. Everyone knows that Terry has other business partnerships. The only problem there was to make sure they weren't my partnerships. I don't have partnerships. I think it may be complicated for him but it's not complicated for me.'

In fact it wasn't complicated for him or us. The proceeds went into our income-sharing agreement as they always did. Barrett hadn't yet made the final breach but he and Lawless weren't talking. I had been based more in the USA, with a lot of our bread-and-butter matches being done by the Midlands matchmaker and former heavyweight, Ron Gray. Jarvis Astaire remained a constant in the equation.

The fight itself, if not the politics behind it, made sense because it was an easy one for Bruno. It was heavily criticised by the press, but it sold. Bugner did a good publicity job but didn't exactly exert himself in training. I suspect he actually put on weight while he was here! Of course, the drum kept beating about his hard work in the gym – and, if we were to believe the William Hill organisation, one punter was so convinced of Bugner's chances that he put £6,000 on him to win. In Bugner's prime it might have been a decent bet, but Joe was 37 and just too old and Bruno won a one-sided fight in front of a crowd of about 25,000. I remember Jim Jacobs coming out with a nice line before the fight when somebody asked him, if Bugner were to win would he replace Bruno as Mike Tyson's next challenger. He said: 'Neither Joe Bugner nor Max Schmeling figure in our plans.'

Schmeling, who is now the oldest surviving world heavyweight champion, was 82 at the time!

The show was Hearn's and Bruno dealt with him as much as he did with us. In the end I heard he was very unhappy with his take-home purse – he was on 35 per cent of the take and gate receipts were half of what he expected, and afterwards Lawless and Hearn didn't want to do business. The result of the fight was just about the only thing that went right. Bruno stopped Bugner against the ropes in round eight.

We put the Hearn episode behind us and got on with the job of making Bruno's second world title fight, with the undisputed champion, Mike Tyson. I was in a good position to make the fight because I had been close to Jim Jacobs, Tyson's co-manager, for many years. He had an apartment on East 43rd Street and every time I went to New York I would stay there. We pencilled in a date in June 1988 and agreed in principle to use Wembley again but, before anything could be finalised, Jim died of leukaemia. Bruno was No.1 contender but Michael Spinks was the undefeated former IBF champion who had given up the belt to take a big money fight with Gerry Cooney rather than take less money for a fight ordered by the sanctioning body. He had beaten Cooney and was putting up an argument, through his promoter Butch Lewis, that he was the real champion. Tyson wanted to clear up the situation before he fought Bruno and in June, in Atlantic City, he knocked out Spinks in one round.

Jacobs' death also allowed Don King into the picture and his influence increased throughout that year. Tyson spent the year in a marriage, to actress Robin Givens, that was failing and King spent the time gradually prising him away from Bill Cayton, who had co-managed Mike alongside Jacobs. To further muddy the waters, Tyson's wife and his mother-in-law, Ruth Roper, also wanted control of his career. There was not a great deal we could do about any of that. Cayton had fought hard to keep Tyson but eventually lost. In one of his later outbursts to the media, he said: 'If Don King gets control of Mike Tyson, he controls boxing. I am not going to let that happen.'

There was nothing he could do to stop it. Somewhere amid all the confusion, Tyson actually underwent a full immersion baptism at the Holy Trinity Baptist Church in Cleveland, King's home town. Of course King was in the congregation. 'I feel so clean, so pure, so reborn,' said the world champion, who would later switch to the Muslim faith while in jail for rape.

Later on in the build-up to the Bruno fight, King would liken himself to John The Baptist proclaiming the coming of Christ. Baptism and blasphemy were separated by a matter of weeks.

As soon as he had settled his dispute with Cayton, which involved Bill having no say in his career but remaining his manager of licence until February 1992, Tyson agreed to fight Bruno at Wembley on 3 September. Within 24 hours, however, Tyson declared he would *not* fight Bruno in London. Jarvis, who had been in New York for the negotiations, flew home. Then Tyson's lawyers reconsidered, Jarvis was forced to return to New York and the rift seemed to have been mended. Another date of 8 October was agreed.

Then, in yet another twist, Tyson broke his hand – actually a hairline fracture of his wrist – in a late night altercation with his old rival Mitchell 'Blood' Green outside a store in the Bronx. He also had an argument with Robin Givens, drove into a tree and allegedly knocked himself out. He asked for a postponement of a fortnight, and then we had to re-arrange everything again. Tyson, whose life was in turmoil, would not come to London and eventually Jarvis re-negotiated the deal, earning some compensation for Wembley with Bruno getting considerably more money for travelling to fight at the Las Vegas Hilton.

Firstly, it was set for January, and finally for 25 February 1989, eight months after our original date. The flip side of the chaos was that the fight became bigger news. We tried to capitalise on the reports of Tyson's erratic behaviour to build up public confidence that Bruno could win the fight.

As 1988 became 1989 a new era in television was arriving in Britain and for the first time the British TV rights to a Bruno fight were bought by Sky, with the BBC obtaining the rights to the next day showing. ITV, who had been covering Tyson's contests, went to court to challenge the deal, believing they had the rights but lost the case. Jarvis also screened the fights in closed circuit venues, as so few people had access to Sky at the time.

Bruno's previously unsuccessful title challenge against

Witherspoon had been wrecked by tension. As the fight drew nearer, we were obviously anxious to attempt to avoid a repeat of that and even used a hypnotist on a daily basis to help him overcome it. But you can't make a man change his psychological make-up as easily as that and even though the hypnotist had another session with him in the dressing room before the fight, it was not enough to turn him into a winner, even on the 25th anniversary of Muhammad Ali's upset victory over Sonny Liston.

Let me say now that Bruno had the ability to beat Tyson. Sure, he was knocked down in the opening 30 seconds but I think he was hit on the top of the head and just took a count. That kind of knockdown comes from tiredness, tension or fear, not from being badly hurt. Then he got on with it and before the end of the first round shook Tyson to his boots with a clean left hook. Even then, I don't think he really believed he could win. And that was Bruno's problem. He didn't do anything for the rest of the fight, just held on, clubbed away while trying to hold but mostly not doing anything. Basically, he let Tyson beat him up until it was stopped in round five. Even so, the British public welcomed him home as if he were a conquering hero with crowds at the airport as he returned. It's a quirk of the national psyche that Bruno was greeted so warmly and at the same time a British winner, Dennis Andries, slipped unnoticed through customs after regaining his WBC light-heavyweight title in Texas.

Bruno left Lawless after that fight. Their contract expired and Bruno chose not to renew it. He said he had made his decision because he felt stifled, because Terry had never realised he had grown from a boy into a man capable of deciding things for himself. 'I wanted to stand on my own two feet and make my own decisions,' Bruno said.

However, he had earned £1 million more for fighting

Tyson in America than he would have done if they had met at Wembley – and that was because of Terry's persistent lobbying. He was paid £93,000 from the closed circuit rights and Terry didn't even charge him commission. Yet a few weeks after the fight, Bruno refused to pay Terry commission from his earnings other than boxing – which his contract required him to do. Lawyers were consulted by both sides, and Bruno was advised that he had to pay.

Soon afterwards he had a far more serious problem than money – during a routine medical in Manchester, Professor David McLeod discovered a hole in one of Bruno's retinas. It could have been the end of his career but the surgery was succesful and after examining his case very carefully the Board of Control allowed him to continue boxing.

After leaving Lawless, he was considering an offer from Barry Hearn when I paid him a visit at his home and spelled out an alternative that would mean him staying with us. I signed him to a three-fight deal. Hearn was furious. He called Bruno 'thick as two short planks' and was, quite rightly, sued. It was a terrible thing to say. He issued a public apology – and we all got on with our jobs.

We brought Bruno back at the Royal Albert Hall in November 1991 with a one-round knockout of a Dutchman, John Emmen. By this time Evander Holyfield was world champion and Tyson was facing the rape charges that would eventually lead to his jail sentence. Bruno's comeback continued at Wembley with a second round knockout of the big Cuban, Jose Ribalta, and then we were extremely pleased with the way he dealt with a solid, strong South African, Pierre Coetzer, at Wembley in October 1992. Bruno won in the eighth round and looked a serious world title contender again and the championship make-up was changing fast.

By then Tyson was in jail. A fortnight after Bruno's win, Lennox Lewis knocked out Razor Ruddock – a Jamaican who had twice given Tyson hard fights – in two rounds. It was a sensational performance which showed Lewis had the temperament to handle a big fight and the intelligence to capitalise on openings which came his way. It was one of those fights that was won in the mind first and the body second.

In November, I was ringside as Riddick Bowe outpointed Evander Holyfield in a terrific 12-rounder before a 17,000 crowd in the Thomas and Mack Center in Las Vegas. It was one of the best heavyweight championship fights in history, with Holyfield under heavy fire and looking ready to be stopped before rallying and rocking Bowe in a dramatic 10th round. Holyfield actually went down in the next, but fought his way back again in a thrilling finish. Bowe didn't want any part of meeting Lewis and so gave up the WBC title – and because of his win over Ruddock, the WBC gave the belt to Lewis in a ceremony in a London hotel in January 1993. Lewis became a fairly obvious target for us in our attempt to obtain a third world title fight for Bruno.

In April 1993 Bruno stopped Carl 'The Truth' Williams in the 10th round of a fairly tough fight at the National Exhibition Centre. The following month, Lewis outpointed Don King's heavyweight, Tony Tucker, in Las Vegas in his first official defence of the WBC title. It was now possible for Lewis-Bruno to happen.

Bruno had been earning good money in pantomime, in TV commercials and in public appearances – and his popularity was as high as ever. He was also a very experienced boxer by this time. The defeats by Smith, Witherspoon and Tyson could not be erased but in a way they could give him confidence against a guy like Lewis, who still had so much to prove. Bruno had not lost to a British boxer in his 11 years as a professional, which helped his state of mind. We didn't play on that, however, preferring to make much of

Lewis' Canadian upbringing and selling Bruno as the 'true Brit' with Lennox as a fake. They traded a few harsh words in the build-up but Bruno actually brought in his lawyers when Lewis called him an 'Uncle Tom', a particularly nasty insult from one black man to another, meaning he had sold his soul to the white race. Bruno was understandably riled.

The fight took place in October 1993 on a cold, horribly wet night in the open air at Cardiff Arms Park, the heart of Welsh rugby union, at around 1 a.m. The rain swept across the stadium all day and rendered the canopy above the ring useless as far as protection went. The undercard fights were carried out on a slippery canvas, which was changed and covered before the championship fight. Both boxers came to the ring in all kinds of protective clothing against the cold, although the rain eased right off shortly before the fight began.

Bruno boxed very well for six rounds. Technically, he had the edge on Lewis, but in the end Lewis showed he had the better mental approach. In round seven Bruno was caught by a heavy left hook and stopped fighting. He took some fearsome shots to the head and just stood on the ropes until the referee, Mickey Vann from Leeds, stopped it. Bruno looked in shock.

It was all very frustrating. Frank could have beaten Tim Witherspoon, and I believe he should have beaten Mike Tyson when he had him hurt. And he had the ability to beat the Lennox Lewis of 1993, the Lewis who turned up that night in Cardiff. He had his chances but blew them.

When it mattered, Bruno did not have the will to win. At that level, when you have two men who have talent and who can punch, the man with the greater will almost always wins. Lewis had that extra something. Bruno didn't. Lewis would be up there with the top heavyweights in history. Bruno won't be. In fact, I believe Lewis would have given even

Muhammad Ali a lot of trouble. He's tall, he's big, he can box, he's quick and he has real heart. Bruno would have been easy pickings for Ali.

I was wrong about Lewis twice. Two years before I believed our unbeaten heavyweight Gary Mason would beat him in a fight for the British, Commonwealth and European titles at Wembley. Lewis had only 14 fights behind him, to Mason's 35. I made the fight because I didn't think Lewis was experienced enough as a professional to beat Mason. I was wrong. He was.

We promoted Bruno only once more, in a terrible fight against Jesse Ferguson at the National Exhibition Centre in Birmingham in March 1994. Ferguson was pathetic. I think he came here for a holiday. Bruno stopped him in less than a round. In Frank's defence, nobody has done that to Ferguson since then and Bruno could punch. He could catch fighters with one shot early in a fight and take everything out of them. Nobody was convinced by it, however, and even Harry Carpenter, who had been one of Frank's greatest allies in his years with the BBC, had to ask him some pertinent questions. Bruno didn't appreciate it.

The BBC's Head of Sport, Jonathan Martin, told us after that debacle they were not interested in featuring Bruno again. This was sad but as far as the BBC were concerned his story had run its course. We continued to stage shows for the BBC with fighters like Johnny Armour and Richie Woodhall until their *Sportsnight* programme ended. In our 33 years of working with the BBC we had provided some real highlights in the sporting history of the nation. One of their spokesmen was once asked to justify why they gave us favourable treatment, and his answer was blunt and to the point. 'Because they've got the best fighters.'

And it was true.

It was a shame because I had been a loyal BBC man and

I did not consider moving channels even when I think I had the opportunity to do so.

After leaving us, Bruno signed for Frank Warren, who was still working with ITV at the time. He beat a Puerto Rican named Rodolfo Marin in one round. Two fights later he fought Oliver McCall for the WBC title. Warren had begun his relationship with Sky and was working with Don King. They deserved each other, as far as I was concerned. McCall had won on a one-punch, second round knockout over Lennox Lewis the previous year, had looked awful in beating Larry Holmes and was reported to have serious discipline problems. Some said he was even developing a drug habit and later he did acknowledge his addiction and go into rehabilitation clinics. Two years later he was to suffer an emotional breakdown in a fight for the vacant title with Lewis, and was in floods of tears as a puzzled Lennox wondered whether or not he was faking. Eventually, referee Mills Lane led him away. It was this dangerous but uneven and unpredictable man that Bruno beat for his championship. As I've said, I had no wish to acknowledge it in any way.

Bruno lost the WBC title to Tyson in the MGM Grand Garden, Las Vegas, in March 1996. He was promoted by Warren and King and still trained by George Francis and from what I heard at the time was unhappy about his purse. It was the fight Sky chose to launch Pay Per View in this country and I think he expected more because of that. Anyone who saw the fight on television, or in the arena itself where there were giant screens, will have seen the state Bruno was in when he came to the ring. He repeatedly crossed himself in prayer. He must have known what was coming. Mentally, he had already lost the fight by the time he climbed through the ropes. He had sometimes crossed himself on the approach to the ring in the past. Once is fine. Each man has his own preparation ritual and if that includes a short prayer in the corner or making the sign of the cross on the way to the ring, if it helps his mind, it's fine. On the way to face Tyson for that rematch, however, Bruno just couldn't stop doing it. It was ridiculous. To me, it looked as if his lip was trembling as well. I think he lost the second fight in the first one. He was cut over the eye in round one and stopped in round three. This time, he hardly landed a significant punch.

One of the main jokes about the failings of British heavyweights over the years has been that they were always horizontal. As the American writer Dorothy Parker once observed: 'If all the British heavyweights were laid end to end I wouldn't be at all surprised!"

But in Bruno's case when he lost he wasn't horizontal – just vertical. He usually stood up to the onslaught when he should have taken a count, but simply stopped punching back when nailed by a big shot. His defence was non-existent in that situation. There was another thing about him – I cannot remember ever seeing him grit his teeth and win a fight from behind. Only once was he in serious trouble and was he able to fight his way back to win. That was against Jumbo Cummings and it was really only one shot, from which he was able to recover during the minute's interval. The rest of the way he was winning. The overall verdict on Bruno was that he was an on-top fighter. He simply didn't have the necessary fighting instincts to claw his way back into a contest when the chips were down.

Bruno contemplated continuing his career but there was really nowhere for him to go and after another report on his eyes he decided to announce his retirement.

Whatever any of us want to say about Bruno, he held the WBC title for six months. He did qualify for three world title fights in his 12 years under us, and won it at the fourth attempt. All of those fights were attended by large gates.

In recent years, I did receive an invitation to his son's

Christening – and I totally ignored it. Could the breach ever be mended? It didn't even bear consideration because his decision to leave me in the manner he did still rankled. He doesn't need me for anything now. He has earned so well it's almost impossible for him to need anyone, financially, for the rest of his life.

CHAPTER 18

Iron Mike

Mike Tyson became the youngest-ever heavyweight champion when, aged 20, he beat Trevor Berbick for the WBC title. He struck fear into the heavyweight division in the years that followed, but in my opinion he wouldn't have hit Muhammad Ali on the arse.

In fact, he might not have beaten Joe Frazier either, because Smokin' Joe had the knack of backing fighters up. That was the secret to unlocking Tyson's style. And George Foreman, in his prime, might have been too tall and physically strong for him. Foreman just chopped people down.

The first time I saw Tyson was in New York when he was 15 years old and competing in a small tournament. He was like a caged tiger, pacing up and down. He looked a strong kid with plenty of menace and an awesome build for his age, but as yet there were no subtle skills. At the time he was training with Cus D'Amato in Catskill, a little town on the west bank of the Hudson River. D'Amato was a single-minded, disciplined man who thought like a philosopher. He had his own ways of doing things and an abundance of theories about the nature of fear and courage. Yet he was broke.

My friend, Jim Jacobs, was bankrolling his gym and the house where he lived with his companion of many years, Camille Ewald, as well as the fighters under his care. D'Amato had been out of the picture since the 1960s when he had the world light-heavyweight champion Jose Torres. His greatest success had been when he guided Floyd Patterson, a one-time problem-child from New York, to fame as the youngest world heavyweight champion in history in 1956. Patterson was 21. They eventually parted company when they disagreed over whether or not Floyd should defend the title against Sonny Liston. D'Amato's business sense told him it was madness but Patterson's sense of honour would not allow him to avoid a man that many were referring to as the uncrowned champion. Later, D'Amato managed Buster Mathis, who fought Joe Frazier for the New York version of the heavyweight title in 1968.

D'Amato was originally from the Bronx. One of his elder brothers, Tony, was a tough, heavy guy who ran a bar and was intimidated by nobody, and he helped Cus survive in the 1950s when he dared to oppose the authority of the mob-run International Boxing Club, which in turn controlled boxing in New York, which was the fight capital of the world at the time. The IBC was controlled by Frankie Carbo, who had been a member of the infamous Murder Incorporated gang in the 1930s and who had been arrested five times for murder but never convicted. D'Amato had once trained Rocky Graziano, lost him to a mob-connected manager and had to stay in the background as Graziano won the world middleweight title. He never forgave Rocky his desertion. Eventually, probably out of his stubbornness rather than bravery or political design, he helped break the IBC. He took Patterson to the heavyweight title by pretending to enlist with them and indeed borrowing $20,000 from the organisation and then, with his brother's help, defied them. The IBC, who were under increasingly close investigation over the second half of the 1950s, found it hard to lay down the law to D'Amato, who simply pleaded his case for innocent independence. His 'stand' created his name as an iron-willed, eccentric purist.

Now when I met him again, through Jim Jacobs, D'Amato had Tyson. In 1982, when Tyson was 16, Cus asked if I would let Frank Bruno spar with him. I don't think Bruno was 21 and in fact probably had less experience inside a ring than Tyson had at the time. Cus outsmarted me for a moment. He asked me to make sure Bruno took it easy on the youngster and of course I said to Frank: 'Look, he's only a kid, don't hurt him. Take things a little bit gently.'

The next thing we knew Tyson was all over him, hammering away and Bruno was mentally flat. He had to take some stick. Then, before I could get Frank to try to put him in his place, D'Amato called an end to the sparring after one round. 'That was all I wanted him to box today,' he said.

Tyson was fighting in small amateur tournaments, some official and some 'smokers' – that is, glorified gym fights that never made the record books.

In some ways he was a man, in others a child. For example, the way Tyson would put his head on my shoulder was a childish gesture but also a sophisticated way of manipulating a person into being his friend and, in my opinion, putting himself in a position where he could use him. It was obvious he could fight even though nobody really knew how good he was going to be, because he was always difficult to control. He's always been trouble. He's inconsistent and unpredictable. As he's got older and more cunning he's got a little bit smarter, but God knows what will happen to him if he ever becomes in need of money. I think he could kill himself, or get himself killed. Jacobs and Bill Cayton both hoped success would help him change and in the long-term their influence would allow him to disassociate himself from his old ways and bad habits.

I was close to Jacobs and he used to talk to me. I learned of several secrets about the young Tyson which show he was rotten from the start. I remember Jim telling me that when Tyson was 16½ they paid off a girl, I think it was $75,000, to drop a sex charge. When he was 18, they paid another girl. I think that time it was $175,000. One local woman claimed Tyson had made her daughter pregnant and Cus and Jim paid her off. Before that, there were problems with Tyson's violence in the school they had put him in.

D'Amato had persuaded the authorities to let Tyson out of the Tryon School For Boys where he had been locked up for his street crimes in Brooklyn and eventually became his legal guardian, following the death of Tyson's mother in 1982. In another incident, Teddy Atlas, who was a trainer with Cus at the time and had looked after Tyson, put a gun to Mike's head in the gym and threatened to blow him away. Tyson had apparently made obscene sexual remarks to a 12-year-old girl and Atlas was furious. Tyson fled and ran to D'Amato in the house, vowed to kill Atlas but then calmed down. They didn't speak for many years. Atlas made some scathing but, in my opinion, very accurate comments from time to time about Tyson's deterioration that were distinctly at odds with the press and publicity machine of Don King, who had promoted his fights from the late 1980s. Yet I was amazed to hear that after his fight with Frans Botha in Las Vegas in 1999, Tyson saw Atlas at ringside and made a point of giving him a hug.

The D'Amato years in Tyson's life have come to be spoken of as some kind of paradise time, when the ageing mentor would impart his wisdom on the eager, impressionable boy.

Certainly, Tyson loved D'Amato and Camille Ewald, who must have done a lot to steady him down and give him some stability. The popular belief has been that Tyson really only went off the rails after D'Amato's death in 1985. The truth, however, is very different.

Cus could only keep some kind of control over Tyson by giving him everything he wanted. Cus worshipped him. Tyson was the only way that he could be great again. And quite fairly, history will credit D'Amato for producing his second 'youngest heavyweight champ in history'. In November 1986, a year after the old man died, Tyson knocked out Trevor Berbick in two rounds in Las Vegas to become WBC champion at the age of 20 years and five months. Afterwards Mike acknowledged his debt to Cus.

Through Jacobs, who greatly valued my opinion, I was involved in the selection of Tyson's opponents, from the start of his professional career. I either picked them myself or approved them. I would contact Johnny Bos, who had been my American agent for years. There was not a match made without my approval. Jacobs and I talked constantly about the way to move him forward and the rate of progress he was making. We didn't have anything in writing because we didn't need to and anyway I wasn't being paid. We were pals. It was simply that he had a lot of faith in my views and I helped because, although he was a fine boxing historian, he was largely ignorant of the here and now of the heavyweight division and the threat that Tyson's peers may or may not possess. It was important that Jim could show promoters that they were not dealing with a dummy and that's where I was able to help him out.

In the long term it helped me get into a favourable position to make the first Tyson-Bruno fight. In the short term it helped establish Tyson as a credible heavyweight.

When Tyson hit his peak for that brief time from late 1986

until, to be generous, 1989, who were the fighters he had to beat? Well, he followed a poor crop of heavyweights who had more or less passed the titles around between them. When the history of the heavyweight division is written, the names of those champions of the first half of the 1980s will not figure high on the all-time list. When Tyson arrived, the whole sport was screaming for mercy, for somebody to deliver it from this succession of under-achievers. Larry Holmes was the best of them but through the 1980s was in his thirties and past his best. Michael Spinks was really a light-heavyweight, who twice got lucky with Holmes and made some good money because of it.

Tyson beat Berbick for the WBC title and then beat Bone-crusher Smith, Pinklon Thomas, Tony Tucker, Tyrell Biggs, Tony Tubbs, Michael Spinks, Frank Bruno and Carl Williams. Tyson could only beat what was put in front of him, but he hadn't *really* been tested. None of those fighters could be called great. Tyson did knock out Larry Holmes in four rounds, but Holmes was 38 years old and hadn't boxed for almost two years. He wasn't yesterday's man – he was the day before yesterday's!

However, as someone said years ago 'in the land of the blind the one-eyed man is king'. Tyson was a welcome new face with an original style. There had never been a heavyweight quite like him. He was a small giant. He's about 5ft 10in tall, in fact only a little bit taller than me, but I was a welterweight. They put him at 5ft 11½in on the official sheets but I don't think he's that tall. At his best he had an aura about him. Unfortunately, he wasn't able to get himself into the mental and physical condition to match the aura for long enough. During his early years as champion he looked invincible. When he was very young, it seemed as if he could stay for as long as he wanted to. Yet even then I knew what Jim Jacobs had told me. I knew he was like a timebomb and it was only a question of how long it took before he exploded.

Once Jacobs had died from leukaemia in the spring of 1988, the attempt to keep Tyson under some kind of discipline was all over. Bill Cayton was not as close to Mike as D'Amato and Jacobs had been and he was in a vulnerable position, increasingly so as King set about the job of making Tyson his fighter. After Tyson's marriage ended in divorce, he allied himself to King. Their arrangement survived the loss of his title to Buster Douglas in Tokyo in 1990, his jailing for the rape of Desiree Washington – a Miss Black America contestant – in 1992, his three years behind bars and on through his comeback in 1995, and only faltered completely when he lost his licence in 1997 following his disgraceful disqualification in the rematch with Evander Holyfield when he bit off a piece of Evander's ear. They fell out and parted company in 1998, by which time Tyson was in his early 30s and well past his best.

Three events were formative in Tyson's demise. The first was his defeat by Douglas 12 months after the victory over Frank Bruno. Douglas, from Columbus, Ohio, was not an exceptional fighter but Tyson fought as if he didn't care any longer. Buster was inspired by the memory of his late mother and was prepared to fight at a level far above anything he had previously suggested he could reach. Even when Tyson knocked him down, he turned on to his knees and got up at nine. And eventually he knocked out Tyson in the 10th round. The still photographs of Tyson on the canvas, pathetically attempting to shove his gumshield into his mouth, were printed around the world.

Afterwards, of course, King attempted to reverse the result by claiming Douglas had been given the benefit of a long count. Everyone knew it was rubbish but King's perception of his own power was blown so far out of proportion that he thought he could get away with even that preposterous a scam. Fortunately for boxing, good sense prevailed – eventually – and Douglas kept the title. King lost control completely when Douglas defended against the Duvas' fighter, Evander Holyfield, on a show staged by the Mirage Hotel in Las Vegas, whose boss, Steve Wynn, was trying to make an impact. Douglas folded in three rounds to Holyfield. Even his own father, Bill Douglas, a middleweight whom we had promoted 20 years before against British champion Bunny Sterling, was scathing of Buster's performance.

The second significant stage in Tyson's downfall was his night out with Desiree Washington in Indianapolis in the summer of 1991, which ended with disputed versions of what happened in his hotel bedroom. He was convicted of rape. Do I believe he was guilty? I have no idea, but by all accounts he at the very least did not treat her as a gentleman should. This much is certainly in his character.

His treatment of other women is on record but on this occasion did he go over the fine line into the crime for which he was convicted? Only the two people who were in the room at the time know for sure and they disagree, but what was important is that the jury believed Desiree Washington and did not believe Mike Tyson. Although as far as I know he has never accepted his guilt in this case, he has said he had been guilty of treating women with contempt on other occasions and probably had it coming. It cost him three years in jail, three years of his boxing career and millions of dollars.

The third landmark in his downfall was his disqualification for biting the ears of Evander Holyfield in their rematch at the MGM Grand Garden, Las Vegas, in June 1997. Holyfield had boxed well in the first two rounds and had withstood several heavy punches from Tyson in the third when the former champion lost the plot completely and ripped a chunk out of Evander's right ear. The sight of Holyfield bounding up and down in pain and anger will be remembered by boxing fans for many years. Even then referee Mills Lane did not disqualify Tyson immediately. It took until Mike bit Holyfield's left ear for the referee to throw him out. That's what makes me absolutely sure that he wanted out of the fight, that he had lost his stomach for the business. He didn't want to get the shit kicked out of him by Holyfield a second time and knew it wouldn't look so bad, or feel so bad, if the result was a disqualification. It's known rather cruelly in the trade as a Mexican swallow – a nickname which came from a perceived habit of some Mexican fighters in the old days to hit a man low in order to be disqualified when things were going wrong.

With those three incidents, Tyson's historical reputation was sealed. They cancelled out all the good things he had done in his prime in the second half of the 1980s.

After being disqualified against Holyfield, Tyson was fined $3 million and had his licence revoked by the Nevada State Athletic Commission. Only in the year which followed that decision when he attempted to unravel his complicated financial position, did he realise what had been going on during the years that he had entrusted his career to King. He eventually sued his promoter for $100 million and also lodged suits against his co-managers, John Horne and Rory Holloway.

Tyson regained his licence with the help of Shelly Finkel and a new legal team in the autumn of 1998. It was another chaotic episode. At first they applied to the New Jersey State Athletic Commission but abandoned that before the result could be given. Tyson lost his patience with a line of discussion and swore at the hearing which created a bad impression. Then they switched to Nevada where a six-hour hearing ended in an adjournment. Tyson admitted he had spent a fortune in the past 12 months on legal fees. He handled the pressure better, with the help of a cynical sense of humour.

'I feel like I'm Norman Bates [the madman in the *Psycho* movies] up here with all these doctors,' he said. 'Trust me, this won't happen any more. I'm sorry.'

I thought it was terrible that the Nevada Commission had fined him $3 million and kept the money but was interested to read about the breakdown of Tyson's $30 million gross purse from the second Holyfield fight. These figures were provided at the hearing. He had to pay the commission their $3 million, another $4.3m went in taxes and somehow training expenses cost him $2.5m. Don King took $9m, which is a joke when he promoted the fight and his co-managers, Horne and Holloway, also took $3m each. In other words King and the two managers took half of Tyson's money. He ended up with $5.2m. The commission adjourned the hearing pending psychiatric reports and then, after considering them, gave him his licence.

Following his return, Tyson had one fight when he looked bad but won against Frans Botha from South Africa, and then was jailed again for assaulting two men in a road rage incident the previous August – a case that was on the table when his licence was given back to him. At the time of writing, he was free again, apparently training and trying to rebuild his career. After the life he has led, he is 33 going on 53, I don't think he has any chance of being anything more than a fraction of the fighter he was.

How good was he in his prime? Of the heavyweights of recent times, as I've already said, Ali would have toyed with him and Frazier and Foreman would probably have beaten him. Maybe Holyfield would have beaten him when they were first matched in 1990. Certainly, he knew how to as he showed when he stopped Tyson in 1996, but by that time Mike's effectiveness had diminished by at least 50 per cent. Holyfield's career achievements are certainly greater than Tyson's were.

I do think Tyson could have beaten Sonny Liston because of his speed – if he had lasted through the first three rounds when Liston was at his most dangerous. Sonny used to tire and Tyson had the style to beat him. He could have backed Liston up. Larry Holmes' stand-up style would always have suited Tyson. He could reach those guys because he had a roll-in style and Holmes was a little easier to hit than most.

Tyson's story, like so many, is one of what might have been. He had so much but used so little. It's a waste. It was a pity for Tyson that Jacobs' health deteriorated so quickly. His death was the worst thing that could have happened for Tyson and I am convinced there would have been a big difference had Jim lived, because Jacobs was stricter and smarter than D'Amato. Maybe if he had Tyson wouldn't be in the mess he is now.

CHAPTER 19

America and Television

In the 1970s I very nearly moved to live in California full time. I bought an apartment in Marina del Rey with a view to moving there and over a period of several years must have spent 40 per cent of my time in the United States. I was looking for success as a promoter and felt I had almost reached the point where I could flit in and out of Britain as the need required. My wife's mother was living in Los Angeles and my wife wanted to be over there. I was thinking in terms of our joint interests at the time, although later that altered when we separated.

Following the death of the Californian promoter Aileen Eaton, a terribly tough person who was nicknamed 'The Dragon Lady', I became involved with Don Chargin in Los Angeles and promoted several shows at the Olympic Auditorium with Don and the young Mexican, Rogelio Robles, but it was a tough sell and we didn't make any money to speak of. Don eventually managed on his own and is still active.

I had been working intermittently in the USA from the

1960s. In those days boxing had a more defined season in Britain – coinciding with football – from late August to early May. In the summer it was dead here and so I kept busy by going to the States. I even had a show in Omaha, Nebraska, with a local promoter named Lee Sloane, who was really a fight fan. In fact, 75 per cent of the people who come into boxing for a living were fans first. I got him Ray Robinson, who was then in his 40s. I remember sitting discussing the possibilities with Sloane and we were talking about who we could get to top the bill. I said to him: 'How would Ray Robinson go?'

He looked at me as if I was mad and said: 'Are you kidding? He would sell the place out.'

He had been there and won a couple of non-title fights in 1949 when he was welterweight champion. So I rang him up:

'Ray, how would you like to box in Omaha?'

'Omaha, Nebraska?' he said. 'Mickey, what the heck are you doing in Omaha?'

He took the fight, the show sold and, as I mentioned earlier, he drew over 10 rounds with Art Hernandez.

In the early 1980s I also ran a series of shows at Harrah's Marina Casino in Atlantic City in partnership with Dan Duva, the driving force behind the Main Events business. His father Lou, who is of course the patriarch and figurehead of their operation, made the speech to welcome me to my induction into the Hall of Fame in June 1999. 'If you want to talk about boxing,' he said, 'there is nobody better to talk to than Mickey Duff.'

It was nice of him. I got on very well indeed with Dan, who died a couple of years ago from a brain tumour while still in his 40s. I always found him totally reliable. He was a shrewd businessman who didn't bother with long explanations. We would discuss an issue and he would say: 'You've got it. OK, done.'

And that was it. His word was as good as a written contract.

Main Events were the company who pioneered Pay Per View deals in the USA, which they began with the first Ray Leonard-Thomas Hearns fight in 1981. It was a huge success.

The Duvas' linked with Shelly Finkel to sign most of the great American Olympic boxing team from the Los Angeles games in 1984. They promoted the debuts of Evander Holyfield, Tyrell Biggs, Mark Breland, Virgil Hill, Pernell Whitaker and Meldrick Taylor on a show at Madison Square Garden in November 1984. Hill left them shortly afterwards, but four of the other five became world champions with Main Events. The odd man out, ironically because they thought at the time he would be their star, was Tyrell Biggs. His career was wrecked by drug abuse – and a bad beating he took in a world title fight at the hands of Mike Tyson in 1987. Biggs was never the same fighter after that, although he went on for some years.

Main Events eventually prolonged its success by its relationship with Lennox Lewis, but Dan's death was a huge blow to them, and they look as if they have lost their impetus. We shall see.

I love Las Vegas but couldn't possibly remain there. It's very enjoyable when you know you are only there for a week or ten days but I couldn't bear to think of living that kind of a life permanently. I could live in California, though, because it's got the weather and the beach. If you get out of downtown, not obviously into the bad areas, it's like a very large health farm. I gave up on the idea of living there only when my marriage soured.

Vegas has a wonderful climate. It's the only place where it can be 95 degrees and you don't sweat because there is always that mountain breeze. You sit by the pool and relax and it feels hot but not usually unbearable. I always used to say 'in Las Vegas you perspire, in Bournemouth you sweat'. I usually stayed in Caesars Palace where, at the time, fights were viewed as a hook to get gamblers into the casino. I loved it all from the start – and of course enjoyed it all the more because I liked to gamble. Funnily enough, I returned to Las Vegas in the summer of 1999 to talk to Bob Arum about a WBC lightweight title fight for Billy Schwer and while it was a pleasure to be there for a whole week, I had almost $5,000 on me and didn't gamble one penny. I didn't think I was capable of such restraint but I felt that at my time of life I don't have the energy to take a bad loss and go away and recover the money in other ways.

If you were a boxing fan in the 1980s then Las Vegas was the place to be. You had Ray Leonard, Marvin Hagler, Roberto Duran, Thomas Hearns, Donald Curry, Mike McCallum and Wilfred Benitez, all between welterweight and middleweight and most at one time or another were fighting each other, mostly in Vegas. Boxing was huge because it was shown coast to coast by ABC, CBS and NBC. The major fighters were literally household names.

Pound for pound, who was the best of them? I would have to say Ray Leonard. It's a toss up between Leonard and Hagler, and Ray won when they fought and so, even though that was at the end of Marvin's career, I would have to give it to him. Leonard had the style to beat him.

Duran lost on points to Hagler, was knocked out by Hearns and was the first man to beat Leonard in that thrilling, close fight in Montreal in the summer of 1980. It was a breathtaking 15-round war which Duran won on a unanimous decision. In the rematch he pulled the infamous 'No Mas' because, I think, he was being outboxed to the point of humiliation. On a good night, Leonard was capable of doing that to almost anybody. In the 1970s Duran was one of the best lightweights of all time and went on to hold world titles in four different weight divisions from 135lbs to 160lbs. I liked referee Mills Lane's description of Duran. He said when you looked into his eyes, you saw nothing. It was like looking into the eyes of a shark, he said. Leonard and Hearns moved up and down the weights, too, but Hagler was a middleweight from first to last. The first Leonard-Hearns fight in Las Vegas in 1981 was magnificent. Hearns boxed his way ahead, but Leonard clawed his way back and stopped him in the 14th round. After 13 and with only two to go, Hearns was still in front on points. When they were old men they fought again at the end of the decade – Hearns knocked Leonard down twice but they gave Ray a draw. They were all great fighters.

One of the American media icons of the time was the commentator, Howard Cosell. He was very conceited, had an extraordinarily high opinion of his own ability and status and was very sensitive to criticism. We were at the weigh-in to, I think, the John Stracey-Hedgemon Lewis fight in a marquee at the back of Quaglino's restaurant in London and I said to him: 'Howard, this is going to upset you but I am the only person in this place who knows who you are.'

He pretended he didn't hear me. He eventually retired from boxing after the one-sided Larry Holmes-Randall 'Tex' Cobb fight in 1982, making a typically pompous farewell statement about no longer being able to stand the hypocrisy and sleaze that had become associated with the sport. Most people applauded his leaving. The truth is his time had come. Cobb's reaction was unforgettable. 'I can do my sport no greater service than this,' he said.

By then, boxing was changing. Since the early 1960s, world titles had been run by the World Boxing Council and the World Boxing Association, which were formed by members from American states or national bodies. It worked quite well. One kept the other on its toes by providing an alternative, although we didn't deal with the WBA until the 1980s because Britain had always been allied to the WBC, which from 1975 was, and still is, headed from Mexico City by Jose Sulaiman. I have dealt with Jose over many years now. He has received a lot of criticism but I am very fond of him. I think he has been forced into political decisions from time to time in order to stay in business but all-in-all has done a good job. The WBC is far from perfect but stands out a mile as being the fairest of the governing bodies.

The situation began to change in 1982 when a group of disenchanted members walked out of the WBA, led by Bobby Lee snr. from New Jersey, and formed the International Boxing Federation. Their point was that the WBA had a Latin bias and was prejudicial against American interests even though most of the major fights were only possible because of American money. Bob Arum spoke out in one of the American boxing trade magazines, I think *Ring*, and revealed the way the WBA were doing business. He claimed that to get anything done in the WBA a 'bagman' named Pepe Cordero had to be paid. Cordero held no official office within the WBA. The article certainly hurt the organisation badly and helped pave the way for the IBF, which naturally looked more favourably on American boxers and promoters.

The IBF prospered because Larry Holmes defected as heavyweight champion from the WBC when they refused to sanction a fight he had more or less made himself against Marvis Frazier, son of Joe. Holmes won in one round and after that defended only the IBF belt. Through Holmes they got television exposure and were able to thrive. They also had a colourful featherweight champion from Mexico, Jorge Paez, who drew huge ratings on NBC television.

In Britain we had always worked with the WBC, but with the rise of Frank Warren in the 1980s, the IBF managed to get a foothold here. And in 1988, when another walkout occurred at the WBA, led by Cordero, the World Boxing Organisation was founded. Cordero, who is dead now, owned it. In America, the WBO managed to get Thomas Hearns and Michael Moorer as two of its early champions, both of whom the TV companies wanted to show. In Britain, Barry Hearn promoted WBO title fights with Chris Eubank their star attraction. There were others, of course, and while purists could complain and write letters to the trade press, the fact of the matter was that the IBF and WBO had proved that privately run companies purporting to be world boxing authorities could become viable business propositions.

Now the situation has become ridiculous and there is nothing legally that the British Board of Control can do about it. The Restraint of Trade laws in this country prevent them from banning any of these organisations, and the Board can do nothing to stop their members from doing business with them, or working for them. On the backs of the IBF and WBO, so many of these privately run organisations have sprung up during the 1990s. We call them the Alphabet Boys because you can't really tell one from another. There is the WBU, IBO, IBC, IBA, WAA, WBB . . . you name it, it's there. I have been making my living out of boxing for 50 years and if you put a gun to my head I couldn't name you all of the world champions. If you told me their names, there would be some that I've never even heard of.

Television is to blame for accepting them as bona fide organisations. If they chose not to do business with promoters on the basis of screening a WBO title fight, or IBO or WBU or whatever, then they would disappear very quickly.

Where can it end? It would be easy for me to write off boxing and say it's finished, but it somehow has a way of rearing its head and coming back again. I wouldn't be at all surprised if some enterprising company comes along, grabs boxing by the scruff of the neck and gives it a fresh face.

The would-be abolitionists are wrong. Banning boxing is not an answer to anything. Fundamentally, it has value because people want to do it and people want to see it. There is always room for improvement and change, but there is no need to get rid of it.

Boxing is a dangerous sport and those who participate in it, unless they are totally stupid, know it's dangerous. I have always realised that heads weren't made to be punched and bodies weren't built to be hit, but human beings weren't built for a lot of the things they do. Horse riding is dangerous – three people were killed in equestrian competitions in Britain in the first eight months of 1999. Driving a car is dangerous. Life is dangerous. Basically, you take a chance whatever you do.

Having said that, I don't think you can have too much medical protection for boxers. The standard of safety in Britain is higher than it's ever been – and rightly so. We have more facilities available now to protect boxers and better safety methods. Medical care has improved over the years, just as it has in every other walk of life.

Recently, there have been suggestions that boxing could be made safer by the introduction of headguards into competition and by increasing the size and weight of gloves. Both ideas are wrong-headed and ill-informed. Headguards are dangerous. Boxers wear them in the gym to protect against cuts caused by punches or accidental head clashes, but boxers who wear headguards are more likely to get hit than those who do not. Firstly, because they obscure vision. Secondly, because they increase the size of the target area. Thirdly, because however light they are, they effectively increase the weight of the head and make movement a fraction slower. Headguards are an extra weight to be moved about and an extra surface area to be struck. In the same way bigger gloves, even the big ones used in sparring, are unhelpful. They protect hands from damage and there is less likelihood of a single punch hurting a boxer, but there is a bigger area of glove being thrown and more chance of a punch landing. There is more glove to avoid. There is also the likelihood of increased cumulative effect of punches because bigger gloves make them hurt less. A boxer is less likely to worry about getting hit by a big glove than by a small one, and is therefore more likely to forget the basic principle that the art of boxing is to avoid getting hit.

Fighting for a living is dangerous, but in my opinion boxers are better now than they were years ago, just as soccer players and tennis players are better than they ever were. Sports progress and learn from the past.

Financially, I think, the rewards are about the same as they were 50 years ago, taking inflation into account. If you compared a boxer like Dave Crowley, who was British lightweight champion in the 1930s, and Billy Schwer, who is our best lightweight now, I think you would find that Crowley's purses were every bit as good as Schwer's – and Billy has earned very well out of boxing.

I think the fact that sanctioning bodies have sprung up like weeds is to the detriment of boxing and as I have said, it does the sport no good at all to have so many world champions that even the most avid fight fan cannot reasonably be expected to name them. But I believe the worst thing that has happened to boxing is the arrival of the multiple titles. The problem is not confined to the number of so-called world championships on offer, for each governing body has now also introduced Inter-Continental titles, which purport to be 'junior' championships, or stepping stones to the world title. They rarely are. The truth is that everything has to have a championship tag so that the sanctioning bodies can claim sanctioning fees. Even if promoters don't want to stage them, governing bodies have the power to make life easy or difficult. It's not hard to understand that governing bodies are likely to look more kindly at the promoters who provide them with the most income, which means by staging Inter-Continental fights a promoter can expect favours when it comes to promoting full world championships.

Frankly, it's terrible. The public are nowhere near as stupid as these people imagine. If I were a ticket buyer and I saw the words 'Inter-Continental' on the bill-poster I would immediately think 'fake'.

Yet for all that's wrong with the business of boxing, I still love it. And yes, if I were starting out today, I would still do it all over again.

We were dealing with the BBC for 33 years and I don't blame anybody for not wanting to deal with us now. I am 70 years old. If they want to work for the future, they don't look for people like me. At my time of life, you can't sign a boxer and take a long term view. I might be here in 10 years, but I might not. Time is not on your side and you get a little bit more impatient for results than you were. Against that, you do bring the value of those years of experience to any new business relationship.

But in my opinion British boxing has got to find a strong opposition to Sky because it has to prevent them from putting on exactly what they want to put on. A lot of what they show is mediocre and fight fans who attend on the night almost seem to be incidental. There was one show recently on which the first two fights happened before doors opened to the public. This was to accommodate overseas television interests.

The BBC and ITV lost interest in boxing around 1995 because Sky came into the sport. If Sky hadn't come in with the kind of financial ammunition they did, then the BBC and ITV might have stayed with it. As it was, they couldn't compete and so backed off.

Now it needs somebody to come along who understands boxing, who has the desire and knowledge of the business, but first and foremost has the financial backing. If you've got no socks, you can't pull them up.

CHAPTER 20

End of an Era

By the turn of the 1990s times were changing. Frank Warren was well established and Barry Hearn had followed up the financial success of the Frank Bruno-Joe Bugner fight in 1987 to set up the boxing arm of his Matchroom organisation. Warren and Hearn had the energy and drive that comes naturally to men in their 30s and were, quite understandably, making headway. I didn't like it and still don't – but I wasn't going to run anywhere. The facts could not be avoided, however. Their power was increasing. Ours wasn't. And, whoever wins, competition makes the world go round.

But now the decade is at an end it's plain to see that we didn't just fade away: we promoted and managed some very good fighters. I hung on out of stubbornness because too many people wanted me to go. Anyway, what else would I do? My business is my life. I have no interests other than boxing. If I'd quit, they'd have won.

I don't want to be everybody's favourite uncle. I made my

enemies and people resented the power we had and some of them didn't like the way we did our business. That's life. I loved the line somebody came out with years ago: 'That Mickey Duff, you know, he's not nearly as nice as he looks!'

While we're on the subject of looks, it might be the best time to point out that the scar on my face which runs down from my left eye on to my cheek was not the result of a dramatic confrontation with an opponent, in or out of the ring. It happened when a cab I was travelling in was involved in an accident. I was cut by the glass from the window and spent a lot of money on repairing the damage in London and Miami.

As well as our shows at Wembley and the Albert Hall, we ran the Anglo-American Sporting Club for 19 years and then merged with the National Sporting Club for the next decade. We revived the Anglo-American when we started National Promotions in the early 1990s and I like to think it set the highest possible standards for dinner boxing establishments of that nature. We did away with the old ideas of eating the meal in a separate room and having silence during the boxing.

Few know that I came very close to signing Lennox Lewis before he turned professional, but Roger Levitt, the business-man who was eventually disgraced in a sensational fraud trial, reportedly gave him £250,000 to turn. I could have matched that but didn't want to. I wasn't prepared to gamble with our money to that extent. It was different for Levitt, whom the courts found had come by his money by illegal means. With hindsight we can all be smart and say a substantial investment from us would have repaid itself many times over but, in 1988, nobody could.

Lewis had won the Olympic super-heavyweight gold medal in Seoul by stopping Riddick Bowe in the final and looked as if he might be a terrific heavyweight. All kinds of things can go wrong, however, and while we had resources, nobody has unlimited money. He had been born here, had been taken to Canada when he was 12 by his mother and had been taught to box there. He had represented Canada in the Olympics in 1984, won a Commonwealth Games gold medal for them in 1986 and then the Olympic gold in 1988. We had no way of knowing what, if any, his commitment to Britain was, whether or not the British public would accept him, or whether or not he would want to spend his career in America. And of course while we could be sure of his talent, at that stage there was no possibility of knowing how much character he had. Now I can honestly say Lennox deserves his success and his recognition as the best British heavyweight of all time. I met him and his lawyer, John Hornewer, for dinner with Jarvis at Caesars Palace, Las Vegas, and had preliminary talks. Hornewer did the talking, Lewis the listening, and the meeting was inconclusive.

Later, when Levitt went bust, Lewis' contract – which actually belonged to the Levitt Group – was up for tender. Frank Maloney, Lewis's manager, had some interest in it and had a say in who it was sold to. He wouldn't sell to us, and eventually it was sold to Panos Eliades, the neighbour of Levitt who is a liquidator by profession. Eliades had no previous boxing experience but has done a good job. So has Maloney, who was not taken seriously when he began but who has now proved to be a survivor and, with Lewis at least, extremely successful.

I promoted Naseem Hamed for one year, 1993, early in his career. He was managed by Brendan Ingle and they had just left Matchroom after their promotional deal had expired. I can't remember seeing a more naturally talented fighter as Hamed, with his daring and his precision, but I didn't think much of him as a person. He's too cocky for my liking. I've always said that he's almost as good as he thinks he is! We promoted a few fights for him but we couldn't do anything for him in terms of television deals. When I discussed him with the BBC Head of Sport, Jonathan Martin, their attitude was negative. 'Who do you think is going to watch somebody called Naseem Hamed,' said Martin. 'This may surprise you but we haven't got too many Arabs living here.'

What a mistake that proved to be. I lost Hamed. He signed for Frank Warren and went on to win his World Boxing Organisation featherweight title two years later. I don't have a problem with Brendan Ingle, who of course has now also lost Hamed. I don't think Ingle's an Einstein and I believe his own teacher was Herol Graham. I know he denies that but before he had Graham, none of his fighters boxed in that style. Now they all do it.

Herol Graham was another story. We tried to promote him in the 1980s but Ingle wasn't easy to work with. He wanted to work with everybody and, as a promoter, you can't look after a fighter that way. It wasn't greed but Brendan always had a few fighters who were difficult to place and he would deal like somebody holding a sale. He would be off to work on somebody else's show if there was a chance of two or three of his fighters getting work. A business relationship with us couldn't work like that. A manager has the right not to be exclusive – and so does the promoter. Graham had plenty of talent and an original style but didn't fight for a world title until he was nearly 30. Even then, he almost beat Mike McCallum, one of the best fighters of the generation.

Of course, the loss of the BBC hurt us. We still had good fighters like Joe Calzaghe, Richie Woodhall, Robert McCracken, Henry Wharton and Neville Brown and I think with a different attitude from the television companies we could have made a whole new generation of boxing stars.

I was pleased with the way we moved Woodhall through to his first world title fight. He had won an Olympic bronze medal at the Seoul Games in 1988 – Roy Jones outpointed him in the semi-finals – and he began with a local business-man backing him. We did a deal and guided him carefully. He wasn't a big puncher but he was a fine boxer in the upright, amateur way. I remember him knocking out an Aus-tralian, Vito Gaudiosi, in just over a minute at Telford to win the Commonwealth title – a rare knockout for him. Gaudiosi was on his knees and put up his gloves to his chin as the referee reached 'eight' as if he wanted to box on. He was so stunned he didn't realise he was still on the canvas.

Woodhall learned the business well with us and defended his Commonwealth title several times, then won the Euro-pean title with a tremendous fight against an Italian, Silvio Branco, in Telford, which was Richie's home town and where he always had fantastic support. He proved he could fight as well as box that night when he stood toe-to-toe and stopped Branco in the ninth round. We knew then we had a world title prospect and the World Boxing Council ranked him No.1. Don King had the title, which meant Richie had to hang around because King wasn't going to do me any favours. I think the championship changed hands twice with Woodhall still at No.1, until King finally gave him the chance against a tall southpaw, Keith Holmes, in Maryland in October 1996. Woodhall didn't like southpaws but could have beaten Holmes. He had injury problems by then – his right elbow had gone and he had keyhole surgery a couple of weeks before the fight, just before he left England. I said we could postpone it but he needed the money, which was understandable – £100,000 paydays don't come along that often, and he had a family to support. We were messed around out there but I don't think he went out in the right frame of mind. Maybe it was the surgery that took it away from him. He couldn't straighten his right arm, which took something away from him. He had such a good left hand that he was able to outbox Holmes but he couldn't keep it up and was stopped in the last round.

Before that I had earned him a big payday without his having to lace on a glove. We accepted a six-figure offer to go to Germany to defend the European title against Salvador Yanez, who I didn't think would be in Woodhall's league. He was a South American who had become a German citizen and was selling a few tickets for a new promoter. We accepted the offer and travelled over there, only for the fight to be cancelled at the last minute. We had fulfilled our contractual obligations and so were entitled to be paid, and I made sure we were.

Woodhall left me after the Keith Holmes fight and signed for Warren, which I don't think he should have done. We had done very well for him, but his contract had expired and he was entitled to do it. He won the WBC super-middleweight title in 1998 when he outpointed Sugarboy Malinga from South Africa. Malinga was about as old as me! Recently Woodhall wanted to leave Warren but now I hear they have patched up their differences.

Joe Calzaghe was co-managed by Terry Lawless and I – and would have won a world title with us, instead of with Frank Warren, if he had been prepared to wait. He had won three ABA titles, training with his father, Enzo, in a gym near their house in Newbridge, south Wales. It was a partnership which worked, just as Woodhall's did with his trainer-father Len, and there was no reason to change something that was succeeding. Calzaghe was with us from the start of his professional career and made his debut on the Lennox Lewis-Frank Bruno show at Cardiff Arms Park in October 1993 – not a bad place to start for a Welshman. Calzaghe won in the first round. He could punch in those days and the only man we found who could stand up to him for more than a couple of rounds was a cruiserweight, Bobbi Joe Edwards from Manchester, whose sister was the athlete Diane Modahl and whose cousin was Chris Eubank. Edwards gave Calzaghe eight rounds because of the weight he carried.

We followed the same pattern with Calzaghe that we had formulated all those years ago, monitoring his matches carefully and moving him up. On one of the shows we did in 1995 for ITV, the idea of which was to match our fighters with Barry Hearn's, Calzaghe won the British super-middleweight title by stopping Stephen Wilson from Scotland in the eighth round at the Albert Hall. I must admit I wasn't over-keen on the idea when it was suggested but I got to like it a little more when our fighters won almost all of the fights. After beating Wilson, who was actually managed by Hearn's associate Tommy Gilmour, Calzaghe stopped an unbeaten Matchroom hopeful, Mark Delaney from West Ham. Delaney was on the floor four times and the referee stopped it in round five.

After that fight I remember the ITV interviewer, Gary Newbon, suggesting to Calzaghe that he still had a lot of things to put right, that he did a lot of things wrong. I think that's the way they were by then – looking for faults to find rather than praising the kid for the progress he was making. Calzaghe left us at the end of 1996 and moved on to Warren, following a British Board of Control hearing. He got out of our contract on a technicality. After the Michael Watson case, when the judge found for him on the grounds that I could not act in his best interests as both his manager and promoter, our counsel suggested to the Board what is now Clause 6.2 in the boxer-manager agreement, in which the boxer is given the right to negotiate for himself in cases where his manager also acts as his promoter. Ironically, it was my own failure to send the necessary letter to Calzaghe, as required by the clause, which left us open for him to leave us.

After he moved to Warren, Calzaghe was going to fight Steve Collins for the WBO title, then Collins retired and he fought Eubank instead. Eubank had to shed a lot of weight and Calzaghe beat him over 12 rounds to win the WBO championship, over which of course Warren has considerable influence. He has promoted WBO title fights regularly for some time. The WBO is still based in Puerto Rico but its original owner, Pepe Cordero, died and passed it on to his family. Then a split occurred and after some in-fighting it is now run by a guy named Francisco 'Paco' Valcarcel, who has a working relationship with Warren.

I managed Henry Akinwande for the first 25 fights of his career, of which he drew one and won the rest. He came to me as a capable but colourless amateur who had won the ABA title twice and boxed in the Seoul Olympics. He won the European heavyweight title with us and moved into the world ratings. He was a big, 6ft 7in Nigerian who was born in London and was disowned by his father when he said he wanted to be a boxer. I could sympathise with him. His best win was on points over Axel Schulz in Berlin. He was clever but with nowhere near the amount of ability of either Bruno or Lewis – and about one-tenth of the charisma. He left us and lived in Florida, working under Don King. He won the WBO championship but disgraced himself when he fought Lennox Lewis for the WBC title. Akinwande looked as if he was locked in some kind of trance and referee Mills Lane threw him out in the fifth round for failing to throw punches. He's still boxing – and winning – in the States, but it will take a long time for him to recover from that flop.

Henry Wharton was a good, exciting fighter, a gipsy from York, who challenged for the world title with us – he lost on points to Eubank, Nigel Benn and Robin Reid. He could hit with the left hook and was very popular but didn't quite have the skills to win the big ones. He left us when his contract ran out and signed with his trainer for a while. He has retired now. His career just petered out when he got to 30.

Another fighter we handled and kept unbeaten, the Birmingham middleweight Robert McCracken, was among the last to leave us and is still unbeaten but past 30 now and, at the time of writing, still waiting for his world title fight. McCracken was always close to Woodhall, way back from their days as youngsters and they used to help each other prepare for fights. When Woodhall fought for the WBC middleweight title in the States, McCracken paid his own way out there to support him. McCracken opted instead of going to Warren to make his base in Las Vegas with one of the new promoters over there, Mat Tinley from America Presents.

Tinley, whose uncle is reportedly extremely wealthy, made his name in boxing with the Irish bantamweight, Wayne McCullough, with whom I was highly impressed when I saw him win silver at the Barcelona Olympics. I always made a point of watching the Olympics to assess the potential professional stars on show and another that caught my eye at Barcelona was the American 'Golden Boy' Oscar De La Hoya. Regrettably, I was unable to sign either. McCullough opted against remaining in Ireland and signing with someone like Barney Eastwood, preferring to base himself in Las Vegas under the guidance of Tinley.

In another era, I think we would have done great business with all of these boxers and they could have been as big as John H. Stracey, Jim Watt, Alan Minter and the others were 20 years before.

A fighter I did enjoy a good relationship with was the welterweight, Gary Jacobs, who came to me after his contract had expired with Mike Barrett. Gary, a steady, methodical southpaw from Scotland who had been around for years, was brought to me by his partner, Graham Sulkin, who had his full confidence. He had a financial interest as his advisor but I called the shots. I have yet to meet a boxer who had the option of becoming a brain surgeon but Jacobs was knowledgeable and had a head for business. I was in his corner when he challenged Pernell Whitaker for the WBC welterweight title in Atlantic City in 1995. Whitaker was one of the slickest boxers of the time, not especially popular because of his awkward style, but very effective. Inevitably, people wrote beforehand that Jacobs was following the path set by Stracey and Lloyd Honeyghan, who had won their world welterweight championships with me in the corner. Gary talked intelligently before the fight and knew the odds were against him but relished the challenge. He didn't want to be satisfied with winning a minor title. He wanted the best or nothing.

'They say Whitaker is the finished article,' he said. 'The finest fighting machine the world, the best in the business. That's why I have held off for so long, to get this chance of meeting the No.1 man. No man is unbeatable and I firmly believe I can prove a point.'

Unfortunately, Gary couldn't pull off another upset but did go the full 12 rounds in a hard fight that was much closer than the judges had it. He was in trouble in the last round but had earned the right to hold his head high. Whitaker admitted afterwards it had taken him four or five rounds to fathom out Jacobs's style.

Jacobs had earned very well in European title fights with us, at Wembley, in Paris and in Glasgow, and his career kept going for a while after the Whitaker fight. In France in June 1996 he was winning clearly against a local fighter, Patrick Charpentier, who wasn't much of a boxer but who could punch. Then Gary was tagged and came apart. He took a bit of punishment and the fight was stopped in the seventh round. Afterwards I said: 'Gary, I think it's all over.'

He was past 30 and had just reached 50 fights. He had a wife and two daughters, was well set and I didn't see any point in his going on too long. He didn't agree and we parted company. He won a couple of small fights, then lost a 12-round decision to a Russian, Yuri Epifantsev, in one of these meaningless title fights at Earls Court in 1997. As he came out of the ring, he passed by me and said: 'You were right.'

We had a good relationship. I always believe in a fighter retiring two fights too early than too late. Gary didn't get hurt and is now set up in business with a fitness centre in Glasgow.

Now my hopes for the future lie with Billy Schwer, who at the time of writing is waiting for his shot at the WBC lightweight title. As they always are, negotiations have been protracted but we have stuck at the task and Billy's reward will come before the turn of the millennium.

I first contacted his father, Billy Snr., at an England amateur international staged by the Anglo-American at the Grosvenor House around 1990. I watched him box and was very impressed. I remembered his father boxing in the early sixties as an amateur when he had come over from Ireland and was first living here. The family were from County Kildare and Billy Snr. won the Irish ABA featherweight title in 1962 when he was also boxing for Vauxhall Motors in Luton. After young Billy had boxed, his father, who was watching from the gallery, was pointed out to me and I went up there to see him. I said:

'Excuse me, my name is Mickey Duff.'

'I know who you are,' he said.

'I am very impressed with your son.'

'Are you really?'

'If he's ever interested in turning professional, I would appreciate it if you would give me a ring.'

I gave him my card and three or four months later they

contacted me. We signed a three-year deal – and that was nearly nine years ago. When he won the British and Commonwealth lightweight titles with a nine rounds win over Carl Crook, a Matchroom fighter, at the Albert Hall in 1992, I was delighted. He lost the championship because of cuts against Paul Burke, a kid who like Crook came from the Preston area. We were furious at the time because our cut-man, Dennie Mancini, insisted he could have stopped the bleeding and Burke was also cut. These things happen and we made the return nine months later. Billy won on points. By then we had taken up the renewal clause in the Board of Control contract, which allows a manager to repeat the length of the original deal. People have criticised this in the past but most managers and promoters lay out a considerable amount of money in the early stages of a fighter's career. We didn't take money from fighters when they were hardly earning anything. Only when they reach championship level can you begin to recoup your investment and the Board contract allows you the chance to do that. Some say loyalty has to be earned, but there is always somebody willing to whisper in a young fighter's ear, particularly if he can fight, when they work out his contract is about to expire. I think the renewal option is sensible.

By 1994 we thought Schwer was ready for a shot at one of the world champions and manoevred him into a position to challenge Rafael Ruelas, the classy IBF titleholder from Los Angeles. Bob Arum and Barry Hearn were to stage it on an ambitious promotion in Hong Kong, with the financial backing coming from John Daly, who had been involved in the 'Rumble In The Jungle' fight between Muhammad Ali and George Foreman 20 years before.

It turned out to be a total disaster. They billed it 'High Noon In Hong Kong' and from the moment we arrived it was obvious there were serious financial problems. Daly had guaranteed Hearn and Arum $1.5 million and they had billed, as well as the Ruelas-Schwer fight, WBO title defences for Steve Collins and Herbie Hide, who were both Matchroom fighters, and a heavyweight scrap between Frank Bruno and Ray Mercer. The boxers' contracts were with Arum's Top Rank organisation but the company behind the project was Hemdale, which was run by Daly. Things went from bad to worse: there were arguments with the people at the fight venue, difficulties with the hotel (who complained that 500 rooms had been booked but not yet paid for); most bizarre of all a local boxing commission sprung up from nowhere and tried to gain some leverage in the show.

Hearn wanted his guarantee to be honoured, Daly's bank refused to loan the money and the whole thing fell apart. Instead of the weigh-in, Hearn and Arum held a press confer-ence to say the cash had not been forthcoming and they were cancelling the show. I was beside myself with anger at the mess. We had travelled out there, our fighters had prepared themselves meticulously and Billy Schwer's family and friends had spent hard-earned savings on travelling half way around the world to support him. Daly said he had put $800,000 of his own money in but the bank would not back him with the further sum of $771,000 which was needed to satisfy Arum and Hearn. Daly said he had arranged the stadium, air fares and pre-fight promotional expenses but the purses for the fighters were a matter for Top Rank as they held the contracts. Arum was not prepared to put his company's money in to salvage the show. Daly looked almost ill as he said:

'It seems I was ready to take the shots but Mr Arum was not. I wish I could have pulled this off but I couldn't.'

I slammed Arum publicly.

'He didn't say he was cancelling the show because he couldn't take the loss, but because he wouldn't. What kind of a promoter is that? I've been in this business 45 years and I've never cancelled a show just because I was going to lose money. I would rather cut my throat.

'If the show had made an extra $1 million, we wouldn't have expected to be paid another penny. Now they find they've made a bad decision, they think they can just walk away from it.'

For once I agreed with Bruno, who was equally furious.

'Top Rank are big promoters and they should have dug deep in their pockets. They've made enough money out of fighters over the years.'

Of course, we claimed for compensation immediately but nothing could take away the stench of one of the most disgraceful promotional exercises I have ever seen. The fighters were all absolutely dismayed. Collins' opponent, Lonnie Beasley, said: 'I'm a meat and potatoes fighter. If you don't box, you don't eat. That's the way it is. I have had to pay for house sitters, baby sitters, air fares for my girlfriend, for my kids' schooling . . .'

I had every sympathy with him. A few thousand dollars might not have constituted a fortune to Bob Arum but it would have been to Beasley, who incidentally never did get his shot at Collins. The fight was re-scheduled for January, then called off again.

As for the Schwer family, they were distraught. Billy's mother was in tears and Billy himself was almost speechless with disappointment. The compensation package for him was a 25 per cent increase in his money when the fight was eventually staged at the MGM Grand Garden Arena in Las Vegas in January 1995. Billy was behind on points as the fight neared the end of the eighth round and he had bad cuts over both eyes. Dennie Mancini had bought Billy a little time by sealing them as best he could but they were not going to hold out for another four rounds. Schwer would have fought on, but I told the ringside doctor, Flip Homansky, who is an experienced man: 'Do what you have to do.'

I was proud of Billy but that's no compensation for a defeat because of cuts. We kept him in the picture with the Commonwealth title until he lost that on a 12th round stoppage against an African, David Tetteh, on a show screened by ITV from Dagenham in November 1995. For a while it looked as if he couldn't go any further but then we gambled everything on a European title challenge in Spain and Billy resurrected his career with a 10th round stoppage of Oscar Garcia, the defending champion. He was behind on points but found a big right hand. Now he's gone on to his second title fight.

I lobbied successfully for Billy at the WBC Convention in South Africa in 1998. When I arrived he was No.8 in the rankings, but I pointed out, in a brief meeting with Jose Sulaiman, that he was the only man in the ratings who had beaten three other fighters in the top ten. I argued very strongly and he was raised, first to No.3 and then on a vote to No.1. I was elated – and Arum, who had the champion, Cesar Bazan of Mexico, and the previous No.1 contender, Stevie Johnston, was very angry. We allowed Bazan to meet Johnston, and for Johnston to make voluntary defences because Billy is the No.1 contender and they cannot avoid him, however long they wait. All they are doing is softening up their man. Finally, with the great help of Sulaiman I agreed step-aside money of $50,000 for Schwer when Johnston defended the title in August 1999 against fellow American Angel Manfredy – and Billy gets his chance next. Eventually, I agreed to forfeit $15,000 of the step-aside fee in return for Johnston fighting Schwer in England.

I like the Schwers and Billy's trainer, Jack Lindsay. They are nice people. When the other fighters left me, Billy rang me and said: 'I am Mickey Duff's last fighter.'

Later when his contract ran out, I rang him to tell him. I wouldn't have argued if he had said he wanted to leave, but he showed what a loyal man he is. 'I know it has,' he said. 'You'd better draw up a new one.'

He came up to see me in my flat. By nature, he's an 'asker' and so naturally he wanted to know if there was a new signing-on fee.

'Bill, I don't need to give you a fee,' I said. 'I gave you one in 1990.'

He laughed:

'Ok, but you can't blame me for asking.'

Then he turned the contract over, said he had got to rush and just signed it, leaving me to fill in the gaps. He trusted me to do it properly and that's the basis of our relationship. If I were hindering him I would advise him to go somewhere else. I make no secret of the fact that success for him now would crown my career. I wouldn't want anything else. Of course if he does, I will stay for as long as he's champion or wants to fight, but he would be the 20th and last world titleholder that I have been involved with.

CHAPTER 21

Epilogue

Ninety per cent of the people in this country probably don't love what they do for a living. I swear to God, if I had my life again I'd do exactly the same. If they outlawed professional boxing tomorrow, I'd find a couple of amateurs and follow what they were doing. Now, of course, I'm at the stage where I know I've almost come to the end of the road. In the words of Marvin Hagler to one of his opponents: 'You have a great future behind you.'

Tommy Trinder, the great comedian of the post-war years, always said there were three stages in life: young, middle-aged and 'doesn't he look well?' I'm in that one now. I'm 70 and when you meet me you're not surprised.

There have been good and bad times, great friendships and fall-outs, the details of some of which have hazed over with the passing years.

I am reminded of an American fight manager of the old days, Willie Ketchum. His real name was William Friedlander, but he was called 'Ketchum' because he used to work as a gopher for one of the old mob managers, who when he heard of a prospect somewhere would invariably send his man off to sign them with the words: 'Go catch 'im, Willie.'

It was modified over the years to Ketchum. One day we were in a coffee shop in New York and another manager walked in. Ketchum lowered his head and it was obvious there was bad blood between them.

'I didn't know you didn't speak,' I said.

'We haven't spoken to each other for 25 years.'

'Really? What was that over?'

Ketchum looked at me and grinned.

'To tell you the truth, I forget.'

I'm sure that's the case with a lot of us along the way. In 1957, incidentally, Ketchum was the man responsible for breaking the stranglehold enforced by Jack Solomons on American boxers competing in this country. Up to then, Solomons controlled the market, but Jarvis Astaire brought in former world lightweight champion Jimmy Carter, who was managed by Ketchum, to fight Willie Toweel of South Africa. Solomons was furious. The gangster, Frankie Carbo, tried to intervene to stop Carter coming but Ketchum said Jimmy owed him money and that this was a good way for the debt to be settled. It wasn't really affecting Carbo and so he left it alone. Carter's career was drifting in the States – he'd had more than 100 fights even then – and Ketchum knew there would be no more big paydays over there. He wasn't trying to do anything significant for anyone but himself but it was a decision that had far-reaching effects. You could say that without it my life would almost certainly have run another course.

It's been a long journey from those days as a child of a rabbi in Poland. I saw my relationship with my father end, I made my living without his help and in a sport for which he had no love. It didn't matter to me because from the day

I first pulled on those gloves in my first schoolboy scuffle, I was entranced by this business. It has given and taken so much, but I think I will leave it having contributed greatly to its history and its huge vault of momentous occasions. I have had enormous help along the way from my friendship and association with Jarvis Astaire. We constantly argue and sometimes it takes him a long time to see the other point of view, but I have never known anybody in my entire life, including my family, with a greater sense of honesty.

I once said that if you can get by in boxing, you can get by in life. In boxing you meet every sort of person imaginable: The smartest, the simplest, the nicest and the nastiest. And I think I'm a combination of them all.

I was very proud of my induction into the International Boxing Hall of Fame in Canastota and also enjoy attending the monthly meetings of the London Ex-Boxers Association, who do an excellent job of keeping old friends – and the odd enemy – talking boxing, when their own active days are done. I still see Solly Cantor, for example, from time to time, which stirs memories of our days in South Africa more than 40 years ago.

I enjoy visiting my son Gary and his wife Orly in Florida and of course love seeing my grandchildren. When my career is finally over I have plans to sell my flat in London and retire in Israel, where I bought property following the death of my father. It would seem appropriate for the great-grandson of the Rabbi of Beltz to spend his declining years in the state that Jewish people have created for themselves. And I like to think that in their way the old men of my youth would have understood the way things have turned out and be as proud as I am of what I have achieved.

How would I like to be remembered by boxing people? As a man who knew his business, as a tough but fair negotiator, as someone who always acted in what he thought were the best interests of his boxers and as a good manager and matchmaker. I don't expect to be remembered as a man who only made life-and-death matches. Hopefully I will be remembered as a man who made matches in the best interests of the boxers I was representing, but at all times with a regard for the general public who were paying money to watch. And I hope, more often than not, I succeeded.

Whatever your verdict, I think you will agree, it's been one heck of a ride from that small house in the town of Tarnow, east of Krakow, where as a terrified child I heard my father say it was time to change all of our lives forever.

I have shared tables with sporting legends and mixed with some of the greatest boxers in history: Jack Dempsey, Ray Robinson, Joe Louis, Rocky Marciano and, of course, the incomparable Muhammad Ali. I have known the bad and the good, have crossed swords with the best boxing promoters of the last 30 years and have dealt with everybody who has been anybody. And somehow I have prospered to the point where I can be confident that my family and I are financially secure. Now, more than 60 years after those confusing child-hood years of displacement and fear, I am lucky enough to be here to share this story with you and to be able to look forward to the only chapter left unfinished: Billy Schwer's world title quest. I would so love him to win, for it would be a wonderful reward for one of the most loyal men I have known – and a perfect way for me to go out.

Career Statistics

Born: Monek Prager, 7 June 1929 in Tarnow, Poland.

Professional boxing career: 1944–48.
Full professional record: 69 fights, 55 wins, 8 defeats, 6 draws
Licensed matchmaker, manager and promoter with the British Boxing Board of Control.

Mickey Duff has been significantly involved – either as manager, promoter or matchmaker – in the careers of 19 world champions. They are listed in chronological order, as follows:

Terry Downes (b. London, England, 9 May 1936)
World middleweight champion 1961
Won title: rtd 9 Paul Pender (USA), 11 July 1961, Empire
  Pool, Wembley, London, England. (Harry Levene promotion)
World title fights: 4
Career span: 1957–64

Howard Winstone (b. Merthyr Tydfil, Wales, 15 April 1939)
World featherweight champion 1968 (recognised by British
   Boxing Board of Control)
Won title: rsf 9 Mitsunori Seki (Japan), 23 January 1968,
   Royal Albert Hall, London, England. (Mike Barrett pro-
   motion)
World title fights: 5
Career span: 1959–68

John Conteh (b. Liverpool, England, 27 May 1951)
WBC light-heavyweight champion 1974–77
Won title: pts 15 Jorge Ahumada (Argentina), 1 October
   1974, Empire Pool, Wembley, London. (Harry Levene
   promotion).
World title fights: 7
Career span: 1971–80

John H. Stracey (b. London, England, 22 September 1950)
WBC welterweight champion 1975–76
Won title: rsf 6 Jose Napoles (Mexico), 6 December 1975,
   Monumental Plaza bull ring, Mexico City.
World title fights: 3
Career span: 1969–78

Maurice Hope (b. St John's, Antigua, West Indies, 6 December
   1951)
WBC light-middleweight champion 1979–81
Won title: rtd 8 Rocky Mattioli (Italy), 4 March 1979, San
   Remo, Italy. (Guerin Sportivo promotion)
World title fights: 6
Career span: 1973–82

Jim Watt (b. Glasgow, Scotland, 18 July 1948)
WBC lightweight champion 1979–81
Won title: rsf 12 Alfredo Pitalua (Colombia), 17 April 1979,
    Kelvin Hall, Glasgow, Scotland. (Mike Barrett/Mickey
    Duff/Peter Keenan promotion)
World title fights: 6
Career span: 1968–81

Alan Minter (b. Crawley, Sussex, England, 17 August 1951)
World middleweight champion 1980
Won title: pts 15 Vito Antuofermo (Italy/USA), 16 March
    1980, Caesars Palace, Las Vegas, Nevada, USA. (Caesars
    Palace/Top Rank promotion)
World title fights: 3
Career span: 1972–81

Cornelius Boza-Edwards (b. Kampala, Uganda, 27 May
    1956)
WBC super-featherweight champion 1981
Won title: pts 15 Rafael Limon (Mexico), 8 March 1981,
    Civic Auditorium, Stockton, California, USA. (Azteca
    Promotions)
World title fights: 6
Career span: 1976–87

Charlie Magri (b. Tunis, Tunisia, 20 July 1956)
WBC flyweight champion 1983
Won title: rsf 7 Eleoncio Mercedes (Dominican Republic), 15
    March 1983, Empire Pool, Wembley, London, England.
    (Harry Levene/Mike Barrett/Mickey Duff promotion)
World title fights: 3
Career span: 1977–86

Barry McGuigan (b. Clones, Ireland, 28 February 1961)
WBA featherweight champion 1985–86
Won title: pts 15 Eusebio Pedroza (Panama), 8 June 1985, Queens Park Rangers soccer stadium, Loftus Road, London, England. (Eastwood Promotions/Mike Barrett/ Mickey Duff promotion)
World title fights: 4
Career span: 1981–89

Lloyd Honeyghan (b. Elizabeth, Jamaica, 22 April 1960)
World welterweight champion 1986
WBC/IBF welterweight champion 1986–87
WBC welterweight champion 1988–89
Won title: rtd 6 Don Curry (USA), 27 September 1986, Caesars, Atlantic City, New Jersey, USA. (Top Rank promotion)
World title fights: 9
Career span: 1980–95

Buster Drayton (b. Philadelphia, USA, 2 March 1953)
IBF light-middleweight champion 1986–87
Won title: pts 15 Carlos Santos (Puerto Rico), 4 June 1986, Brendan Byrne Arena, East Rutherford, New Jersey, USA. (Top Rank promotion)
World title fights: 5
Career span: 1978–95

Duke McKenzie (b. London, England, 5 May 1963)
IBF flyweight champion 1988–89
WBO bantamweight champion 1991–92
WBO super-bantamweight champion 1992–93
Won title: ko 11 Rolando Bohol (Philippines), 5 October 1988. Wembley, London, England. (Mickey Duff/Terry Lawless promotion)

World title fights: 10
Career span: 1982–98

John Mugabi (b. Kampala, Uganda, 2 September 1961)
WBC light-middleweight champion 1989–90
Won title: ko 1 Rene Jacquot (France), 8 July 1989, Mira-
    polis, Cergy-Pontoise, Paris, France. (Acaries Brothers
    promotion)
World title fights: 5
Career span: 1980–99

Henry Maske (b. Treuenbrietzen, East Germany, 6 January
    1964)
IBF light-heavyweight champion 1993–96
Won title: pts 12 Charles Williams (USA), 20 March 1993,
    Dusseldorf, Germany (Cedric Kushner/Wilfred Sauerland
    promotion)
World title fights: 12
Career span: 1990–96

Frank Bruno (b. London, England, 16 November 1961)
WBC heavyweight champion 1995–96
Won title: pts 12 Oliver McCall (USA), 2 September 1995,
    Wembley Stadium, London, England. (Don King/Frank
    Warren promotion)
World title fights: 5
Career span: 1982–96

Henry Akinwande (b. London, England, 12 October 1965)
WBO heavyweight champion 1996–97
Won title: rsf 3 Jeremy Williams (USA), 29 June 1996, Indio,
    California, USA. (Don King promotion)
World title fights: 3
Career span: 1989–present

Joe Calzaghe (b. London, England, 23 March 1972)
WBO super-middleweight champion 1997–
Won title: pts 12 Chris Eubank (England), 11 October 1997,
  Sheffield, England. (Frank Warren promotion)
World title fights: 5
Career span: 1993–present

Richie Woodhall (b. Telford, England, 17 April 1968)
WBC super-middleweight champion 1998–
Won title: pts 12 Sugarboy Malinga (South Africa), 27
  March 1998, Ice Rink, Telford, England. (Frank Warren
  promotion)
World title fights: 4
Career span: 1993–present

ko   knockout
pts   points decision
rsf   referee stopped fight
rtd   retired

Index

agents 178–179
Ahumada, Jorge 122
Akinwande, Henry 253, 271
Albert Hall 52, 57, 107
Allen, Eileen 171
Andries, Dennis 216
Angel, Johnny 32, 44
Anglo-American Sporting Club 76, 79, 109–110, 247
  opening night 31–33, 43–44
Antuofermo, Vito 133, 144, 146
Archer, Joey 44
Arguello, Alexis 2, 140–141, 195–196
Armour, Johnny 220
Arthur, Bobby 127
Arum, Bob 2, 97, 124, 134, 162–164, 197, 240
  Hong Kong cancellation 163, 257–259
Astaire, Jarvis 24, 52, 85, 169, 215
  Anglo-American Sporting Club 31; partnership with 41–42, 47–49, 52, 56, 107; relationship with MD 46–47, 67, 264; charges over contractual agreement 175–178
Atlantic City 236
Atlas, Teddy 227
August, Bernt 97

Avoth, Eddie 117
Ayala, Tony 182

Baker, Mike 133–134
Baksi, Joe 24
Baldeyrou, Raymond 139
Barnard, Ivor 31
Barone, Joseph 'Pep' 71
Barrett, Mike 57, 145, 192
  partnership with 52, 57, 107; charges over contractual agreement 175–178; on Bruno/Garner fight 210–211
Basilio, Carmen 2, 40
Batten, Jimmy 142
Bazan, Cesar 260
BBC 110–111, 220–221, 244, 249
  Bruno fights 202, 204, 215, 220
Beasley, Lonnie 259
Beech, Sid 16–17
Benavides, Jesse 199
Benitez, Wilfred 131, 135, 238
Benn, Nigel 172–173
Bennett, Lonnie 122
Berbick, Trevor 103, 212, 224, 228
Berliner, Victor 22
Biddles, George 97, 99–100, 114

Bidwell, Doug 111, 148
Biggs, Tyrell 237
Bivins, Jimmy 2
Blin, Jurgen 114
Blocker, Maurice 187
Bloom, Joe 21
Bodell, Jack 56, 61, 114
Bodinetz, Harold 21, 24, 48
Bodinetz, Morris 21–22, 24, 48
Boggis, Arthur 62–63
Bogs, Tom 117
Bohol, Rolando 198–199
Bonavena, Oscar 92
bookmakers business 157
Boon, Eric 46–47
booths, boxing 18–19
Bos, Johnny 179, 204, 210, 228
Botha, Frans 233
Bouttier, Jean Claude 119
Bowe, Riddick 218, 247
Boxing News, mismatch allegations
    176–177, 178
Boza-Edwards, Cornelius 178, 195–197,
    269
Brady Street Boys Club 15
Braitman, Dave 24
Branco, Silvio 250
Brandman, Henri 173, 202
Braverman, Al 165
Breland, Mark 190, 237
Brenner, Teddy 164
British Boxing Board of Control 66, 88,
    105
    grant licence to MD 22–3; restrictions
        on MD 58; dispute with Spanish
        Board 137–138;
    charges of monopoly and exploitation
        176, 177
Brown, Bundini 103
Brown, Joe 'Old Bones' 62
Brown, Neville 249
Brown, Paul 112
Bruno, Frank 116, 176, 201–223
    split with MD 201–202; early career
        202–206; eye surgery 202, 217; v
        McCall 201, 221; temperament 204,
        209, 216, 219, 221–222; v Bugner
        212–213; v Coetzee 207; v
        Witherspoon 208–209; v Tyson
        215–216, 221–222; v Lewis
        219–220; career statistics 271

Bruno, Laura 201–202
Bryan, Del 183
Buckingham, Snowy 47, 49
Bugner, Joe 92, 95–96, 111–116, 155
Bugner, Marlene 116
Bumphus, Johnny 187–188
Burke, Paul 257
Burnett, Jesse 124
Burns, Sam 26, 49, 52, 60, 111, 148

Cabrero, Danilo 194
Caesars Palace 154–156
Calzaghe, Enzo 251
Calzaghe, Joe 172, 251–253, 272
Camacho, Hector 196
Canizales, Gaby 199
Cantor, Solly 25–26, 29, 264
Caplan, Benny 15
Caplan, Bill 149
Carbo, John Paul 'Frankie' 71, 225, 263
Cardew, Jimmy 30
Carpenter, Harry 210, 220
Carpentier, Georges 87
Carr, Curley 48
Carr, Rita 48
Carter, Jimmy 265
Carter, Rubin 'Hurricane' 68–69
Cayton, Bill 159, 214, 215, 230
Cedeno, Frank 142
Chacon, Bobby 196–197
championships, proliferation of 243–244
Chargin, Don 140, 149, 178, 235
Charles, Ralph 128
Charnley, Dave 62–63
Charpentier, Patrick 255
Chichester, Sir Francis 76
Christle, Joe 202–203
Christle, Mel 203
Christle, Terry 203
Chuvalo, George 84
Clarke, Ray 179–180, 204
Clay, Cassius *see* Muhammad Ali
Clay, Sonjie 85
Coetzee, Gerrie 206–207
Coetzer, Pierre 217
Cokes, Curtis 128
Collins, George 183
Colombo, Allie 79
Comer, Jack 'Spot' 28–29, 30
Conteh, John 111, 119, 120–125, 268
Conteh, Tony 123

Cooney, Gerry 156–157, 214
Cooper, Henry 53, 54, 55–56, 60, 61
    v Ali 83, 85–87; v Bugner 113–114
Coopman, Jean Pierre 101
Cordero, Pepe 240, 241, 253
Corletti, Eduardo 113
Cornelius, James 103
Cosell, Howard 239
Cotton, Billy 61–62
Coulon, Johnny 3
court cases 170–172, 174–175, 194
Cowdell, Pat 195
Crick, evacuation to 9
Crook, Carl 257
crowd trouble 146–147
Crowley, Dave 16
Cruz, Stevie 194
Cuello, Miguel Angel 124
Cummings, Floyd 'Jumbo' 204, 222
Curry, Don 181, 184–186, 238

Dagge, Eckhard 133
Daily Mirror, libel action against
    170–171
Dakin, Roland 144
Dalby, W. Barrington 110
Daly, John 257–258
D'Amato, Cus 163, 224–228
D'Amato, Tony 225
dangers of boxing 242
Davis, Howard 138–139
De La Hoya, Oscar 164, 254
del Rio, Santiago 192–193
del Valle, Rafael 199
Delaney, Mark 252
Delannoit, Cyrille 39
Dempsey, Jack 78–79
Deutsch, Sindel (father of MD) 5, 6, 7, 8,
    10–13
DeVorce, Paul 192
Diaz, Juan 'Monito' 141–142
Dillon, John 170–171
Dimes, Albert 29–30
Dokes, Michael 'Dynamite' 206
Douglas, Bill 231
Douglas, Buster 230–231
Downes, Terry 35, 37, 41–42, 48–52, 79,
    80, 267
Drayton, Buster 205, 270
Duff, Mickey
    childhood in Poland 5–7; leaves Poland

8; childhood in England 8–10;
evacuation 8; early employement 10;
alienation from father 11–12; as
amateur boxer 14–16; adopts name
15–16; as professional boxer 16–20;
becomes matchmaker/manager
21–23, 24, 25–26; marriage 24–25,
26–27, 160–161; becomes British
citizen 87; gambling 153–158; work
in USA 237–237; career statistics 267
Duncan, Eddie 121
Dundee, Angelo 51, 56, 94–95, 102–103
Dundee, Chris 35, 55, 90, 94–95
Dunn, Richard 95, 96–98, 100, 115
Duran, Roberto 131, 138, 142, 182,
    238–239
Durham, Yank 115
Duva, Dan 168, 236–237
Duva, Lou 188, 236–237
Dwyer, Pat 64

Eastwood, Barney 191–194, 195
Eaton, Aileen 235
Edwards, Bobbi Joe 251–252
Edwards, Jack 195
Eguia, Esteban 192
Eklund, Anders 206
Elbaum, Don 44–45
Eliades, Panos 248
Ellis, Jimmy 86
Emmen, John 217
Epifantsev, Yuri 256
Erskine, Joe 53, 54, 56, 60
Eubank, Chris 171, 173, 174, 241, 253
Ewald, Camille 225, 228
exploitation of fighters, charges of
    175–178
Ezra, Ronnie 24

Fahrat, Ben Salah 50
Famechon, Andre 67
Famechon, Johnny 66–67
Famechon, Ray 66, 67
Ferguson, Jesse 220
Fernandez, Perico 136–137
Ferrer, Roger 210
Fields, Ross Eugene 168–170
Figueroa, Juan 205
films of fights 159
Finkel, Shelly 182, 232, 237
Finnegan, Chris 100, 111, 117–119, 121

Finnegan, Kevin 111, 119–120, 145, 148
Fiske, Jack 170
Fleischer, Nat 88
Flint, Jimmy 178
Folley, Zora 55–56, 91
Foreman, George 93
Foster, Bob 118, 121–122
Fragetta, Dewey 40–41, 76, 179
Francis, George 111, 120, 121, 123, 124,
    149, 209–210, 221
Fraser, Frankie 34
Frazier, Joe 92, 93, 109, 115
Frazier, Marvin 240
Fullmer, Gene 2, 40
Futch, Eddie 122

Gainford, George 40–41, 42, 43
Gains, Larry 57
Galaxy, Khaosai 2
Gallouze, Farid 192
gambling 153–158
Garcia, Oscar 260
Gardner, Chuck 210
Gardner, John L. 142
Gateshead, religious college 9–10
Gaudiosi, Vito 250
Gavilan, Kid 47–48
Getty, J. Paul 79
Giardello, Joey 43
Gibbs, Harry 113–114, 133, 139, 205
Gilmour, Tommy 252
Gilpin, Cliff 184
Givens, Robin 214, 215
Gizzi, Carl 113
Glasgow, Jim Watt fights 136, 137,
    138–139, 141
Glass, Sam 170
Glendenning, Raymond 110
glove size 242–243
Goldstein, Ruby 40
Gomez, Wilfredo 194
Gottert, Joachim 90
governing bodies of boxing 239–241,
    243–244
Graham, Herol 173, 249
Gray, Ron 213
Graziano, Rocky 225
Greb, Harry 159
Green, Ben 48
Green, Dave ('The Fen Tiger') 131–132,
    178

Green, James 'Hard Rock' 149
Green, Kenny 17
Green, Mitchell 'Blood' 215
Griffith, Emile 63
Gross, Reggie 211–212
Grossmith, Bernie 48
Grossmith, Harry 48, 157
Guardino, Frank 94
Guinaldo, Antonio 137
Gunns, Carl 148
Gutteridge, Reg 74

Habib, Tony 26
Hackett, Desmond 64
Hagler, Marvin 2, 120, 146–147, 149,
    150, 151–152, 238–239
Hall, Dick 113
Hamed, Naseem 248–249
Hamsho, Mustafa 147
Harada, Masahiko 67, 68
Harnett, Doug 19
Harris, Ronnie 145
Hatcher, Gene 188
headguards 242
Hearn, Barry 116, 167, 217, 241
    Hong Kong cancellation 163, 257–258;
        Bruno/Bugner fight 212–213; WBO
        influence 253
Hearns, Thomas 152, 238–239, 241
Henning, Jack 16, 17
Henriques, Basil 14
Hernandez, Art 43, 236
Herrera, Carlos 134
Hill, Virgil 175, 237
Holloway, Rory 232, 233
Holmes, Keith 250
Holmes, Larry 102, 156–157, 229,
    240
Holyfield, Evander 166, 218, 230,
    231–232, 233, 237
Holyk, Andre 136
Honeyghan, Lloyd 132, 181, 183–190,
    270
    v Curry 181, 184–186; v Vaca
        188–189
Hong Kong, promotion cancelled (1994)
    163, 257–259
Hope, Maurice 94, 132–136, 268
Hope, Pat 133
Hopkin, David 37, 177
Horne, John 232, 233

Hornewer, John 248
Hulls, Sydney 23
Huntman, Benny 46–47
Hutchings, Fred 183
Hutchins, Lenny 124
Hyams, Jack 22

Ingle, Brendan 248, 249
International Boxing Federation (IBF)
    240–241
International Boxing Hall of Fame,
    induction 1–3

Jacobs, Alf 17
Jacobs, Benny 53–54
Jacobs, Gary 254–256
Jacobs, Jim 135, 159, 213–214, 225
    and Tyson 227, 228, 230, 234
Jacopucci, Angelo 146
Jenkins, Lew 2
Jenkins, Rob 127
Jimenez, Daniel 199
Johansson, Ingemar 87
Johnson, Bunny 98
Johnston, Stevie 260
Jones, Billy 'The Fox' 31
Jones, Colin 66, 182, 185
Jones, Mike 139
Jones, Roy 250
Jordan, Don 71
Jordan, Jack 31
judging system 166–167

Kasler, Archie 32
Kaylor, Mark 205
Keenan, Peter 74–75, 137
Ketchum, Willie 262–263
King, Don 101–102, 103, 138, 164–166,
    182, 196–197, 208
    and Tyson 214, 230–231, 232, 233
Klein, Bill 16, 46
Knight, Billy 145
Kray, Charlie 31
Kray, Reggie 31, 32–37, 74
Kray, Ronnie 31, 32–37, 74
Kushner, Cedric 192

La Motta, Jake 39
Laing, Kirkland 181–183
Lane, Mills 221, 232, 239, 253
LaPorte, Juan 192

Las Vegas 237–238
    Caesars Palace 154–156
Lawless, Terry 129, 132, 134, 136, 141
    partnership with 107, 126–127, 128,
        129, 137; falling out with MD
        142–143; charges over contractual
        agreement 175–178; as trainer 181,
        184; and Bruno 201, 202–204, 205,
        206, 210–212, 216–217
Layne, Alfredo 194
Lazar, Davey 16, 19
Lazar, Eddie 16
Lazar, Harry 16
Lazar, Lew 16
Leahy, Mick 43, 59
Lee, Bobby, snr. 240
legal actions 170–172, 174–175, 194
Legge, Harry 18
Legra, Jose 66, 67
Leonard, Ray 2, 131, 134, 182–183, 238
Lesnevich, Gus 23, 24
Levene, Harry 55, 57, 60
    partnership with 41–42, 52, 56–58;
        matchmaking for 106, 107; rivalry
        with Solomons 108–109
Levers, Dick 20
Levitt, Roger 247, 248
Lewis, Butch 214
Lewis, Hedgemon 130
Lewis, John Henry 57
Lewis, Lennox 166, 168, 217–220, 221,
    237, 247–248
Lewis, Ronald 'Butch' 165–166
Lewis, Ted 'Kid' 79
Leyton Baths 21, 24, 29, 30, 50
libel cases 170–172
Limon, Rafael 'Bazooka' 196
Lindsay, Jack 260
Liston, Charles 'Sonny' 70–76, 113
Liston, Geraldine 71, 75
Little, Tommy 62
Liverpool, promotions in 105–106
London, Brian 55, 56, 88–89, 113
London Ex-Boxers Association 264
Longo, Peter 49
Lopez, Alvaro 'Yaqui' 123
Louis, Joe 2, 76–78
Louis, Martha 77
Lucas, Frankie 148
Lyle, Richard 115–116
Lynas, Jimmy 49

McAlinden, Danny 114
McAuley, Dave 199
McAvoy, Jock 57
McCall, Oliver 201, 221
McCallum, Mike 173, 238, 249
McCearn, Neil 154
McCoy, Jackie 130–131
McCracken, Robert 254
McCrory, Milton 66
McCullough, Wayne 254
McDonnell, Jim 194, 207
McGowan, Lavon 192
McGuigan, Barry 191–195, 270
McKenzie, Clinton 197–198
McKenzie, Duke 197–200, 270
McLeod, David 134
McTaggart, Dick 116
McVey, Sam 3
Maddison, Les 15
Magri, Charlie 141–142, 176, 178, 198, 269
Main Events 236–237
Malinga, Sugarboy 251
Maloney, Frank 168, 173, 248
Mancini, Dennie 175, 257, 259
Manfredy, Angel 260
Manning, Jack 36
Mantle, Johnny 117
Marciano, Rocky 79–81, 87
Marin, Rodolfo 221
Marley, Mike 170
Marsh, Terry 198
Martin, Jonathan 220, 249
Martin, Lenny 120, 121
Maske, Henry 174–175, 271
Mason, Gary 220
matchmaking 106–107
Mathis, Buster 225
Mattioli, Rocky 133, 134
Maxim, Joey 40
medical care in boxing 242
Mendy, Ambrose 172–173
Menetrey, Roger 119, 127
Mercante, Arthur 139
Mercedes, Eleoncio 141–142
Merritt, Jeff 165
Middleton, George 43
Mildenberger, Karl 61, 89–91
Miller, Ray 40
Milligan, Mike 22
Mills, Freddie 23, 24

Minchillo, Luigi 136
Minter, Alan 111, 119, 132, 144–148, 269
mismatch allegations 176–177, 178
Mitchell, Brian 207
Mizler, Harry 15, 22
monopoly allegations 175–178
Monzon, Carlos 119
Moorer, Michael 241
Moss, Peter 108
Mugabi, John 'The Beast' 149–151, 174, 271
Muhammad Ali 56, 83–104
  v Liston 75, 84; ban on 84–85, 91–92; v Cooper 83, 85–87; religious beliefs 84–85, 92; v London 88–89; v Mildenberger 89–91; v Frazier 92, 93; v Bugner 92, 95–96, 155–156; v Foreman 93; physical deterioration 93–94, 102, 103–104; v Dunn 96–98, 100
Muhammad, Akbar 186
Muhammad, Elijah 89–90
Muhammad, Herbert 89, 94
Murray, Jim 136
Mwale, Lottie 148, 170

Napoles, Jose 127–130
National Promotions 247
National Sporting Club 247
Navarette, Rolando 196
Neill, Bobby 117, 185, 186
News of the World 175–176
Norman, Sam 157
Norris, Jim 55
Norton, Ken 92–93, 101, 102

Office of Fair Trading 174, 176, 178
O'Grady, Sean 139–140
O'Halloran, Jack 112–113
Oliva, Patrizio 183
Olivares, Ruben 68
Omaha, Nebraska 236
O'Neal, Ryan 130
organizations, boxing 239–241, 243–244
Owen, Johnny 137–138
Oxford and St George's Boys Club 14–15

Pacheco, Ferdie 93–95, 170
Paez, Jorge 240
Page, Greg 206, 208, 210, 211
Palermo, Frank 'Blinky' 71

Palomino, Carlos 130–131, 135
Parkin, Bob 18
Parlov, Mate 124
Parnassus, George 42, 128
Pastrano, Willie 35, 51–52
Patterson, Floyd 71, 225–226
Pazienza, Vinny 190
Pedroza, Eusebio 2, 192–193
Pender, Paul 51
Pep, Willie 66, 109–110
Perry, Cornelius 59
Peyre, Jose 59
Pinna, Piero 198
Pitalua, Alfredo 138
Poland, childhood in 5–7
Powell, Charley 60
Powell, Dennis 58
Powell, Ike 43
Power, Colin 198
Prager, Danielle (granddaughter) 158
Prager, Gary (son) 26, 27, 36, 158–160, 264
Prager, Helen (aunt) 9
Prager, Lewis (brother) 5, 8, 9, 13
Prager, Marie (wife) 24–25, 26–27, 35–36, 160–161, 235
Prager, Monek *see* Duff, Mickey
Prager, Natalie (granddaughter) 158
Prager, Orly (daughter-in-law) 264
Prager, Tyla (mother) 6, 8, 10–11, 158
Prescott, Johnny 56, 61, 113
protection for boxers 242
Pusateri, Mike 79

Quarry, Jerry 92, 114

Ramsey, Bobby 30–31
Rankin, Jackie 19
Rappaport, Dennis 139
Read, Leonard 'Nipper' 36
Regis, Ulric 112
Reiche, Frank 119
Rhiney, Henry 181
Ribalta, Jose 217
Richardson, Charlie 34
Richardson, Dick 56, 90
Richardson, Eddie 34
Roberts, Les 136
Robinson, Steve 200
Robinson, Sugar Ray 32, 38–45, 236
Robles, Rogelio 140, 235

Rodriguez, Juan Francisco 137–138
Rogers, Leonardo 124
Rokach, Moise 6
Rokach, Norman (half-brother) 6, 12
Roper, Ruth 214
Rose, Lionel 68
Rosi, Gianfranco 184
Royal Albert Hall 52, 57, 107
Rudd, Irving 2
Ruddock, Razor 217–218
Rudkin, Alan 68, 106
Ruelas, Rafael 257

Saad Muhammad, Matthew 125, 170
Sabatini, Rodolfo 137
Saddler, Sandy 109
safety standards 242
Saldivar, Vicente 2, 65, 67
Santemore, Walter 205
Sauerland, Wilfried 174–175
Savold, Lee 23
Schmeling, Max 213
Schmidtke, Rudiger 119, 121
Schulz, Axel 253
Schwer, Billy 3, 256–261
Schwer, Billy, snr. 256
Scott, Harry 68
Seki, Mitsunori 65
Sellers, Nat 22
Serwano, Art 157
Shavers, Earnie 93, 165
Shepherd family, evacuation to 9
Shoreditch Town Hall 48
Shufford, Horace 184
Sibson, Tony 120, 147, 148–149
Silverman, Sam 30
Simmons, Henry 25
Simmons, Marie *see* Prager, Marie
Sinclair, Max 25
Sinclair, Rita 25
Singletary, Ernie 147
Sky television 244
Sloane, Lee 236
Smith, Andy 111, 112, 132
Smith, Harold J. 168–170
Smith, James 'Bonecrusher' 205
Solomons, Jack 22, 23–24, 26, 58, 88, 107–108, 263
Somerville, Joe 63–65
Soto, Cesar 199
Spada, Luis 192–193

Spinks, Leon 101, 102
Spinks, Michael 214, 229
Spinks, Terry 59, 116–117
Starling, Marlon 190
Steele, Richard 152
Steele, Tommy 52
Stracey, Dave 127, 129
Stracey, John H. 119, 127–131, 132, 176,
    268
Sulaiman, Jose 139, 240, 260
Sulkin, Graham 254–255
The Sun, libel action against 171–172
Sunday Times 170, 175–176
Swift, Wally 59

Tarnow (Poland) 5–7, 9
Taylor, Bernard 194
Taylor, Meldrick 237
television 244–245, 249
    Bruno fights 202, 204, 215, 220–221;
        USA 237, 238, *see also* BBC
Terrell, Ernie 91
Tetteh, David 260
Thomas, Eddie 18, 66
Thomas, Ivor 19
Thomas, Pinklon 208
Thompson, Billy 46
Tibbs, Jimmy 86, 210
Tiger, Dick 48–49
Tillis, James 'Quick' 207, 210
Tinley, Mat 254
Tonna, Gratien 119, 146
Toole, Terry 142
Top Rank 134, 163, 258–259
Torres, Jose 141–142
Toweel, Willie 263
Trainer, Mike 134–135
travelling booths 18
Tubbs, Tony 208
Tunney, Gene 78
Turpin, Randolph 39–40
Tyson, Mike 210, 213–214, 224–234
    v Bruno 215–216, 221–222; v
        Holyfield 230, 231–232; jailing 231,
        233

Urtain, Jose 114

Vaca, Jorge 188–189
Valcarcel, Francisco 'Paco' 253
Van Rensburg, Johnny 26

Vann, Mickey 219
Vary, Danny 20, 31
Velensk, Conny 117–118
Villemain, Robert 46–47
Vines, Harry 138
Viscusi, Lou 115
Volbrecht, Harold 187

Walker, Billy 53, 56, 58–62
Walker, George 58, 59–60, 62
Waltham, Teddy 90–91
Warren, Frank 116, 149, 167–168, 221,
    246, 249, 251
Washington, Desiree 231
Waterman, Peter 47–48
Waters, Bob 163
Watson, Michael 172–174
Watt, Jim 127, 136–141, 269
Weinberger, Bill 154–156
Wembley Stadium 52, 57
Wepner, Chuck ('Bayonne Bleeder') 113
West Ham Amateur Club 15
West Ham Baths 20
Wharton, Henry 253
Whitaker, Pernell 237, 255
Whiting, George 34–35, 41
Wicks, Jackie 54
Wicks, Jim 'The Bishop' 54–55, 85–86,
    113
Wilburn, Al 19
Williams, Carl 'The Truth' 218
Williams, Cleveland 91
Williams, Edward Bennett 134
Williams, Eugenia 166
Wilson, Peter 41, 42
Wilson, Stephen 252
Winstone, Howard 2, 65–66, 110, 117,
    268
Witherspoon, Tim 165–166, 208–209
Woodcock, Bruce 23–4
Woodhall, Len 251
Woodhall, Richie 157, 220, 249–251, 272
World Boxing Association (WBA)
    239–241
World Boxing Council (WBC) 239–240
World Boxing Organization (WBO) 241
World Sporting Club 108
Wortham, Troy 173
Wynn, Steve 231

Yanez, Salvador 251